The view from the audience...

'That perfect combination of laugh-out-loud funny and genuinely moving, Paul A Mendelson's latest is a feel-good novel of considerable substance that will be loved by fans of 'The Thursday Murder Club.'

Petra Fried, BAFTA-winning producer.
The Misfits. End of the F***ing World.

It is funny and touching, as is all Mendelson's work. I was a bit nervous initially about the subject matter in the light of Covid, but I have to say that feeling left me very quickly as I became immersed in the concept of an actors' home and the diversity of brilliantly distinctive characters.

David Lister. *The Independent.*

When Elspeth Quest, MBE and great lady of the British theatre, goes reluctantly to stay at Dustingford Residential home for geriatric thespians, all guns blazing, the result is hilarious. This is a heartwarming, very funny story of a group of mostly loveable, always entertaining characters. Writer of May to December, So Haunt Me, and My Hero, Paul A Mendelson's observations on performers are real, heartening and laugh-out-loud-on-London-Transport funny!

Carolyn Pickles. Actress.
Broadchurch. Harry Potter. Canterville Ghost.

A warm, funny and engaging novel from a legendary comic writer. The book has it all: pages of snappy, laugh-out-loud banter punctuated with rug-pull moments of real depth and emotion, all leading up to a show-stopping climax.

Daniel Peak. BAFTA-winning writer.
Not Going Out. Code 404. Horrible Histories.

A truly charming read. You'll either love or hate the novel's heroine, Elspeth Quest, but you'll never forget her, as she leads her fellow ageing performers to one final bow.

Francine White. Show business journalist.

Witty, touching and profound. No murders but plenty of 'corpsing'. Mendelson's best yet.'

Paul Harrison. BAFTA-winning director.
Ballykissangel. Touch of Frost.

their exits and their entrances

paul a. mendelson

The Book Guild Ltd

First published in Great Britain in 2022 by
The Book Guild Ltd
Unit E2, Airfield Business Park
Harrison Road
Market Harborough
Leicestershire, LE16 7UL
Freephone: 0800 999 2982
www.bookguild.co.uk
Email: info@bookguild.co.uk
Twitter: @bookguild

Typeset in 11pt Minion Pro

ISBN 978 1914471 155

Printed and bound by CPI Group (UK) Ltd, Croydon, CR0 4YY

British Library Cataloguing in Publication Data.
A catalogue record for this book is available from the British Library.

MIX
Paper from
responsible sources
FSC® C013604
www.fsc.org

To M. You've been my rock since our youth.
There's no one with whom I would rather grow old.

author's note

The events chronicled in this book occurred in that heady, carefree winter of 2019, before the dreaded virus that has affected the world hit families, hospitals and care homes throughout the United Kingdom.

The owners and managers of the famed Dustingford Hall residential home have since assured this author that – owing to their own perspicacity, diligence and foresight, the relative remoteness of their particular institution and the sheer belligerence of the residents – they are, thankfully, still in the majority of similar establishments that remain, to this day, creditably unscathed.

Perhaps certain occurrences outlined in this tale may even have unwittingly contributed to their due diligence.

The author is in constant touch with Dustingford Hall and is assured that this will remain the case.

All the world's a stage,
And all the men and women merely players;
They have their exits and their entrances,
And one man in his time plays many parts,
His acts being seven ages.

William Shakespeare *(As You Like It)*

act one

Early November, 2019

scene one

Her minicab is on the final and particularly tiresome curve of a bumpy, tree-lined drive, when she notices the tap dancer.

An elderly yet enviably flexible man, he stands in the shade of a huge oak, neat trilby set back on his balding head, moving in tartan carpet slippers to music existing only in his mind and appearing graciously to acknowledge a partner who remains equally imaginary.

The passenger can't discern whether the man is of colour or simply obscured in morning mist from the nearby sea and really could not care less. Yet, she would have been hard-pressed to dream up a more appropriate image for the hell into which she is slowly being delivered.

Turning her attention to the grim Victorian mansion looming ever more darkly out of the sea's wintery breath, with dripping, alopeciac ivy and more turrets and gables than it knows what to do with, she suddenly recalls a scene from some old black-and-white British film and becomes convinced that this monstrous pile had served as a location. A Dickens, a Bronte, some lesser Du Maurier? She wonders for a moment if she had been in it.

The cab driver, a perspiring, overweight man in his mid-thirties, with a vague smell of the provinces and baked beans about him, is snatching in the mirror what he assumes are surreptitious looks at his imperious passenger. Finally, the old lady can stand it no more.

"Yes. I am," she says.

"Yes, you are what?" responds the bemused driver, who snatches surreptitious looks at all his passengers, as it makes his job in this small and stultifying coastal town just a fraction less tedious.

"Never mind," she says and turns her attention back to the hideous building, outside whose grand and firmly closed doors they are now arriving. "Wait here," she orders when the minicab comes to its gravelly stop.

The driver nods, as the alternative would be to let her attempt to retrieve her luggage from a moving Toyota. It takes a good five minutes before he deems it appropriate to ask the old woman exactly what they are waiting for.

"Staff, obviously," she sighs. When this is reciprocated with an even louder sigh, she instructs the man to get out of his cab and ring the bloody bell.

From a tired but clearly once expensive handbag, the woman produces a trusty compact and proceeds to repair whatever damage the disquieting train ride from London and a car journey down pitifully neglected country lanes has inflicted. Taking an objective gaze at the reflected image before her, she has to concede that she is still a fine-looking woman, despite a life of indescribable torments equal to those suffered by any of the characters she has played, Cleopatra and Hedda included. But ah, the triumphs. These are what she clings onto; these are what make life bearable, hers a show that must go on.

When the huge face suddenly smudges itself against her window, or this is how it seems, she wonders for a moment whether this patently notable life might be in peril of premature truncation. The inquisitive apparition must indeed be the recently sighted tap dancer, a conclusion confirmed by the

4

bobbing head that indicates his lower limbs are still dancing happily, even as his brain attempts to recognise the new arrival.

She waves away his puzzlement and hopefully his person with an elegant, albeit regrettably veined and liver-spotted hand. This intruder – who can perhaps be forgiven for not recognising her, as she concludes he is clearly demented – smiles exceedingly warmly and continues to buck-and-wing his way round the side of the great house and out of view.

Turning her attention back to the cab driver, she notices with some disgruntlement that he is still alternately knocking on the door and yanking the stiff metal bell chain on the adjoining wall. A bronze plaque nearby reads 'Dustingford Hall', as if no further description is necessary. Which, for most of those likely to come here, is probably the case.

"The buggers must be out," he calls back to her.

Before she has time to respond to this absurdity, although she doubts right this moment whether she even has the energy, the man resolves to kick open the heavy door, return swiftly to his cab and remove one grumpy, time-wasting passenger, along with her bootful of luggage.

Remembering to retrieve her walking stick from the seat beside her but choosing to collapse it in one deft movement, as soon as it has served its purpose in assisting a reasonably poised debarkation, the woman, who is quite tall and only slightly stooped, gives one of her best strides as she makes her painful way to the door.

The cab driver would be quite content to dump her three well-travelled, matching suitcases on the threshold and take his leave, but one look from his passenger tells him that he can whistle for a bloody tip if this is his attitude. So, he hoists them up again from a pitted stone doorstep that appears permanently moist. Wondering for a moment how the old woman could have managed on the train with such a cumbersome load, he shuffles his way into the unwelcoming darkness.

Had its lighting been a touch more generous, the Dustingford Hall entrance lobby might almost be considered festive, abounding as it is in a variety of sumptuous reds. On walls, carpeting and a profusion of solidly, if not exactly recently, reupholstered Edwardian chairs. Today's visitor, however, can just about make out the inexpensively framed and mostly monochromatic photos of several smiling dead people that apparently pass as decoration, testimonials to the indisputable fact that once a resident has spent time in Dustingford, they would never stay anywhere else.

Noticing a small and rather discreet desk, perched below a montage of persons she barely recognises, the visitor looks around for a bell to smack. Her attention is caught by a small, stooped figure some distance away, walking painfully slowly with the aid of a Zimmer frame towards a waiting lift.

"Dear God!" mutters the observer. She turns to check whether the driver is equally appalled but finds him staring only at her.

"Sixteen pounds fifty," he says. "Sorry, I'm right out of change."

"Fortunately, I have plenty," says the woman, dipping into her purse and handing the man the exact fair. When he continues to stare, she turns away and attempts to recognise some of the nonentities on the nearest wall. She barely registers the thuds as her suitcases hit the ground and the front door is bashed open, as her mind has moved firmly on.

Now that she is certain she is quite alone, the woman allows herself a slump. It is as if all her bones are settling back into the default state of her own weary and well-worn body, the way a body itself sinks into an old, hollowed-out mattress on which it has slept for decades. She resolves, as these bones creak, to ensure that the mattress with which they provide her today is good and firm, as she has no intention of sinking any farther.

Were the dozens of characterful (and supporting characterful) eyes that beam out so hopefully, yet unblinkingly, from the walls, in the undying hope of prospective new audiences, suddenly to cast themselves down onto this newcomer – whom they might expect in due course to be joining their posthumous ranks – they would witness a less than imposing figure, somewhat scared and alone yet not wholly without its trademark defiance.

"*Miss Quest?*" enquires a voice from a newly opened doorway.

The addressee gains at least two vertical inches as she swivels majestically to face the tardy arrival. "Obviously," she responds.

The man, whose age would give him away as 'staff', even if his conventionally smart, chain store suit might not, offers what she assumes in his world could pass as a smile (although it would only fully register as such in the tightest of close-ups.) With his gaunt face and tall, slim build, he has what one would, at first, take as a military bearing but might subsequently revise to simply having a broom up his arse. Even his hair seems tight. The thin moustache, above equally thin, taut lips and below frowningly narrow eyes of an undistinguished grey, appears to have been cultivated in the hope it might give the otherwise bland and sallow face some character. To the older woman, who has known some fine moustaches in her time, it looks as if its previous home has been a pound store Christmas cracker.

"I'm Gavin Silk." She nods, awaiting amplification. "Director. But not quite in your sense. Ha." She nods again. "I'm very glad – *we* are very glad – that you have decided to reside with us at Dustingford Hall."

At this point, Elspeth Quest – *the* Elspeth Quest, for this is indeed the name adopted many decades ago by Dustingford Hall's newest resident – notices an elderly couple assisting each other down the main staircase. It is as if they are roped together and are only just managing to avoid a potentially catastrophic topple into a bottomless crevice. A descent made all the more precarious by their thickly bespectacled eyes veering away from the crucial steps to gaze quizzically, and with forgivable excitement, in the newcomer's direction.

"I have not *decided to stay*," she corrects the man overloudly. "I'm just here while my place in London is being *underpinned*."

Gavin Silk appears momentarily confused. He is normally on top of these things. Before he can take the matter further, a young man, dressed crisply in a white shirt and tight black trousers, skips down the stairs past the struggling couple.

"Traffic jam! Excuse me, Mr B, Mrs B," he says, in what must clearly be a local accent, smiling warmly at them. "Beep beep!"

"Ah, Jason," says Silk, "just in time." He snaps his fingers towards the suitcases. "This is Miss Quest."

"Welcome to Dusty Hall, Miss Q," says Jason, beaming at the new arrival as he lifts all three bags as if they are filled only with memories. "I'll take you to the 'Quest' Room."

Elspeth Quest finds herself relaxing slightly at this first unexpected sign of warmth, despite the overfamiliarity, until she remembers where she is and swiftly resumes her disdain.

"Just take the bags, Jason," grunts his boss, who has had no such hiatus. "Room sixteen."

Gavin Silk now segues into his customary and distinctly cursory 'introductory tour', which involves little more than his pivoting on his shiny Clarks, with a long, bony arm outstretched. She notices that the man's shirt cuffs are slightly frayed, which doesn't surprise her in the least.

"It used to belong to the de Courcey family," he intones, in a bored voice. "I imagine they used less red. We are, as you know, a fully staffed residential home. You'll be introduced to our dedicated and highly experienced care team in due course. We do, as you may also know, have a sister *nursing* home in an adjoining county, which caters for those in your profession who are unfortunately more infirm, physically and/or mentally, and less able to stroll around and enjoy our well-maintained house and grounds and all the many pleasures Dustingford has to offer, such as crochet classes and geriatric yoga. They also have a rather impressive, but sadly unappreciated, dementia wing. Shall we—"

He is interrupted in this oft repeated and robotically delivered introduction by a sudden clattering. They turn towards the adjacent lift as the doors grind open and a small, coughing figure emerges unsteadily, its face and phlegm completely obscured by what appears at first, and on subsequent confirmatory glances, to be a large, wooden owl.

"Dear God!" exclaims Elspeth Quest. Not for the first time and unlikely to be the last.

Silk appears unfazed. In fact, he seems quite relieved. "Ah, Mr Dodds. And how are you today?"

The owl bearer waddles over to Silk and this new arrival. "Couldn't be fitter, Mr Silk," he announces from his obscurity. "Couldn't be fitter."

The man, who is noticeably smaller than the director, is also considerably older. Elspeth would put him at around the eighty mark, old enough to know better than to walk around with a ridiculous wooden bird on his hand. Especially one that, like its bearer, has clearly seen sprucer days. Although, she would have to admit that, with its intricately carved feathers and expressively sad but thoughtful eyes, it is a beautifully handcrafted specimen of something that really didn't need crafting in the first place.

The owner of the owl, this Mr Dodds, appears to be waiting rather anxiously for something. After what seems to Elspeth like a lifetime, the younger man sighs deeply, as if in defeat, and says, "And how *is* Mr Chips?"

On cue, the wooden bird opens its mouth unnaturally wide, swivels its huge green eyes in their sockets and begins to cough quite violently. When this subsides, which can't be soon enough for Elspeth Quest, the creature appears to talk.

"I've not been well," it confesses, in a croakily high-pitched and strangely unlocatable regional accent.

Elspeth – who knows a catchphrase when she hears one, even if she despises them – is silently quantifying the exact pointlessness of ventriloquists and her own misfortune in being anywhere near one, when the bird suddenly utters a disturbingly loud neighing sound. Even the moustached block of ice beside her gives a perceptible start. Before either of them can comment, the elderly vent does it for them.

"Now what was *that* all about, Mr Chips?" says Cyril Dodds.

The owl head slowly turns, and the eyes shift upwards towards their inquisitor. "I think I'm a little horse!" At this, the mouth opens wider, and the eyes actually appear to smile. "*Hotcha!*" exclaims the owl triumphantly, giving what has to be its definitive laugh.

The elderly performer is smiling too, in apparently selfless amusement, until he notices the look of undisguised contempt on the face of the newcomer. His new expression reveals to Elspeth that this strange little man has clearly recognised her, which only makes his aberrations even more unforgivable. What Gavin Silk suggests next, as Elspeth herself might say and most probably will in time, is simply piling Pelion upon Ossa.

"Mr Dodds, would… the two of you… care to show our new resident around? Whilst I take care of the necessary paperwork?"

"We would be honoured, Mr Silk."

"I would prefer to do it after I've inspected my room," protests Elspeth.

"Your room isn't ready yet," says Silk, a touch snappily, in Elspeth's opinion. "You *are* rather early. And I assure you," he adds, "it won't need 'inspecting.'"

Elspeth swiftly makes the decision to offer this impudent nonentity one of her famous withering stares, rather than a verbal put-down. The effect of this, however, is diminished by an uncomfortable pecking on her arm, causing her eyes to shift focus and her nearest hand to smack the repellent wooden creature's beak firmly shut.

Undaunted, Mr Dodds beckons her onwards. "Walk this way, Elspeth… 'if I walked this way…', you know the rest! Ha ha!"

If there is one thing Elspeth Quest loathes more than ageing ventriloquists, it is people who laugh at their own jokes. It is for the audience, in her informed opinion, to make such judgment. Currently, she is that audience and she is not laughing. Yet, she is obliged to concede that right now – with the smarmy 'director' disappearing at some speed back into his office, and the layout of Dustingford Hall still a mystery – she has little choice other than to follow the small man and his wretched wooden excrescence.

Elspeth wonders yet again how it has come to this. That she, once beloved of thousands, should feel so utterly alone.

Of course, she has been alone before, over many years and in many places, but at least she had some choice as to the how and with whom.

Taking a breath that sounds very like another of this morning's portfolio of sighs, she once again summons up Doctor Theatre – that unpaid and invisible miracle worker, that Mother Teresa amongst healers – who has seen her through fever, fractures, Delhi belly and even breaking waters, with full houses and often even fellow performers totally oblivious.

Permission granted for the little homunculus to conduct her down a long and disturbingly clinical corridor, towards whatever horrors lurk within.

scene two

Following has never come easily to Elspeth Quest.

Even as a child, she was more accustomed to leading, whether it was her school friends into trouble or her ill-chosen parents to distraction and dreams of a mercifully early grave. She thinks of her father now, as she watches the bobbly-cardiganed back of her annoyingly perky escort.

Were he here – and admittedly, he would be around 108 – her old man would undoubtedly tell her that he had always known she would end up like this. The acclaim, the awards, the celebrity would mean nothing to him. He did, in fact, live long enough to taste them and they remained bitter on his tongue. As an electrician himself, one might have assumed he would at least have been impressed with all that theatrical lighting, but this was not to be. Someone once remarked to Elspeth that there are folk in this world who would rather be right than happy. She had always felt that this described her father to a T. Although, she still occasionally wonders why this person bothered mentioning such people to her.

Elspeth realises that pairs of eyes are staring at her. And not just dead ones. As Dustingford residents make their painfully slow way along the corridor, mostly in the opposite direction, they pause briefly – although, at this velocity, a pause hardly merits the descriptor – to nod in greeting and in wonder.

Mr Dodds, of course, knows them all.

"Nice enough day, Henry, although wise move with that woolly scarf … see the old foot is moving better now, Noreen." He turns back to Elspeth. "The wonderful thing about this place, Elspeth, is that you can ask folk *how* they are, but you don't need to ask 'em *who* they are!"

Elspeth would dispute this with every fibre of her being, if indeed she could be bothered. A further sigh will do for the time being.

"To the Green Room," cries Cyril Dodds. "And don't spare the horses!" adds Mr Chips.

"What fresh hell is this?" mutters Elspeth Quest, as they round a final corner.

*

The Green Room is, of course, totally red.

Elspeth Quest has known more Green Rooms, those backstage waiting and lounging areas in theatres and studios, than she could possibly count, yet the fingers of one expressive hand would cover those which might literally fit the description. She has no idea where the term originated. Vowing to herself that she will one day look it up, she realises this is simply the latest item – and hardly the most important – on a vast list of things she must one day do but now knows with some certainty that she never will.

"*Da da!*" yelps Cyril Dodds, by way of announcement.

The room itself – whilst accommodatingly spacious and high-ceilinged, with decorative moulding, cornices and non-slip rugs in all the right places – has clearly seen better days. Perhaps in keeping with its clientele, the first impression it gives is of an ingrained tiredness. Scattered around, like some sort of museum retrospective, are a selection of worn, but most probably still comfortable, armchairs drafted in from various eras, some cleverly propped with a selection of very still and almost lifelike old people. Random occasional tables are piled high with recent newspapers and well-thumbed copies of *The Stage*. Teacups abound, and built into a wall is the obligatory and massive smart TV.

Against the other walls are a well-stocked, but currently firmly shuttered, bar and several huge, free-standing mahogany bookshelves. These are filled floor to ceiling with volumes pertaining to that special industry in which all the residents once found themselves and to some extent are convinced they still reside. An old, upright piano leans against a wall, with a less than upright pianist sitting on the accompanying stool, frozen in place like a calcified figure from Pompeii, as if poised forever in pre-performance mode.

At the rear of this central hub is a sizeable glass conservatory, leading to a wide, neatly paved terrace. Beyond it, down some judiciously railed steps, is a well tended and imaginatively planted garden, where wooden 'in memoriam' benches abound like shrubs, alongside the occasional figure smoking themselves to death.

Whilst the piano might be silent, the room – despite hosting these several motionless occupants – is actually slightly less so. There are elderly residents quietly, or not so quietly, reading, whilst others chat, play cards or chess and occasionally hum songs to themselves that they might even at one time have made briefly famous. Despite the more obvious differences and degrees of mobility, there is a distinct homogeneity here, lacking perhaps in other such establishments, in that the guests all spring from the same (or at least similar) rarified pools. Pools they will happily wade back into, if only nostalgically, at the drop of a stick.

Elspeth, of course, assesses this in an instant yet finds it remarkably dispiriting. Especially when, one by one, the room's occupants, distracted by the old ventriloquist's noisy entrance, turn somewhat creakily to inspect the newcomer.

"This is what you might call our inner sanctum," explains her unwanted guide.

"Inner rectum more like," adds Mr Chips. "Who goes there – friend or enema?"

Elspeth Quest finds herself turning to address the wooden owl directly. "Could you possibly just shut the fuck up for one blessed second?" she snaps, quietly but firmly, then realises what she just did.

"You heard the lady," says an almost gratified Cyril Dodds, as the owl recoils and theatrically snaps shut its chastened beak. "Play dumb!"

Without waiting for some further insult, the elderly man turns to address a potentially less hostile crowd. "Ladies and gentlefolk, may I have your *attenzione* please! We have a brand-new arrival in our midst. A legend in her own lunchtime, no less. So, let us all give a hearty Dusty Hall welcome to Dame Elspeth Quest!"

As the assembled company begin gently and courteously to applaud the newcomer, 'hearty' clearly proving too onerous a note, Elspeth feels obliged to correct her erstwhile host. "I'm *not* a dame," she whispers, with a smile that can't quite conceal a hint of absolutely justifiable bitterness.

"*Not a dame?*" says Cyril Dodds, in unnecessarily loud surprise. "Are you sure? Sometimes we forget, you know… okay. Sorry peeps, the lady is not a dame. But there's still nothing like her!"

Elspeth, who can't recall when she last felt quite so mortified, although early Stratford rep and quotes from the wrong Shakespeare spring hazily to mind, decides that her best move is stage left towards a vacant armchair, in which she can hopefully sink and sink, until all that remains is the odd strand of thinning grey hair.

She has hardly made this descent, which is less embracing of her brittle bones than she might have wished, when she hears her name spoken in an unexpectedly robust, yet patently surprised, greeting.

"*Elspeth?*"

Elspeth shifts uncomfortably in her chair to stare upwards at the occupant of a far less yielding piece of furniture. The woman, clearly of a similar age although perhaps less worn, is smiling warmly down at her. Her small, round face is quite still, but her agile hands are moving at incredible speed as she continues to knit an object which, to her observer, could be anything from a very large scarf to a very small mobile home.

When there is clearly not the slightest hint of recognition emanating from the person whose name she has just spoken, this kindly looking lady appears perfectly sanguine at having to jog a long-buried memory.

"It's me, Diana," she says. Confronted with equal if not greater blankness, the woman amplifies. "Appleyard. Diana Appleyard? Your understudy?"

"I *never* missed a performance!" responds Elspeth instantly, for the benefit of anyone who might be in earshot and not totally deaf.

"No. I know," says the understudy, with just the slightest tinge of regret. And she would indeed have to be saintly not to bristle at the infinitely more famous woman's subsequent observation.

"Didn't know they let understudies in here," mutters the star.

"I did do some good work, out of town," says Diana Appleyard, silently berating herself for feeling obliged to make a stand.

Cyril Dodds, whose hearing is as unimpaired as his curiosity, offers up the simple, qualifying rule for Dustingford eligibility. "One proof of professional performance is all you need, Elspeth. We don't have to audition to play our part here."

More's the pity, thinks Elspeth, looking around at the staring faces, but wisely, she reserves this thought as subtext.

"Even if they said your delivery was a bit wooden," adds Mr Chips, who clearly couldn't resist. "*Hotcha!*"

Elspeth feels her hand being taken gently by a slightly warmer one. As her arm begins to rise, she looks with some bewilderment into the still sparkly blue eyes of her erstwhile understudy.

"I believe there are some people here you *will* recognise," says Diana Appleyard, easing her upwards.

Elspeth, whose radar for malign inflection is notoriously acute, can detect nothing other than genuine thoughtfulness in the other woman's tone. And so, she deigns to be guided towards a trio of gentlemen propping up the firmly closed bar. They look as if they are patiently awaiting opening hours and have formed the exact same tableau since closing time the previous evening.

"Now here's somebody I'm sure you know," beams Diana. "Gerard Bunting?"

The elderly man – although locally there is a total absence of men not fitting this description – has character written all over him. In other circles, this might be considered a compliment. In Elspeth's world, this simply means you would never find him playing the lead. He is of medium height and seriously rotund, with the ruddy countenance and Falstaffian belly of an A-list drinker. He smiles at Elspeth, as if at an old friend. Elspeth, who thinks she may have had words with him as a stationmaster or small-town mayor, isn't going to go through the same rigmarole again.

"Er... yes, of course," she says, with what she hopes is a knowing smile. "Hello, Gerald."

"Gerard. Savile Theatre, love. *Hay Fever.* No longer there, sadly."

"Aren't you, darling? Well, it happens to us all."

"I meant the theatre."

Diana drags her former colleague – who does indeed now recognise the hardly unknown actor and is vaguely perturbed that she hadn't – a few inches along the bar towards a cadaverous gentleman with a walking aid. But Elspeth can stand this torture no longer. What's more, the excessive heat in the room, clearly on max to preserve the health of the inmates, is causing her to fear that she might simply pass out and be accidentally stamped upon by an errant surgical boot.

"Would you mind, dear, if I took a peek at your lovely garden?"

"We'll come with you," says Cyril Dodds, who seems to be bloody everywhere.

"*No!* Thank you. That's quite alright." She looks the wooden owl straight in its bulging eyes. "*Stay!*" she commands.

And now she walks, with as much dignity as she can muster, through the crowded room. Residents shuffle awkwardly to the sides, as if at a parting of the red Axminster.

A passing member of staff, bearing a tea tray, observes her making her break towards the conservatory and freedom. "Are you alright there, love?" asks the woman, with a concerned smile.

"I can still bloody exit," says Elspeth Quest, MBE, pushing open both glass doors. Yet she just manages to overhear her former understudy at the bar, attempting indulgently to smooth things over.

"It's always difficult at first," says Diana Appleyard.

"She was like this in 1973," mutters Gerard Bunting.

scene three

Bedroom sixteen, which is on the side of the old house farthest from the sea and has an unimpeded view of the car park, could best be described as functional.

The most colourful items in the room are the swanky old suitcases Jason has just lugged in and set down beside the single bed.

The deep red of the floor below, which dominates to the point of overwhelming, is nowhere to be seen. The walls and fabrics here are of a pale blue, perhaps to reflect the coastal location, whilst the furniture – a stained beech wardrobe, an easyish chair, a mirrored dressing table, a small chest of drawers – are an attempt to keep the feeling light and welcoming. As are the neatly framed Turner greatest hits prints hammered into the largest wall, just above the small television set. The fact that they all fail miserably is simply because no bulk-bought and uniform items can hope to replicate the individually tailored warmth and comfort of home, so there is almost no point in trying. The management relies on its clientele to assist them in making the accommodation more personal, without of course hammering any new holes in the walls.

Yet the room is spotlessly clean – or soon will be – and perfectly well-aired. As Jason has been heard to say to one of his colleagues, these may not be bedrooms to die for, but they're just the job to die in.

This is the thought that goes through the head of the tense young woman in the crisp, light grey uniform, as she completes the final dusting. She gives one last whisk to the naked surface of a dressing table that she imagines will soon be totally trashed with powders, paints, brushes and more face stuff than you can shake a lipstick at. Having never worked at other residential homes, she can't swear that this lot use more make-up than normal folk, but she's still bloody certain that they do. Even some of the men, bless them.

The young employee, who still looks like a teenager but knows that she isn't, catches her reflection in the mirror as she wipes away a last stubborn smudge. She would never admit that above the trimly unfetching and neatly ironed uniform is a face that smacks of danger. Yet even she can detect a wildness in the darting blue-green eyes, almost overshadowed today by sooty Gothic mascara. And rebellion in the spiky jet black hair that looks like it, too, came from a cheap bottle but she knows is all her own. The darkness where the morning's eyeshadow ends, accentuated by her otherwise pale skin, is equally natural but less alluring. She has, in fact, been offered several generous suggestions from the older folk downstairs as to how she might minimise this. Longer sleep being amongst the more sensible options.

She has no idea, as yet, who will be occupying this room, nor of course for how long, but she hopes that the person will be kind, despite their circumstances. She does understand that, for many of them, this is so far from the place they want to be. It is a sentiment with which she finds some sympathy, but you just have to make the best of it, don't you? Until you find your own way through.

She stares out of the small window, as if searching for something she can't articulate. It probably isn't the ambulance that she can now see trundling up the drive.

A knock on the door sets her dusting with heightened rigor. "Come in," she says.

The stocky man slips in through a small gap and swiftly closes the door behind him but not before checking that the corridor is empty and his entry unnoticed. He appears slightly too young and robust for a resident, yet possibly a good few years older than one might envisage a member of staff.

"Hello, petal," he smiles. The accent is from way north-east of here, unsullied by the softer south.

"Hi, Stanley," says the young woman, downing her cloth, her taut face softening in the glow of his.

The weathered visitor looks around, as if watchers might be hiding under the carefully made bed. "All quiet on the western front?"

Another of his myriad expressions she can't quite unravel but sort of understands. "New one's still down there," she says, pointing to the floor. "Who's the ambulance for?"

"Old Mrs Turks. You know, the one who juggles. Well, did. She seemed perfectly fine until a few days ago. All her balls in the air. Funny how they…" He doesn't finish and the girl notices a brief spasm of sadness in his leathery face and crinkled, smiley eyes, which she knows isn't just for the juggling grandma. Yet barely two seconds later, the same eyes are twinkling again and a mischievous look takes over. "Let's go for it, then."

He rips open his old tweed jacket with an almost theatrical flourish, like Clark Kent on a mission. Around his waist is a well-worn canvas toolbelt. Sharing pockets incongruously with the impressive array of seasoned chisels and spanners, are an iPod Touch and two tiny speakers. He sets these up on the small chest of drawers.

"Borrowed 'em off my grandson," he explains. "You should hear the bloody noise that comes out." To prove the point, he touches the screen exactly where he has been instructed. The sound of electronic dance music is ear-splitting. "Off you go, Lisa, pet."

The young woman gives him a grateful peck on the stubble and opens the door. Checking there is still no one patrolling or prowling or hobbling, she swiftly nips out.

Stanley smiles and picks up the discarded duster.

*

It takes a few anxious, corridor-hovering moments before next door's aged occupant acknowledges the knock and bids Lisa enter bedroom eighteen.

The contrast between the two adjoining rooms could hardly be starker, nor this particular chamber, glimpsed through the gently opening doorway, less so. Posters, photographs, framed sheet music and playbills from three continents splatter the walls, until barely a patch of sea-blue or mass-produced Turner can be glimpsed. Being a corner room, it is far grander than its neighbour, with a second, smaller window framing the sea below, as it sweeps with the strutting élan of a prima donna around the adjacent bay.

In a wheelchair, staring haughtily out over the dewy lawn towards the cliffs, is a once tall and still hugely imposing woman in her mid-eighties. Instantly recognisable from the multiple representations of her decking her room like wallpaper, this striking, hazel-eyed figure of, in her day, unfashionably mixed parentage, is still clearly every lined and wrinkled inch a star.

The music thumping out from next door sounds as if it is attempting, Joshua-like, to bring the party wall tumbling down.

"Hardly Noel Coward, is it?" says the woman, in a voice so deep it could be that of a man.

"Hardly," agrees her young visitor. "Who's Noel...?"

"We don't have time for that," mutters the resident, waving the notion away with a dark, heavily ringed hand, as she swings

22

her carriage around. For the first time, she looks up at the anxious young woman, her expression stern. "Now, what do you have for me?"

Lisa moves further into the room, towards the slightly shrivelled but still seriously intimidating legend. She tells herself that she has to radiate confidence, stand fearlessly proud. Yet she finds it so hard to address this mesmerising, clearly once beautiful face, with the reddest lips she has ever seen, made-up today, as every day, as if the curtain is just about to rise once more.

Finally, the young woman mumbles something and is harshly instructed to speak up or get back to the other room. The old lady doesn't mention that her hearing is not all that it was. It is none of the girl's business and admitting it only makes it true.

"It's one I wrote myself, Miss Marguerite. It's called 'Sand.'"

"How appropriate. Come closer, girl. I need to hear you above that fuckin' din."

Lisa had thought that, after a few months of working in Dustingford, she would grow quite accustomed to old people swearing. It is hardly as if any of the words so freely and lavishly deployed here are strangers to her own vocabulary. Yet it still feels disquieting and wrong, like a vicar wearing a Black Sabbath T-shirt. She tells herself that there is absolutely no logic to this, as she knows that she is unlikely to stop using the 'f' and 'c' words in her own eighties. But then she reminds herself that she has serious doubts she will ever reach the heady days of octogenarian cursing. There was even a time… her mind is wandering. *Concentrate*, Lisa!

The young woman moves close enough to the old lady to smell the by now familiar blend of lavender, Max Factor and the sadly inevitable rot of age – each constituent more than a little overplayed.

Lisa knows she mustn't blare so loudly that she forgoes any

sweetness in her voice, throaty as it already is by nature and – if she is totally honest – by nicotine, but the pounding through the walls, whilst unfortunately essential, is hardly her backing of choice. Yet when she finally does sing, it is with an appealing huskiness that still manages to embrace some distinctive purity of tone. Like crusty pastry around a temptingly sugary core.

"*Sand,*" she sings, "*loving you is like sand. You slip through my fingers, you don't leave a trace. You'll say that you'll stay, but you just wash away. Like sand... sand...*"

The old lady says nothing. She simply raises a hand sheathed in rings and Lisa knows immediately to stop. She stands there, barely able to look at the figure in the wheelchair, as if she has suddenly been stripped naked and has no idea what part of herself to cover first.

"Voice improvin' marginally," says the star, once known only as Marguerite. "Breathin' still problematic. Song execrable."

Lisa brightens, her face flushed with relief. "Oh, I'm so glad you like it, Miss Marguerite. It just came to me. In my sleep. Not that I sleep that much."

"Obviously."

Lisa feels like she is on a roll. The words tumble out of her, perhaps in a hurry to arrive before something else more troublesome comes along. "I'm trying for a sort of timeless Taylor Swift/Nora Jones type vibe. Er thing."

"And I'm tryin', with little apparent success, for a Lisa type thing. Now sing it once again. And this time, girl, hear it with your heart, not just with whatever is in your bloody head."

As Lisa, who had thought that she was doing all this teacher is demanding of her – and more – prepares doggedly for that definitive rendition – the one that will, who knows, elicit a nod or even a smile from the scarily stern legend – she hears the door of neighbouring, and still unoccupied, room sixteen fly open. The thumping electronic dance music immediately subsides.

Through the walls, Lisa can hear the conversation. She is

pretty sure, by the look on the older woman's face, that despite everything, the ears still remain her least swiftly decaying feature.

"*What do you think you are doing?*" splutters Gavin Silk, who Lisa guesses is glaring not at Stanley but at the speakers.

"Just securing the old curtain rail, *MR SILK*," explains Stanley, at a volume sufficient to give next door a clear heads-up. "Want it to look nice for your new guest."

"That didn't sound like your sort of music."

"I'm a man of hidden shallows."

Even Marguerite has to grunt at this as the two women stare towards the wall.

"*Where's Lisa?*"

The women have no idea whether the handyman (and co-conspirator) is shrugging or pointing. But Marguerite swiftly hands Lisa a silver-backed hairbrush from the nearby dressing table.

They don't have long to wait.

"*You're meant to be attending to number sixteen!*" says the infuriated director, as he stands in the doorway, taking in the Renoiresque scene before him.

"She was helpin' me, Mr Silk," explains Marguerite, in an unraised voice that even Lisa finds scary. "You do know that I need extra assistance these days."

"I do, Miss Marguerite. And there are people here to give this to you." He looks at Lisa, who begins to scratch her arms almost uncontrollably. "*Qualified* people." She forces herself to desist and, with a nod to her employer and barely a glance at the room's occupant, walks out into the corridor.

Marguerite sighs. "You really should be a little easier on her."

"Do you have children, Miss Marguerite?" enquires the man.

"You know I haven't."

"Then kindly don't advise me on how to deal with mine."

scene four

In the distance, the tap dancer is still in his own special world.

His routine appears, to her admittedly inexpert eye, unchanged, but the stark backdrop of chalky cliffs and a sea that seems constantly to rage adds an extra precariousness to the scene. Yet not sufficient to hold her full attention, as she stands on the expansive and admittedly well-tended terrace.

It might add spice to some people's life, but Elspeth Quest has always hated Variety. Smacking of 'show business' with all its superficial, mass-appeal gloss, this quite categorically is not the business or, more accurately, vocation, she has always been so proud to call her own. She has as much in common with a tap dancer or ventriloquist as with the Rumanian cleaning lady who, so many months ago, she had to lay off. This place in which she has now so cruelly found herself – and is in imminent danger of losing herself – only confirms her distaste for that world and how astute she has been all these years to afford it only the narrowest of berths.

"Soft, what light from yonder window breaks?"

Elspeth stays on the terrace, rooted for a moment in shock, then composes herself and slowly turns her head just slightly round, as if waiting for the speaker to walk into frame. She knows this voice. Has always known this voice.

"I thought it was you," says the man, approaching slowly.

The once luxuriant blond hair still abounds, although now unsurprisingly pure white. Posture remains remarkably sound, considering. Of course, he was always tall, so even the loss of an inch or two would not detract too onerously from so regal a bearing. Nor indeed does a small but noticeable paunch. The presence, despite the simple and inevitable erosion of time, is still formidable. And there remain those wonderful, glinting, and only slightly faded, teeth.

"Hello, Rex," says Elspeth, offering the gift of a very slight smile. She is not going to admit that it is good to see him, although it is so good to see him.

"I had no idea you were coming here, darling."

"Don't they give you a cast list? How remiss of them. Anyway, I haven't 'come here'. I'm just… passing through."

"Ah," nods the elderly actor, in genuine sympathy. "Respite care. I'm so sorry, Elspeth, have you been poorly?"

"I am never poorly." She stares at him for a moment. *How well I know that basilisk stare*, he thinks, and not just from stage and screen. "Have you… been ill?" she enquires.

The man suddenly leaps, with surprising élan, onto a low brick boundary protecting a flower bed brimming with cyclamen and winter aconites. Adopting a swashbuckler pose, invisible rapier outstretched, he gives one of his best Rupert of Hentzau scoffs. "Rex Markham – invincible hero of two dozen seminal, oft repeated but seldom surpassed action movies?" After a moment, as if the stills photographer has given his all-clear, a sadness comes over the elderly man and he steps a tad more gingerly down from his battlement. "Plumbing isn't all that it was," he shrugs. "Truth be told, love, rather lucky to be here at all."

"Oh, poor Rex," tuts Elspeth. "And you were once so renowned… for your plumbing."

The silence between them is on the cusp of discomfort, each wanting to ask so much of the other that neither knows where to begin, when a tall, silver-greying lady in a warm down jacket strolls round a corner of the building. On seeing the pair, she pauses, as if uncertain whether to intrude. Yet almost immediately, this elderly newcomer's stare appears to switch focus to take in another equally grey and puffy presence approaching from the opposite direction. Rex graciously acknowledges them both with a polite nod, which they ignore, choosing instead to retreat around their respective corners and continue their journey elsewhere.

Elspeth Quest, who has observed this wordless playlet with an amusement quite absent from the day until now, stares at the remaining actor. "You are *not* telling me...?"

Rex nods resignedly. "Two ex-spouses on the same bill. How's that for blind casting? I hear they call them 'Rex's Exes'. Couldn't make it up, could you?"

"How very nostalgic for you."

"Gives being 'between wives' a whole new meaning. Thank God you're here, Elspeth."

"God had nothing to do with it. Unless he causes subsidence." Rex just stares at her. "My London place. Not my bones. Or my womb."

A young woman – little more than a girl, sparky in an off-centre way but with a curiously pale, ravaged look – calls Elspeth's name as she approaches.

"Miss Quest?"

"Yes?" challenges Elspeth, displeased by the baggy-eyed interruption.

"Er, your room's nice and ready now. I'm Lisa. If you'd like to—"

Elspeth gives the girl, and indeed the whole terrace, one of her best sighs. St Joan, Anne Boleyn and Mary Queen of Scots. The fates have ruled. "I suppose I must."

As she follows the girl, at a stately pace, she hears Rex call out, "Make sure it has a star on it."

Elspeth begins to turn back to him but then decides against it. So, she doesn't notice him remove a silver cigarette case from his jacket pocket, as he shakes his head in amused but not displeased wonder.

She does notice an old gentleman stooped over a Christmas rose bush. It is only as she passes that she realises he is addressing each of the flowers by the title of a song. 'Rose of Washington Square', 'Second Hand Rose'. She really wishes he wouldn't.

scene five

The room is every bit as shitty as she had expected it to be.

Admittedly, Elspeth's moving finger comes up free from dust when she pointedly writes it across the cheap dressing table and every other unit she can reach, but this is small comfort, having writ, when even a layering of grime might afford the place some character.

Lisa Silk watches patiently. This isn't the first time she has observed an old bugger inspect her and her colleagues' ill-paid handiwork. She supposes that she should feel something for people on their last staging post before death, and she does genuinely believe, despite everything, that she has the requisite quota of empathy, at least for the more kindly residents. She has a suspicion with this one, however, that even when she was as young as Lisa, the woman was no cheerleader for the congeniality team.

When she senses that just one more tut or sigh will have her grabbing for the only standing piece capable of braining an old woman – in this case a metal lamp from the local John Lewis – Lisa deems it prudent to move things on. "It doesn't have a sea view, but it's still very nice…"

"Why *exactly* don't I have a sea view?"

"Because the last person to die here didn't bloody have

one," is what Lisa feels like saying. Instead, she mollifies the old grump. "I'm sure when one comes up… anyway, once you set out all your little bits and pieces—"

"I'm *not* staying!" insists Elspeth Quest, which makes a wrong-footed Lisa Silk wonder why the hell the woman is making all this fuss in the first place.

"Oh. Sorry. I thought—"

"I'm not interested in what you thought." Elspeth Quest wanders around the room in a manner that nails for her audience exactly how little room there is in which to wander around. "Dear God, I've had bigger dressing rooms." To her delight, she finally finds a microscopic spec of dust on her smallest and least arthritic finger. "And cleaner ones."

"I just bloody cleaned it!" roars Lisa, who by this time has had all she can take of this – and most probably every – elderly actress. Currently resident, recently shrouded or still to roll up. Mindful of the precariousness of her own position, however, she instantly mellows. "Sorry… well, when you've unpacked your cases – in your own time, no rush at all – we'll take them and store them away for you. It'll feel a whole lot roomier – you'll see."

Elspeth sits on the bed and bounces gently. "Young lady, I am not a simpleton. Nor, perhaps unfortunately, am I deaf." She bounces some more. Lisa awaits the inevitable. "Far too soft."

"The last person was a big lady."

"Well, I need a hard mattress. For my back. I can tell you the optimum make if you wish."

When Lisa responds, it is in the very softest, lightest of tones.

"What did you say?" asks Elspeth.

"We can sort that out!" yells Lisa, because these days you have to grab your pleasures where you find them. When Elspeth can summon up no suitable response beyond a glare, Lisa makes for the door. "I hope you'll be very happy here, Miss Quest. For a while."

She leaves Elspeth staring at the standard lamp with

remarkably similar homicidal thoughts.

It is only when Lisa has skipped out of view that the latest resident of bedroom sixteen notices in the corridor a rather slight and fairly nondescript woman staring at her through the still open door, in what could only be interpreted as open-mouthed wonder.

This unabashed observer is most probably of a similar age to Elspeth Quest but wearing it as unremarkably as her dull, fawn jumper and thinning, sludge-grey trousers. Only the eyes appear to have any spark – they are as wide as an ostrich's and seem incapable of blinking. When Elspeth stares even more pointedly back, on her way to closing the door, the tiny woman scuttles away at a speed that quite impresses the new arrival.

As soon as she hears the door click shut, Elspeth Quest wishes that she had left it open. Yet to open it now would appear foolish even to her and perhaps exhibitionist to anyone who might be passing. But it is only when the room is completely her own that the situation in which she now finds herself feels unnervingly real.

She glances round at her suitcases, as if their presence might persuade her that she has just arrived somewhere wonderful on holiday, but even her unquestionable skills at transportation aren't up to this particular job. And she rarely goes somewhere wonderful on holiday. Well, perhaps once she did. In better days.

Elspeth grabs hold of the largest case and attempts to heave it onto the bed. She has managed to enlist the aid of people far younger and stronger all day and she simply can't do this anymore. So, she sets it gently back down with its fellows and shuffles somewhat creakily across the small room to the easy chair by the window.

As she sits, looking out at the few cars and straggly trees, Elspeth Quest wonders if a view of the sea would at least make things more palatable and whom exactly she might have to kill to attain one.

scene six

The diminutive and rather drab lady who had spotted Elspeth through the temporarily open gap in the doorway to room sixteen has managed to retain her incredible burst of speed all the way down the stairs and through the empty dining room to the terrace, save for a little sit-down in the lobby and just the briefest of naps.

Of course, the good, solid walking stick helps.

She can only pray that in one of the rapid successions of violent jabs she gives it for increased propulsion, she doesn't get the metal tip caught in the muddy gaps between flagstones. It has happened before, and she was lucky that it was only her former stick that had snapped beyond repair. But Zelda Gatley has always been a creature of impulse, impressionable and prone to over-excitement since her rather bleak Black Country childhood, and there is absolutely no mileage in changing now.

To her delight, she finds lovely Rex Markham on the terrace with veteran character actor Gerard Bunting and rather sweet but un-famous Diana Appleyard, adding steam and smoke to the salty late afternoon air. She doesn't notice, or perhaps chooses to ignore, the heavy sighs that appear to sink three sets of shoulders on her arrival.

"Have you *seen* who's here?" she squeals, in an energised

Midlands accent, tinged with just the vaguest hint of even less appealing antipodean. "Gerard, Rex, Diana, have you *heard*?"

"Elspeth Quest," says Gerard Bunting, who knows it would have been a kindness to let the excitable woman attain her climax but really doesn't have the energy.

"Oh," says Zelda Gatley, who has been hoping that the celeb in question had perhaps only recently arrived and gone straight up to her room unnoticed. Which, of course, had been poor Lotte Anstruther's room until last Tuesday, you know, that shrewish butcher's wife from the long-running soap, but mercifully, she came to a less bloody end in real life.

"*The barge she sat in, like a burnished throne, burnt on the water,*" says Rex.

"Yes… indeed," agrees Zelda. She assumes that this is a quote. At least she hopes it is.

"She did it at the Vic. I was offered Antony, you know, but I was giving my fearless French resistance fighter. In Budapest."

"Oh, yes, I saw that!" says Zelda, excitedly. "The film, I mean. Not the Vic thing – although, of course, I saw that, too. Twice!"

"Tell me, Zelda," asks Gerard Bunting, staring at the overly enthused woman, "did you ever work with Elspeth Quest?"

For a moment, Zelda Gatley appears rather flustered. But, of course, whilst the residents of Dustingford survive on memories, not all memories survive on them.

"Er…quite possibly, Mr Bunting. There've been so many, you know. One forgets. Yes, I'm sure I have." She can feel three pairs of eyes on her, expecting further amplification. "I was touring in Australia when she became – you know – big. I do hear she's rather tricky." She looks at Rex, who to be honest is never that hard to look at. Even now. "Have you and Miss Quest ever… er…?"

"Oh yes, Zelda. La Quest and I have 'er'-ed. First time was at Stratford. *Romeo and Juliet.* Our stars crossed."

Zelda had thought that by now she was totally familiar

with all the expressions that might pass across the wonderfully sculpted face of this ageing, but still so very handsome, romantic lead. Hasn't she been studying them for some time? But this current one is new to her. How might she describe it? Wistful? Sad, perhaps. Regretful. Whatever, she knows that she has touched on something, a matter she most definitely needs to probe and investigate further. But, as ever, with subtlety.

"Well, you know what they say? DCOL."

"DCOL?" repeats Diana Appleyard, who has felt rather out of this conversation and is still recalling her own, less entrancing, encounters with Elspeth Quest.

"Doesn't Count On Location," explains Zelda, as if to an idiot. "Or, in your case, Diana, I suppose – DC in DR – Dressing Rooms!"

"Don't let the exes hear that!" grunts Gerard Bunting.

"Oh! Oh no! Goodness!" laughs Zelda. "Well, must get ready for dinner. Chef told me he is doing his Cod Mornay tonight."

"Mornay's at seven, all's right with the world," says Rex.

"Er… yes," agrees Zelda with a knowing nod and scuttles off in cane-propelled urgency to find anyone who might not yet have heard about the new arrival.

"ARFA," says Gerard Bunting. The others stare, awaiting explanation. "All Right For Australia."

The others shrug and resume their smoking.

scene seven

Elspeth Quest has not moved from her chair.

Not even when one of the home's qualified carers popped in just to welcome her and assure her, in that perky yet concerned voice they all use, that they had been sent the complete works from her GP and she would be ever so well looked-after, pharmaceutically, emotionally and spiritually. Elspeth had played such a carer once, in an old B-picture, but she had turned out to be homicidal and ended up setting the home and herself on fire.

The sun is completely down. Of course, she hadn't been able to glimpse that much of what had promised to be a rather passable winter sunset, as the management had deliberately ignored her room specifications. So far as she can ascertain, the only excitement to be savoured from her particular viewpoint is the occasional ambulance and, judging from the wardrobe, the odd local funeral director. Although, in her opinion, having observed the nearby town on her drive here, everyone has the right to look funereal in this part of the world.

She wonders whether there are pre-ordained visiting times for friends or relatives, as in hospitals. In her case, of course, this is relatively academic, as she hasn't yet informed a soul as to her whereabouts nor does she intend to. The news will get around soon enough. She had thought of telling her agent, but she is not actually certain whether he still is her agent or indeed whether he is still alive. There was talk last year of a guest appearance in an episode of *Casualty*, but malicious mutterings of insurance and reliability had put paid to that.

Elspeth Quest has never been stupid or naïve. She knows that the real reason for her unemployment, when so many of her peers and inferiors are still in work, is because she falls under the blanket description of 'difficult'. As most directors these days are clearly about twelve years old and part of what she has heard referred to as the 'snowflake' generation, she has had to accept that her form of interrogating the text, insisting on full backstory for her character and occasionally rewriting her scenes is no longer acceptable. In her day, 'demanding' was considered a compliment rather than a stain. Although, perhaps her storming out of a meeting two years earlier shouting that in her next life she'll be coming back 'as a fucking, one-legged transexual from Namibia' might have been reported back to the kindergarten where such people gather.

It is as she is rewinding such thoughts, whilst simultaneously experiencing first rumbles of a hardly unexpected hunger, that she hears a jaunty whistling from the corridor. Elspeth Quest is not partial to jaunty at the best of times, so she is already primed for bile when her door swings open, and a large mattress appears to walk through.

"Who are you and why didn't you knock?" she addresses the object.

"Oh, sorry, love. Didn't see you in the dark. Miss Quist, isn't it?" says Stanley Grainger, poking a large but friendly head out beyond the edge of the mattress.

"No. It is not," she replies, wondering why the man, who is clearly no youngster himself, should be smiling at her like an idiot or like someone who believes that he is addressing an idiot and therefore has to go with the territory. "It is Quest, as you well know."

"Oh. Aye, you're not wrong. My apologies. Quest. I thought you'd be having your supper."

"Why should you think that?"

Stanley nudges the nearby light switch with his shoulder. "Throw a little light on the situation. There, that's better. Well, cos it's gone 7.00, love. Chef likes his residents to be regular... on time, I mean!" He smiles to himself. "Mind you, regular's good, too!" He pauses, as if awaiting a response. Elspeth knows about such pauses. And how you need to ride the laugh and continue just below the crest. But there is no crest, and she isn't laughing, so Stanley takes his cue and carries on. "Do you mind if I put this down, pet?"

He sets the new mattress on its side, with some relief. Resuming his whistle, he proceeds to strip the freshly made-up bed and remove its apparently flabby and now clearly unwanted accoutrement. His legs nudge the suitcases.

"Here, you haven't unpacked!"

Elspeth merely shrugs. This is not a conversation she needs to have and the man, far too old in her opinion to be lugging heavy mattresses, is not someone with whom she might wish to have it. What happened to the cocky youngster she first met in the lobby?

"Aye, well," continues Stanley, who is quite accustomed to his new residents being a touch overwhelmed and unresponsive, "no hurry, dear. You've got all the time in the world."

"Not necessarily," says Elspeth Quest.

"Oh, come on," he laughs, "you're a spring chicken compared to some of 'em."

"I meant that this... stay... isn't permanent. My house in London..."

She can sense that the man isn't listening, even though he is now obscured by her old and wanting mattress, which he proceeds with some deftness to shift into the corridor and set down against the opposite wall. On his return, as he is settling in the new bedfellow, he decides to chat.

"So, what line were you in, Miss Quest?"

"Line?" she says, ignoring the past tense.

"Singer, contortionist, magician's assistant? We've got 'em all here. Sadly, it's not looking too bright for our lady juggler. Elsie Turks. Nice woman. Seemed so well. We even had one of them performing midgets, lovely little chap, but I can see you're not—"

"Haven't you ever been to the theatre?" She wonders why she is bothering.

"Have I ever? *Who hasn't?* Panto with the kids, every year without fail. And now the grandkids, bless 'em." He looks at her and smiles. "Here, it's coming up again very soon, isn't it? Before you know it! Everyone loves a show at Christmas, don't they?" She feels the question doesn't merit an answer and the follow-up even less so. "You ever done panto, Miss Quest?"

Stanley happily fills the silence with his whistling and starts to refit the bedlinen. Elspeth finds herself observing the man's dexterity and the curious delicacy of his movements, even with hands that are clearly gnarled and broadened by years of physical work. She ponders on their cleanliness, then thinks how bored she must already be to pay attention to such mundanities. Especially as performed by so basic and unremarkable a person.

"Oh, and every year I take mesel' up to London for one of them musicals," he continues. "Have to take out another mortgage, mind, if you want to see the bloomin' stage." He laughs again. The man does appear unnecessarily cheerful. "So, you're a theatre actress then, pet?"

"I'm an actress. I go where the muse takes me."

"Oh aye. Telly. I should watch more, but there's always something better to do, isn't there? Maybe when I retire." He looks up from his work and shakes his head at her. She chooses not to react. "But I don't intend to do that neither. Not as long as they need me. Hey, that's a song, isn't it? From one of your shows." To her surprise but not enchantment, the man begins to sing 'As Long as He Needs Me'.

"I believe I *shall* go down to dinner," says Elspeth, rising from her chair.

"That's it," says Stanley, a huge grin widening his face and showing a set of uneven but strong northern teeth. "Usually works! Oh, and the name's Stanley. Stanley Grainger. I do hope you'll be happy here. The staff are very caring. Most of them. And if you want owt doing, Stan's your man. See, yours isn't the only business where you need a catchphrase!"

Elspeth sighs as she reaches down for her handbag. From her purse, she selects a pound coin and hands it to him.

Stanley looks at her as if for the first time. He gives her a smile, which is full of warmth yet tinged with a certain melancholy that even Elspeth picks up. "No need for that, petal," he says. "They pay me enough here."

"Please knock before you come in again," says Elspeth Quest, dropping the coin back into her purse.

"Will do. Now you enjoy your supper. Cod night tonight... and it's cod night from me!"

He stands aside, as Elspeth wraps her green woollen cardigan around herself like a protective shield and manoeuvres past him towards the door.

The moment she enters the corridor, she hears the cheery whistling resume. It trails her all the way to the lift.

scene eight

It is an accepted fact that the British Isles is host to a vast assortment of rest homes, many of them solidly respectable establishments, in which reasonably contented elderly residents enjoy nourishing, if not over-imaginative, meals in relative silence or quiet conversation, often lost in their own thoughts and unreliable recollections.

The staff at Dustingford Hall occasionally wish they worked in such a home.

The dining room in this particular venue is occupied entirely by veterans of stage, screen and variety hall, folk who interpret the term 'resting' in a particularly individual and vocation-specific manner, choosing to vie with each other in terms of credits and anecdotes, as if still simply waiting for that call which will inevitably change their lives.

The tables here are larger than one might find in other homes, as the more company-spirited, refectory-style units appear to suit the residents best. Ancient programmes and yellowing press cuttings are casually passed along crispish white tablecloths in the same sharing, reciprocal manner as condiments, whilst occasional bouts of sleight-of-hand and close-up magic are still practised with the dexterity one might employ to bone a fish. Perhaps sensibly, the interior designers have chosen to festoon the neutral walls with framed posters from bygone triumphs rather than images of residents who are simply bygone.

Rex Markham doesn't notice Elspeth Quest's arrival on the threshold of this large and bustling room. He is in mid-reminiscence and his companions know better than to interrupt him. Despite the chatter filling the air, the old actor's rich, distinctive baritone, quavering only slightly, appears to cut through, even though he is barely raising it above an acceptable level.

"They were going so badly these rehearsals – *Oedipus,* I think, not sure – but lovely Peter got the cast together and said, 'I want you all, one by one, to come onstage and say something – anything – that will really *terrify* me.'"

Elspeth immediately locates the still familiar voice and looks across the room towards the long table beside the French windows. She recognises that old understudy woman, Deborah Somebody (?), listening intently and believes she knows the solemn, cadaverous man seated next to her. Wasn't his name Jack, no, Jeremy? Jacob? Probably still is. She has no idea who some of the others might be and is not particularly interested.

"So, they each stepped forwards and they effed and they blinded and they screamed and threatened, all bulgy eyed and drooling lips – then it was Jonny's turn to be scary. So, he – Jonny – just saunters to the front of the stage, draws languidly on his ciggy and says…" At this point, Rex gives his definitive Gielgud. "'We open in two weeks!'"

The fellow diners, most of whom have already heard this story a good many times over the years and occasionally over this very table, still chuckle in appreciation. As if the constant regurgitation of corkers such as this are necessary contributors to that most essential and enlivening of pursuits – the continual reinforcement of how fortunate they all are to have been, and indeed to have survived, in this maddeningly gloriously precarious and unique business. A noble trade to which, at whatever level of fame and to whatever degree of ability, they have for several decades most assiduously devoted themselves.

So why, wonders Elspeth Quest, as she quietly takes in this particular tableau, this geriatric crowd scene, does a feeling of overwhelming sadness suddenly hit her, like a cruelly activated and over-harsh spotlight?

For a moment, she thinks that it must simply be because she is standing here, alone and unremarked in the doorway, observing a communal gathering at which she is currently a total outsider. Yet, as she has not the least desire to be an insider, she soon tells herself that there has to be something else going on. A tang, maybe of overcooked Cod Mornay and understated desperation, that she picks up with the sensitivity she is assured has forever been the very hallmark of her craft.

Or perhaps it *is* just her.

Elspeth Quest walks slowly and somewhat regally down the aisle between tables, ignoring the mumbles and mutterings, looking neither left nor right but towards the rear of the large room. Here she can see, drawn across the French windows, material of a rich but faded red velvet that instantly reminds her of her beloved theatre, yet which her cruel brain just as swiftly terms the 'final curtain'. A friendly voice beckons her, which is exactly the response she was going for.

"*Elspeth!*" calls Rex Markham. "We've saved you a place, darling."

"Plaice? Thought it was cod!" rasps a gravelly cockney voice from further along the table, which evokes appreciative laughter that the newcomer chooses to ignore.

As she sits herself down opposite him, Elspeth nods gratefully to her old Romeo, yet within the acknowledgement is a sense that she would have expected nothing less.

Before she has even fully settled, an elderly resident seated next to her, his mouth still partly filled with boiled potato, begins to address her in a voice she can only assume isn't his own but can't quite fathom whose it could possibly be.

"Of all the Gin Rummy joints in all the towns in all the world, she walks into mine," says the man.

Elspeth turns to inspect the speaker, as if he is something that has just crawled onto her plate, if indeed she had a plate, which is a situation she intends to address quite smartly, as she really is rather hungry.

The first feature she notices about this person spouting gibberish and food particles is the hair. It is a strikingly abundant and untamed meld of black and silver-grey yet combed into such an unusual shape that it looks as if a small wolf has fallen asleep on his head.

"And who might you be?" asks Elspeth Quest, although she couldn't be less interested nor indeed disposed even to attempt recognition. She tries to attract the attention of a member of staff, any member, but they are clearly doing their level best to avoid both her stern eye and rapidly snapping fingers.

Having given his famed, albeit food-muffled, Humphrey Bogart, the man – who by now has digested his potato and is onto the last scrapings of cod – offers up his Sean Connery. "The name's Prince. Barry Prince." He offers Elspeth a shaky hand, which could be drink, age or Parkinson's and which he already half expects her not to accept. "Licensed to spill."

Rex fills Elspeth's empty glass with water from a jug she feels could be cleaner. "Man of a thousand voices," he says. "Some of them almost recognisable." He lowers his own voice to a stage whisper that magically carries even further than his normal tones. "'Variety', love, but we occasionally allow him to bask in our legitimate glow."

Elspeth shrugs. She is too busy anyway, indicating her empty place setting with a directorial hand to anyone within notice and finally receiving a weary nod from a young woman whose diner-avoidance training is only in its starter stages.

"Elspeth?" says that understudy person, whom the new

44

arrival had noticed parked right next to her as she sat down but is choosing to ignore, at least for the time being. "*Elspeth*," persists the amiable lady, maintaining her genuine, gentle smile, "do you know Jacob Bloom?"

Elspeth can sense her neighbour's head nodding vigorously across the table towards the lugubrious figure seated to the left of Rex Markham. She believes she does vaguely know the man and that closer acquaintance might not enhance her life.

"Welcome to Heaven's Gate," comes the voice of Bloom.

"Our very own ray of sunshine," laughs Rex, giving the wraith of a man a hug. "If there's a volcano in Sumatra, this gentleman will mark himself safe on Facebook."

"Sumatra today, Dustingford tomorrow," says Jacob Bloom, his mournful face like that of a dyspeptic bloodhound.

Elspeth – who has never been anywhere near Facebook, Twitter or indeed the entire internet and is amazed that any person at this table could be the least bit computer-savvy or social media literate – looks around the dining room in case it is as infested with mobile devices as today's theatre has now sadly become. Indeed, she herself is quite notorious for having some years ago called out a man in row C of the stalls that the next time his mobile phone rang it would be from inside his rectum, which is a line that the playwright himself might have quite relished, had he in fact been writing three hundred years later.

Fortunately, such devices are currently absent from her disapproving gaze but that annoying little woman in the shapeless cardigan isn't. She is aiming determinedly for Elspeth, holding a half devoured fish plate in her small and quivering hand.

Before the woman can reach her quarry, however, the path is firmly blocked by Gavin Silk, who has emerged, as if on wheels, from the kitchen. For some reason, despite his faux military bearing, the unsmiling director reminds Elspeth of a praying mantis. Or dear Christopher Lee as Dracula but with less charm.

"Miss Quest, I wonder if I might have a word?"

"Can't it wait?" protests Elspeth, who is expecting her cod any day now.

"I'm afraid not."

Raising herself from her seat with a sigh, she almost bumps into Zelda Gatley, who for some reason is now hovering like an incontinent dwarf beside her.

"What are *you* waiting for, my sodding autograph?" asks Elspeth.

"Oh, would you, Miss Quest?" responds Zelda, staring into the revered actress's face, as if she can't quite believe her good fortune. Yet when Gavin Silk suddenly turns back to glare directly at her, the excitable little woman instantly shuffles away and scurries back to her table.

Cary Grant, or at least the Dustingford equivalent, stares at Elspeth's barely touched fish. "What's a nice plaice like you doing in a girl like this? I know, I *know* it's cod. Work with me, guys."

Before she can fully rise, Elspeth feels her wrist being gripped across the table in a cold, but surprisingly firm, hand. "Elsie Turks had an aneurism during the night," says Jacob Bloom, staring unblinkingly at her. "I'd be surprised if she lasts the week."

"Did she have a sea view?" asks Elspeth Quest, as she follows the director out of the room.

scene nine

Gavin Silk's office could not be less theatrical.

There are no homages to past glories or celebrated residents, no deep red plush or framed photos of the man himself with beaming celebrities. Two towering, three-tier metal filing cabinets dominate the nondescript room, as if warning residents that their deepest secrets are filed alphabetically within, their darkest proclivities indexed and outlined.

In the shadow of all this metal is a small yet austere wooden desk, with equally stern chairs on either side. The pens and desk furniture sitting on top are arranged with such anal precision that it would take a saint to resist the temptation to give them just one swift, delicate nudge.

The only concession to idiosyncrasy, or perhaps personality, is a line of highly polished glass bottles of increasing size on a windowsill, each revealing a meticulously, if not over-imaginatively, handcrafted sailing ship in its transparent gut. This must be the man's hobby, concludes Elspeth as she follows him into the room. Curiously, rather than in one dramatic stroke humanising him, this only causes her to like him even less.

Silk moves briskly round to his chair, indicating with a limp hand that Elspeth should do the same on the visitor side. She remains standing for a moment, as if this will somehow afford her the edge that she is only too aware she neither has nor will probably ever regain. She finally decides to take the proffered seat, whilst offering a defiant shrug.

"I think it's best to get the formalities out of the way, Miss Quest," he begins, with what for him might pass as a polite smile. "We don't want them... lingering."

"As you wish," says Elspeth.

"I do. We have all your medical details, you need have no concerns on that score. So, just to confirm. The Trust – that is the Actors Benevolent – have very generously agreed to *fund* your residence here at Dustingford. In its entirety. For as long as you..." The man pauses, displaying an unexpected modicum of tact but perhaps a fraction too late and with a tad too much relish, "As long as you care to reside."

"Is that all?" says Elspeth. She feels a hot flush overtake her body and she certainly hasn't had one of these for a while. The shame and mortification hormone, if there is such a creature, is kicking in with a vengeance.

"Bar the paperwork."

He unlocks the sole drawer on his side of the desk and pulls out a thin folder. Flipping it open, he removes a single sheet of headed notepaper and slides it across to her.

Before he can offer her the writing instrument of his choice, Elspeth dips her hand into the neat assortment on his desk, as if searching for the perfect specimen, and rearranges them haphazardly to the best or worst of her ability. One look into the man's pained face confirms that he would like to pick up the bronzed paper knife from its exact horizontal position on his Moroccan leather letter rack and slit her geriatric throat.

She discovers her name printed on the bottom of the page. "I do have an MBE," she mutters, tapping the blankness where this honour should have been recorded.

"Well deserved, I'm sure," nods Gavin Silk, without any

promise of amendment. "I gather you've had... financial difficulties."

She glares at him, reading into the blankness of his expression a disgust at what he can only assume must have been her profligate thespian ways. "Let us say that not everything is as guaranteed to attract so much interest or indeed dividends as an Elspeth Quest performance," she responds.

"In your heyday."

"You don't like actors, do you, Mr Silk?"

Silk makes a chapel of his hands and slowly manoeuvres his bony chin onto it, which is something Elspeth had believed only characters in television period dramas were wont to do, as she is fairly certain she has never observed anyone doing it in real life.

"What you did before you came here, Miss Quest, you and all your fellows," he says, talking to anywhere that isn't her face, "is no concern of mine. What does concern me is your health, your comfort and the smooth running of this home."

Elspeth, who has had more than enough of this cold fish and is yearning for the one hopefully still on her plate, rises with some discomfort from her chair. "Then I'm assured that my 'circumstances' will remain between the two of us," she says, then adds somewhat puzzlingly, "*Including* the duration of my stay."

"The 'duration'?" repeats Gavin Silk, then nods as he begins to understand. "It's no one else's business. Although, didn't someone say, 'time makes such fools of us all'?" Ignoring her glare and unaware that she has an abiding hatred of people quoting at her, especially when she is unable to attribute, he moves briskly on. "Now, house rules. You must sign out before you leave the grounds at any time. And all visitors do need to register at reception."

"There won't *be* any visitors," insists Elspeth.

The director appears genuinely surprised. "No family, no friends?" No response. "Not even an agent? Some of you people still retain them, you know. We had one lady only last year who got to die rather nastily in a *Silent Witness.*"

"Well, bully for her," says Elspeth Quest, grabbing the door handle. Still gripping it, she executes one of her famous half turns. "I died as Cleopatra. I died as Hedda Gabbler. The next time I die, Mr Silk, it will be as Elspeth Quest, MBE!" She opens the door. The last words he hears, as she strides back to her table, echo dramatically through the empty corridor. "But I want a fucking sea view before I go!"

Silk shrugs and slips the Quest file into the nearest of the twin towers. He wishes he had a section specifically for infuriating old women but then realises that this would consume an entire filing cabinet of its own.

scene ten

In the chill light of morning, the view from Elspeth Quest's small, land-bound window is even more depressing.

It isn't so much the rain, drizzling as it is onto the dismal car park and its ragged complement of unimpressive cars, belonging most probably to Dustingford staff. Nor the fact that the sea hasn't as yet decided to divert its timeless course to greet her. What sinks her spirits further into her own personal slough of despond is the sight of that elderly bloody tap dancer walking out of the door, holding up a hand to check the skies and opening his umbrella.

"Oh Christ, he's going to do his Gene Kelly," says Elspeth Quest, closing her window so at least she can't hear the inevitable whistling. Yet she feels compelled to continue watching him, as if to convince herself of the worst: that this is in fact reality and, as such, unlikely to get less real any time soon.

From a pocket of her oft worn but still smart, navy blue blazer, a pocket made deeper from constant and rather angry thrusting, she removes a tiny bottle of Gordon's Gin and grants herself a much deserved swig.

She gazes around the room and is saddened by how spare and impersonal it still looks. Of course, the dressing table, sadly bereft of its essential garland of lights, displays the bare minimum of assistance that an actress of Elspeth's age and reputation would demand (which, in truth, compared to that of 'civilians', is still an impressive armoury.) Yet aside from this basic slap and warpaint, all she has to show so far are a second-hand Jane Austen, her old travel alarm and a small Roberts radio. Some of her more precious and revealing items are in storage, which she can't really afford. Yet she knows that the very act of selling (or even a more charitable unburdening) would have served only to confirm to her, and indeed to the world, the mortifying permanence of her situation.

This is how it ends.

A brisk knock on the door sends one shaky hand through her thinning grey hair and the other to the depleted miniature, a recently retrieved souvenir from a rare and most welcome location job some years ago. It drops swiftly back into her pocket.

"Come!" she calls, expecting a servant of some sort, most probably recruiting her for an ever-so-much-fun macrame class or Pilates for chronic arthritics.

Elspeth Quest is rather surprised to observe a wheelchair easing its way around her door, although she surely knows by now that such vehicles are hardly a radical means of transportation in these parts. What stuns the actress far more is the actual occupant of this particular wheelchair. A person who clearly is just as shellshocked to be gazing up at her.

"Good morning," chirps Lisa Silk cheerfully, fingers gripping the handlebars, oblivious to the sudden frost or perhaps simply not surprised by anything anymore.

The two old ladies continue to stare wordlessly at each other, pairs of disbelieving eyes connecting but barely blinking, like an octogenarian Gunfight at the O.K. Corral.

"Well, aren't you ladies going to say hello to each other?" laughs Lisa, amiably. Unlike her father, she does genuinely find her old residents amusing rather than merely irritating. Although, she would admit they can quite intensely be the latter when it suits them. But then so can her father, and he's only forty-six.

The elder of the two women finally breaks the silence. "We *know* each other," clarifies Marguerite.

Lisa senses immediately that this isn't going to be one of those tear-jerking reunions like you see on reality TV programmes or at least you used to when she was a kid and she watched TV at home. Before everything became real life.

The seated woman turns her head to glare up at Lisa. "You didn't tell me it was her."

"You didn't ask me, Miss Marguerite. And, anyway, I've forgotten her name."

"It's Miss Quest, to you," snaps Elspeth, recovering with characteristic aplomb from her recent shock. "Hello, Marguerite. Is this still what they call you?"

"This is still who I am. Settlin' in, Elspeth?"

The young woman senses Elspeth suddenly turning to stare oddly at her, as if she might know something untoward, although there is no reason why a chambermaid should be privy to anything that might merit suspicion.

"I've no need to 'settle', Marguerite," says Elspeth, returning haughtily to the fray. "I just think of it as being out of town for a while. Like Grimsby." She moves towards her dressing table, as if she has something pressing that can only be done this minute or the opportunity will be lost for all time. "Now, if you'll excuse me—"

"Yes, you must be frantic," nods Marguerite. "So, I won't take up longer than I need." To Elspeth's surprise, her unexpected guest now nods her head quite maternally towards the curious and far younger woman, who is shuffling uncomfortably beside them in the narrow room. "She wanted to ask you somethin'."

Lisa appears to have set aside every sign of her recent cockiness. She presents to Elspeth as almost sheepish. The elderly actress prays that the girl isn't going to tap her for money.

"Go on, girl," says Marguerite.

"Okay." Lisa points to the shelf by Elspeth's bed. "I-I see you've got a radio there, Miss, er, Quest," she says, her voice diminishing for some reason to a whisper. Elspeth shrugs. She knows that she has a radio. "Would you mind putting it on for a bit, y'know, really loud?"

"Why on earth would I do that?"

Marguerite sighs, either because she feels it ought to be obvious or she really doesn't have the reserves of energy necessary for explanation.

"I'm givin' the child singin' lessons."

"And she's so bloody awful, you don't want me to hear," says Elspeth with a nod. "How very thoughtful of you." Lisa doesn't even bother reacting, as it's simply one of her old ladies being a bit mean. This happens a lot, quite often out of the blue, and she tries not to take it personally. But Elspeth's follow-up confuses her. "Don't you think that's rather ironic, Marguerite? In the circumstances."

"What circ—" asks Lisa.

"It doesn't matter!" snaps Marguerite, without taking her eyes off her old acquaintance. "The girl shows… promise. But her father is dead against it."

"What does her father have to do with it?" asks Elspeth Quest. "And how the hell would *he* know, unless the girl's caterwauling can be heard throughout the town?"

"It's Mr Silk," explains the girl quietly. "My dad's Mr Silk."

Since she began working at Dustingford Hall, Lisa Silk has become quite adept with a heavy-duty brush and some extra strong bleach. She wishes she had them to hand right now, just to scrub away the smile rising on this old witch's smug little face.

"Ah. And don't tell me," says Elspeth Quest, perhaps not entirely unaware of the young girl's musings, "the silly man fails to acknowledge your God-given talent. A classic trope. Poor Johann Strauss apparently had the same problem. His old dad took the whip to him when he discovered him secretly practising the violin. Except, of course, Johann Junior was gifted."

Another one talking gibberish, thinks Lisa but says nothing. Marguerite, however, wheels her chair so close to her old acquaintance that she is almost looking up the standing woman's nose.

"So, are you goin' to do it?" she challenges.

Elspeth manoeuvres her way past the elderly performer, causing Marguerite to swing her chair round in the narrow room in order to hold the moving actress in her eyeline. When she reaches the little radio beside her bed, Elspeth grabs the item theatrically, raises it up and then, in one swift move, chucks it into a nearby drawer. She slams it closed with a flourish, then swings her attention back to the gawping young girl.

"Your first lesson in professional theatre, dear. 'Never piss off the people who can piss back'. George Bernard Shaw."

Marguerite snaps her fingers under Lisa's quivering chin, her signal to be wheeled back to blessed normality.

Elspeth resumes gazing out of the window and waits for the familiar anger to subside.

scene eleven

In the Green Room, Rex Markham's former wives play Gin Rummy with a vengeance, slapping each card down with the sort of flamboyant 'have-at-you!' flourish that the great man himself might have been proud of in his more swashbuckling days.

Indeed, one of these rummy old ladies had even been known to buckle the odd swash with him, at a time, unfortunately, when this hero of so many highly profitable and instantly forgettable films had still been married to the other.

Curiously, whilst this can often encourage each woman to treat her counterpart with casual venom, it has also bonded them in the most unusual way. They do, of course, have names by which they are addressed in daily conversation and both performers have had distinguished stage and film careers of their own. Yet almost inevitably, they are bundled together in this particular venue in a manner with which they are both uncomfortable yet somehow resigned. It is rumoured that they each still carry a torch for the man in question, whilst their batteries are slowly but inexorably running down. Which might be why both regard the advent of one Elspeth Quest with such notable apprehension.

When he spots the pair from the doorway, Rex veers with an

expertise born of considerable practice to the bar at which Jacob Bloom and Barry Prince are standing.

Jacob is kindly reading aloud from the day's *Times* to the aged impressionist, who has cataracts in serious need of treatment. Barry is starting to wish that his ears were similarly afflicted, as he is pretty certain that his personal reader, whilst selfless with his time and energies, is rather too focused on mass disaster and personal tragedy when it comes to his selection.

Rex just catches the words, "I don't even know where fucking Gabon *is*, Jacob!" rendered in a voice approximating the later Michael Caine, as he completes his hastily rerouted journey.

"Anyone seen Elspeth?" he asks. "She doesn't seem to have been around all day."

"Perhaps she died," suggests Jacob Bloom, helpfully. "After all, that is why we're here."

Rex simply looks at Barry, who shrugs. Rex isn't certain whether the other two men's paths had converged before Dustingford, but he and Jacob Bloom go back a long way.

Whilst this Eeyorish gentleman may have grown gaunter and more stooped over the years, Jacob has maintained the same level of just manageable despair (or manageable at least to him) since his early days as a reliable, if slightly typecast, character actor. Everyone in the home, and indeed all those with whom he has worked over the decades, appear to be aware that he had come from an extremely orthodox East End Jewish family, a dynasty of venerated Rabbis and scholars and that a shameful desire to follow his own particular calling had led to total 'excommunication' or whatever people of his occasionally unforgiving faith might term it.

A partner or significant other has never been mentioned nor indeed enquired about – 'keeping myself to myself' could well have been listed as one of the more verifiable skills on the Jacob Bloom CV. What was widely recalled, however, is that when a newcomer would find himself seated next to Jacob at a rehearsal room or studio canteen, observers would take bets as to how long it would be until that unsuspecting person would politely shuffle away or quietly lose the will to live.

The simple mention of Elspeth's name has been sufficient to create a discreet but animated buzz around the room. Residents, unless they are hard of hearing or addressing someone who might be, are speaking in hushed tones. Zelda Gatley, however, is noisily beside herself as she hurtles across the room on her stick and sinks herself into the over-accommodating armchair next to Diana Appleyard.

"So, Diana," she practically yells, only her tiny head fully visible, "what was she like?"

Diana Appleyard knows that the only way she has even the remotest chance of dialling the nervy woman down to the just-about-bearable is to lower her own voice considerably.

"Who, dear?"

"Pardon?" says Zelda Gatley, so that clearly didn't work. Diana sighs and repeats the question, only louder. The expected response arrives with a certain disdain. "You *know* who, Diana."

"Zelda," explains Diana, patiently but firmly, "I'm afraid I make a strict point of not talking about other people." Zelda, who makes a strict point of doing little else, just stares at the woman. She realises, with a tinge of surprise, how very pretty this rather quiet, slightly plump lady is. Or must have been once. No, still is, the appealing roundness of her face contributing perhaps to the relative absence of those oft rampant furrows of age. Such a shame she never really... "And anyway," persists Diana, "no one knew Elspeth Quest well. Not really."

"Except her husbands," corrects Zelda, in case the other woman has forgotten.

"Not even them," says Diana Appleyard, with perhaps a hint of sadness.

"Any kids?" asks her inquisitor, then changes it to 'children', as if this makes the enquiry less intrusive.

"Zelda, are you writing a book?"

Zelda Gatley laughs at this, but it is such an odd, nervy laugh that it leaves Diana wondering if she might have actually hit upon something. Then she reminds herself, whilst simultaneously feeling ashamed for being so judgmental, that the little woman is barely literate.

"Well," concludes Zelda, bright enough to recognise a brick wall when she has been conversing with one, "I do hope she turns up later. For The Programme."

"Ah yes, The Programme," says Diana Appleyard. She shakes her head, a touch despondently. "Has a whole week gone by already?"

The two women look towards the massive TV set in the corner of the room, a generous gift from the governors of the BBC. A few residents have taken up their regular position just inches from the screen, watching anything that happens to come on. Subtitles flick across for those who are hard of hearing and in order to maintain an acceptably unobtrusive sound level for others who regard daytime TV as the devil's plaything.

Zelda suddenly grabs her stick and hoists herself nimbly upwards, eager to unlock more Elspeth Quest memories before they fade and die forever. She spots Gerard Bunting across the room, settled in his usual comfy chair. For a moment, Zelda Gatley thinks that she might rather like a usual comfy chair but, for this to be so, she would usually have to settle in it and she knows that this is not going to happen any time soon.

The elderly actor is doing his now regular *Daily Mail* crossword but, as she moves closer, even Zelda with her wonky radar can detect a greater than usual frustration. The trusty HB pencil that normally finds its way to his teeth for tiny taps now appears to be taking up permanent lockdown against one of his ageing gums. Another frustrated shake of his head and he could sever the instrument altogether.

Zelda Gatley feels that it might be comradely to join the

poor man – whose work she is pretty certain she has enjoyed onstage and especially on TV in the past, albeit never in leading roles – and help him out a bit. Not that crosswords are really her thing, but you never know.

Before she can claim her seat, however, Cyril Dodds is there, with his wooden friend.

"I was married forty years and never a cross word," he says, parking himself next to Gerard Bunting and rearranging the dummy on his knee.

"The wife wouldn't let him open his mouth. *Hotcha!*" chirps the owl.

The frustrated crossworder glances wearily over to the neighbouring chair. "Hello, Cyril."

"Sorry about Mr Chips," says the ventriloquist. "His blood pressure is through the roof today." At this, he deftly whisks the dummy's head up and away from its body, then allows it to drop sharply down again into its neck. Zelda Gatley whoops but the intended audience for this little display just sighs. "Need any help, Gerard?" asks the man kindly, finally sensing the tension. "With the puzzle."

"No, I fucking don't!" When he catches both Cyril Dodds and an inanimate wooden bird recoiling in horror, Gerard lowers his voice to a grumble. "They're making the clues a lot harder these days. I used to do the *Guardian* crossword, you know, Cyril. Every day for forty-five years." Cyril nods. Of course he knows. "I don't even *like* the fucking *Daily Mail*."

The ventriloquist decides to leave the old actor to it, but even Zelda, whose perception is no match for her curiosity, notices that the departing man appears concerned. As indeed does the object of that concern, whose distinctly idle pencil seems fated to fracture.

The familiar sound of a wheelchair instantly excites Zelda Gatley all over again.

She swirls to find that rather strange Lisa girl almost beside her, wheeling the legendary Marguerite, all of whose records Zelda Gatley once owned. She recalls that she even had a signed copy of the woman's landmark musical comedy LP. It will probably be worth quite a lot of money when its famed signatory dies. But sadly, not for Zelda.

"Ah, the blooming Marguerite," greets Cyril Dodds. "An honour, my dear lady, as always. Nobody seems to have seen your new neighbour today."

Zelda smiles excitedly. Now they are right back on track. And see, she's not the only one who is interested. Even lovely Rex has turned his head in their direction.

"Lucky them," sniffs Marguerite.

"Well, I hope she comes down for The Programme," says Mr Chips.

Lisa taps the wooden owl affectionately on his beak, which causes the dummy to nuzzle up to her. Mr Chips's head is actually resting on her breast, but Lisa isn't certain whether this is simply because its master happens to be sitting down or that the old man is very cunningly copping a proxy, linden-wood feel.

"I'm sure she wouldn't want to miss that, Mr Chips," says Lisa, edging just a couple of inches away.

"Highlight of the week, eh, Chipsy?" says Cyril Dodds.

"Even better than a firm bowel movement," opines Mr Chips. "And I can think of no higher praise."

The others nod. The men at the bar turn to bow and smile at Marguerite, out of a genuine respect. Marguerite nods graciously back, as if no less is her due.

Yet, despite the chattiness and bonhomie in the room, the camaraderie of erstwhile fellow toilers in the once verdant fields of film, TV, theatre and variety, even Lisa can pick up something forlorn and wistful in the air. A yearning sadness that fills the room like dry ice on a stage, softening and muting the brightness.

For some reason, the residents currently present in the scarlet and crimson Green Room all turn their eyes towards the large TV screen, which is now showing, in all too vivid detail, a subtitled repeat of a classic David Attenborough programme from 1982.

scene twelve

Elspeth Quest is speaking very quietly on her phone.

The sturdy suitcases remain unpacked beside her bed, save for immediate necessities, as if making a firm statement that she is only passing through. Elspeth can see the ironic side to this, as she knows that even when she is somewhere through which she is only passing, she always insists on first unpacking her suitcases.

"Why do you people always want to know my name?" grumbles Elspeth into her mobile. "It doesn't bloody matter what my name is! Well, alright, *David*, call me… Marguerite. Marger-ite! Yes, it is unusual. No, it isn't French. Well, it might be. You sound very young for a—. I am well aware that Samaritans come in all ages. And colours and creeds. *And* sexual orientations. You could identify as Doris, for all I care… mm? How am I today? Well, I'm feeling full of the joys of sodding spring, *David*, I just had to pick up the phone and tell somebody before I simply burst with—"

There is a knock on her door. Elspeth swiftly downs the phone.

"Come in!"

Stanley slowly pokes his head around, as if testing the room for rain. The intolerably amiable smile with which he left number sixteen the previous afternoon is beginning to signify to Elspeth as a permanent fixture on his face. He takes in the suitcases and the look of defiance accompanying it.

"Oh dear," he says, "doesn't look like much has changed since yesterday."

"You've learned to knock. That's new," says Elspeth. She picks up her handbag, like a meaningful prop. "I told you, Mr, er, I'm just… passing through."

"It's still Stanley, Miss Quest. Stanley Grainger." She turns away, as if suddenly mesmerised by the car park below. "Is everything okay, Miss Quest?"

"What do you mean, *Mister* Grainger?"

"Well, the residents, they noticed you haven't come down for your meals today."

"They don't miss much, do they?" She shakes her head. "So, they sent you to investigate."

Stanley moves gently towards her, balancing a tactful lowering of his voice with a respect for her personal space. She backs away towards the window.

"I know it's hard at first," he says, angling his body a few degrees sideways to adjust a wall shelf he feels isn't quite up to his specifications. "But once you start—"

"Talking about the old days." She looks into the slightly glowering sky, as if lost in a fog of nostalgia. "Larry and Jonny and lovely Rafe, backstage at the Vic."

"That's it!" he enthuses, delighted with his unfailing prowess at cheering up these old dears. "Bet you've got a boxful of stories from way back."

"Actresses I've screwed, actors I've fucked."

"*Exactly!*" says the satisfied handyman, before absorbing what the old dear just said. He picks up one of the cases. "Shall I put these on the bed?"

"Yes, alright. If you insist," she sighs, still staring out of the window.

"I do. I insist. Oh, come on, Miss Quest – it is 'Miss', isn't it? I know some of you ladies like to hang on to your stage names – you might as well unpack. *Even* if you're not staying that long."

Elspeth turns in order to stare fully into the man's eyes. They're rather kind eyes, she decides, despite her not being attuned or terribly open to kindness right now. In a shade of grey that should be dull yet curiously isn't. Eyes that are scrunched up in a craggy, weatherworn face that appears moulded over years by smiles and laughter, the way the cliffs beyond have been permanently configured by an unrelenting sea. It is an intelligent face, she realises, almost disconcertingly so, despite a lack of culture or education (of which he appears almost proud or at best indifferent). She suddenly wonders whether he knows something.

"Very well, then. Thank you. And there's no 'if' about it."

Stanley hoists the other cases to join their fellow. He makes light of it but notices how surprisingly heavy they are. Or perhaps, more concerningly, how his own proud muscles aren't quite what they used to be.

"Hey, petal, I know!" he says, offering her his friendliest smile. "Why don't I get one of our lasses downstairs to bring you up a lovely sandwich? As you're just… settling in." She says nothing, despite her grave doubts as to the loveliness of room service in this establishment, so he continues with what she now realises has to be the main thrust of today's mission. "But a word to the wise: you don't want to miss The Programme tonight."

"What programme?" she enquires in justifiable bemusement.

Stanley Grainger's jovial countenance takes on an expression of delighted smugness that makes her want to knee him in the groin. A move she hasn't executed since a foolhardy middle-European film producer in the swinging sixties pinned her against a backdrop that was meant to be Versailles.

"You'll just have to come down and see for yourself, won't you?" he grins.

Elspeth smiles back but it isn't a kind one. "When you're an actress, Mr Grainger," she explains, "you become an expert on the human voice. And I suspect I've just heard the one you use on your grandchildren."

For the first time, she notices a hardness cloud what she had hitherto assumed was a perpetually sunny countenance. "If you were an expert on the human heart, Miss Quest, I think you'd recognise the difference. And I heard what you said to young Lisa. About the singing. Enjoy your unpacking."

He turns away from her and does what Elspeth considers a disgruntled stomp to the door. She stares after him for a few seconds, more thoughtfully than she might wish, then shakes the unwelcome intrusion out of her head and begins resignedly to undo her case. After a moment, she looks back towards the door, sensing that for some unknown reason Stanley Grainger has returned to stare at her.

He hasn't.

But, yet again, someone has.

Perhaps not truly returned, as this particular undesirable is utterly new.

The small man, looking unusually dapper in an outfit which appears to Elspeth to be distinctly Indian, with a natty mandarin-collared Nehru jacket and loose cotton trousers, is most certainly staring. He is also inclining his head politely forwards, with palms together, in a manner she associates with that particular subcontinent. The most disconcerting aspect of all this, however, is that, so far as Elspeth can discern, this curious man, with his pale skin, cerulean eyes and wispy grey hair, is no more Indian than she is.

"Yes?" she says.

The voice, when it emerges pipingly from the would-be visitor's tidy frame, is as incongruous as his garb. And just as puzzling.

"Detective Inspector Malhotra of the New Delhi Police. At your service, ma'am."

Elspeth can feel her mouth opening very slightly of its own accord – on the cusp of shouting '*who?*' – when a cloudy recollection insinuates itself into her bemused brain.

"I *know* you!" she says eventually. "You're-you're Derek Hirst."

The man gives her a sad yet indulgent smile, as if she has made a forgivable error with which he is sadly all too familiar. "What we have here, ma'am, is a curious case of mistaken identity," he says in his best North Indian accent.

"Oh, Jesus, spare me!" sighs Elspeth Quest in her richly modulated, if perhaps a tad fractured, southern counties accent.

She remembers now or thinks she does. It was a long-running BBC radio series, wasn't it? In the sixties, based on a moderately successful string of novels featuring the enigmatic, vaguely Sherlockian Detective Inspector Mal-whatever-his-bloody-name-was, of some obscure Indian police force. Broadcast at a time when nobody appeared to object to a Caucasian giving what was commonly known as his 'Peter Sellers'. Especially on radio, where no make-up was required. Or wardrobe, she assumes, although the silly old bugger certainly has one now.

"Well, it's very nice to meet you, Inspector," she says, indulgently, "but I really have to—"

"She didn't die a natural death, you know."

"I'm sorry? Who didn't?"

"Mrs Turks."

"Oh well, never mind," says Elspeth Quest, who would like the little man to trot along now so that she can get on with, well, with anything other than this nonsense.

"Elsie Turks, Britain's premier lady juggler," continues Detective Inspector Malhotra of the New Delhi Police. "She passed away in the local hospital this morning. But I believe – using all my deductive skills, my 'Delhi-ductions' as I am humbly terming them – that Elsie Turks was *murdered!*"

It is at this point that entranced radio listeners several

decades back would have expected – and indeed would have been provided with – an appropriately dramatic musical sting. And it is when Derek Hirst (aka Detective Inspector Malhotra etc, etc) provides one, with only his reedy voice as instrument, that Elspeth Quest decides that even The sodding Programme, whatever the hell it is, has to be better than this.

scene thirteen

The smokers, whose activities are frowned upon by the care staff and thereby rendered infinitely more enjoyable, are taking and tainting the after-dinner air, when Zelda Gatley comes beetling around the corner on her magic stick.

"It's starting. It's starting. Five minutes!" she yelps breathlessly, in what for anyone else would be regarded as alarming overexcitement but at Dustingford is accepted as normal for Zelda. The smokers have no time to respond, should they even wish to, as the geriatric dynamo is off and away.

They quietly grind out their cigarettes and adjourn to the Green Room. Had she remained for just two seconds longer, Zelda might have noted a reassuring surge in spirits, albeit considerably less maniacal, on their own weary faces.

Meantime, the Paul Revere of Dustingford is rousing residents still in their bedrooms, rallying weary staff clearing up in their kitchens and most probably unsettling the recently dead. Her only updated script revisions being 'four minutes – three minutes – two minutes'.

Several of those being corralled think Zelda Gatley will give herself a heart attack. A few amongst that number would be okay with this, provided it were painless and swift. A slightly smaller number would settle for swift.

Elspeth Quest, her curiosity having inched just a nose ahead of her indifference, is already making her way rather grandly down the sweeping and perilously steep staircase. She is suddenly jostled quite hard against a bannister as that annoying little person, whose yelps have been echoing around this Victorian monstrosity, scuttles by.

"Demented bitch," says the great actress, as herself.

*

When she arrives in the Green Room, Elspeth notices that it has been transformed.

All the chairs – comfy, semi-comfy and osteoporosis-friendly – have been rearranged to face the large TV. Curiously, the great machine has been switched to rare stand-by mode, as have the residents, most of whom are parked in untypical silence. Yet they appear neither relaxed nor sanguine. Elspeth can almost smell the anticipation. In some cases, there is no almost about it.

Scanning the crowd, she spots Marguerite, sitting regally in her own permanent chair. Elspeth instinctively looks around for that young woman, Louisa or someone, the girl to whom the elderly diva appears inexplicably attached and who so bizarrely wanted Elspeth to ramp up her own little radio to cover the squawk of her singing. She wishes somebody could have done that with Marguerite, but she knows that this is just malice, coupled with more than a shred of envy. She is quite content with both.

As it happens, it is the young man, Jason, the one who initially took her cases, who has most probably done the wheelchair honours this evening. He stands a short distance from Marguerite and appears to be as riveted by the blank screen as his charge and her strangely silent fellows.

The silence, which is indefinably creepy, is broken by Rex

Markham, currently Dustingford's most celebrated (male) resident, with a discreet cough.

All eyes – rheumy, bespectacled, cataracted, macular-degenerated or just world-weary – are on him as he rises slowly, and with some dignity, from his chair, using both arms for the conventional 'lift-off' but with a flourish that is all his own. It is clearly his turn – or perhaps his regular duty – to do the ceremonial switching-on of the television. As ever, thinks Elspeth, the old ham is making a meal of it.

"Get on with it, Tyrannosaurus Rex!" cries Mr Chips and garners one of those precious laughs that keep his Svengali, the great Cyril Dodds, both going and annoying, in equal measure.

As the massive television bursts instantly into over eight million state-of-the-art pixels, an androgynous young male and vapidly toothsome female bound smiling onto the screen to an orgasmic explosion of audience love. Elspeth can only watch in bemusement as this perpetually grinning, banality-spouting combo bid the cameras – and what she can only assume is a vast constituency of semi-morons around this once proud island – an excessively friendly and deeply insincere welcome.

Elspeth Quest has never been exposed to a programme such as this, so she has absolutely no idea of its content. Yet even were she to be its most passionate devotee, she might still not have been anticipating this evening's uniquely Dustingfordian reception.

*

Lisa, the young woman whose absence Elspeth has just noted, sits in Gavin Silk's small but far from cosy office, reading a printed form.

She is doing her best to ignore the familiar face staring across at her, from the official side of the desk. Commander of his fleet of naffing ship in bottles.

"I don't bloody believe this!" she says finally, shaking her head but refusing to meet his gaze. She returns to examining the form once more, perhaps until she does bloody believe it.

"Every member of staff receives one," says her father, as if this makes the situation more palatable.

"'Punctuality, discipline, ability to take orders,'" reads Lisa. "Crap, only got a 'C' for that one – must try harder."

She looks up at the man, her employer, and stares unblinkingly into his eyes until he feels impelled to amplify.

"You do know, Lisa, that I went out on a limb to secure you this job?" She tries to speak but this is clearly a monologue. One of his monologues. "That college in town isn't ring-fencing a place on its Health and Social Care course for Miss Lisa Silk." He pauses for effect. "Not with your... history."

"I wish Simon Cowell was my dad."

"I have no idea who he is."

They hear a sudden roar and clattering from the large room across the hallway.

"*They* do," says Lisa Silk, nodding towards the door.

*

The Green Room is exploding.

Whatever talent (or universally agreed lack of it) that might be emanating from the huge television this evening, this is utterly drowned out by spontaneous barracking and jeering from the floor, alongside a violent clatter of walking sticks, spoons and boiled sweets, as they hurtle in anger towards the offending screen. These are accompanied, in a small but significant number of cases, by ballpoint pens, spectacles, cigarette packets and rolled-up copies of *The Lady*. At least one set of false teeth can be observed bouncing off the not-so-smart TV.

Despite the machine's impressive volume being ramped up to the max, in order to accommodate average-age-eighty hearing, the programme's already strident soundtrack is thoroughly overwhelmed.

Some basic acknowledgment that these unknown performers, however limited their abilities, are trying their damnedest and exhibiting remarkable guts in front of harsh judges and a vast, unduly opinionated viewing audience, is nowhere to be seen in this particular establishment, a noble industry's third and final act for its due-paying professionals.

Elspeth Quest witnesses the alarum with mounting incredulity and just the slightest frisson of pure terror. Amidst the raucous, spittle-strewn shower of head-shaking abuse, she attempts to make out individual utterances.

'Go back to nowhere!', 'Bring on the hook!', 'Call that talent?', 'Bollocks!' and 'Bloody amateurs!' rank amongst the most discernible. Elspeth is quite convinced that – were she a lip-reader – she would decipher more imaginative but perhaps even less genteel outpourings.

She is certain that no one has really noticed her arrival, involved as they are in this dispiriting but not entirely inexplicable display. That young girl, the director's pallid, goth-like daughter, appears to have followed her in and is now sidling up towards Jason. She looks to be on the verge of tears. This is of no concern to Elspeth and anyway, the lad seems to have the comforting well in hand, randy little sod.

Yet, as she looks around – taking in the animated faces of the elderly men and women, some of whom Elspeth once knew and even, in better days, worked alongside and those others whose different, and possibly less elevated, paths she was never destined to cross – she feels an almost overwhelming sense of sadness.

Elspeth Quest realises, with the heightened sensitivity which has been both a boon and a curse in her life, that she is picking up nothing less than the nostalgic bitterness of regret, the sour scent of long-avoided but inevitable closure to dreams.

All roiling with fervour beneath the excessively cacophonous jollity on show. She still can't help feeling, however, that some of this sadness could also be her own.

Suddenly, she senses someone standing behind her, upstage right. Expecting it to be the home's slightly reptilian director, she edges slowly away. Yet, when she turns, she finds that it is only that irritating handyman Stanley Grainger. The ageing odd-jobber is nodding to her, then indulgently out towards the bloodthirsty throng, who now appear to the actress to resemble nothing less than crowds at a major gladiatorial fixture, as the Emperor gives his merciless thumbs down.

It is only when she looks back at Stanley – and wonders for a moment why the hell she has experienced the need to do so – that she recalls something the chirpy man had said when they first met. Dear Lord, was it only yesterday?

And suddenly, everything falls into place.

*

As Gavin Silk walks with his daughter to the small car that Dustingford has provided for his use, the pair notice a slim figure strolling in the grounds, clasping her cardigan tightly round her thin chest. She appears miles away, lips moving without sound, lost in her thoughts. Which, of course, is not unusual for some of his residents, yet he finds himself surprised that it should be so apparent in this, his newest and potentially trickiest one.

"Miss Quest?" he ventures, moving tentatively towards her. When there is no response nor hint of recognition, he edges into her eyeline and tries again. "*Miss Quest!*" She turns with a start that startles him, too. "Is everything alright, Miss Quest?"

Elspeth Quest says nothing but merely nods. Gavin Silk returns the nod or rather nods to himself in reassurance that the woman hasn't suddenly become the aged nocturnal wanderer of his nightmares.

Lisa, however, continues to stare at the new resident, even after her father has seated himself impatiently at the wheel of his car. Something appears to have changed in the actress's face and demeanour, something subtle yet potent. She appears less crabby, more, well yes, enlivened. The eyes, already a quite striking blue, barely diminished by age, give off a spark that is almost electric. Even the lines on her face appear to have begun a process of smoothing or at least untightening.

It is as if the woman has just received some good news, which makes the far younger woman wonder if a sea-view room has suddenly become available and Lisa hadn't noticed the ambulance.

"*Lisa!*" calls her father, anxious to reach home, ships, bottles and relative sanity.

The daughter sighs, prospects of home not quite so nourishing. It is only as she has her hand on the passenger door that she hears what could almost be a rustle of late autumn sea breeze but she picks up as a delayed response, murmured pensively low.

"I think so, Mr Silk. I really do think so. Goodnight."

scene fourteen

The tap dancer is doing a sunny dance.

Not that the majority of his routines don't embrace that essential element of joy, silently transmuting it into something wondrous, albeit just slightly creaking of late. But these days there is more often a gentle wistfulness built in, an indefinable sadness, which today is notably absent. A rare November sun shines coolly down onto the glistening lawn, as the elderly entertainer cranes his dark, balding head up towards it, like a particularly expansive sunflower greeting the day.

Jacob Bloom watches the man in curious fascination from his usual seat at the breakfast table. He knows why the solitary hoofer always appears to be dancing as part of a team, even though he is quite alone. The old actor thinks that he understands. Despite the heartening uplift of the performer's soundless number, Jacob finds that this insight touches him more than he could say.

From what is now apparently *her* chair, Elspeth's focus is closer to home.

Quietly, barely touching her breakfast, she observes her new companions. Rex, Jacob, Barry Prince, Gerard Bunting and that understudy person are all here, as ever, occupying their spaces and making their usual conversation. Anyone with a modicum of perception might note that – whilst she clearly does listen and even graciously nod to odd snippets of chatter, which are quite predictable and not overly stimulating – Elspeth Quest is simply waiting, like the dowager lioness in a pack, ready to pounce.

"Remember in rep," says Rex (which brief intro Elspeth firmly believes must signal the commencement of myriad Dustingford conversations, perhaps even this very morning), "how we used to pray for a play with a nice juicy dinner scene, a 'practical meal', otherwise we might not eat all day?"

The others all nod and mutter. The names of old and mostly forgotten dining room dramas pass like the breadbasket up and down the table, alongside names of equally moribund repertory theatres.

"I thought you guys ate the scenery," says Barry Prince as John Wayne.

One of the kitchen staff – a jolly local woman in her late forties, Nancy Fowler by name – is passing with a refill of warm milk. She stops for a moment, trying to work out exactly who the old guy is doing this time. Sometimes she gets them, sometimes not. She rather likes his Al Jolson, even though she supposes that she shouldn't these days, but she's shaking her head at the current effort. Barry Prince notices and calls out, "John Effing Wayne, darling!" The woman nods, smiles her usual 'of course!' and moves happily on. The stories she comes back home with to her family, she could write a book – she honestly could!

"I was kosher in those days," sighs Jacob Bloom, still gazing out of the window. "I used to pray for a Wesker."

The others glance at him and then at each other, as if they are not quite sure whether the man is joking.

A sudden slamming down of heavy cutlery on a barely touched breakfast plate, combined with the overly violent scraping of a chair, causes the occupants of this table – and indeed of all the tables – to cease their grumblings and reminiscences and turn to face whoever is creating the din.

Across the crowded room, some elderly residents are

instinctively checking their hearing aids or changing their glasses, whilst others are holding onto their toast in case this is a relatively serious interruption and they may have to move.

"Tell me," demands Elspeth Quest, for astonishingly it is this celebrated newcomer who has just, in a rather abrupt and non-Dustingford manner, launched herself upwards and is calling the assembled ex-performing artistes to attention. "*Tell me*," she repeats, with that famed projection, which over the decades has carried her words and sighs so effortlessly to the very rears and peaks of London's most cavernous theatres, "is it obligatory for residents of this godforsaken Victorian excrescence to dwell for evermore in the distant sodding past? Please, I really want to know – is it a vital part of our fucking therapy and our sodding palliative care?"

The listeners are too stunned to respond. And surely the questions were rhetorical?

Unlike possibly any other home of its kind for the retired and elderly, it isn't the robust turns of phrase employed by an otherwise dignified elderly lady that have caused such alarm. These people have sat in too many rehearsal rooms; stood in the back of too many stages and film sets; listened to far too many angry, frustrated, bullying or simply bored producers, directors, fellow performers and crew to care how many letters a word may have. It is the *content* of this rabid outburst that shakes them, the ferocity of its delivery that locks their well-worn jaws mid-chomp.

As they continue to stare, Elspeth abandons her lukewarm breakfast and undrinkable coffee to stride dramatically off through the half-open French windows and into the empty conservatory.

Rex looks at the others in some bewilderment and shrugs.

Eventually, he and his neighbours pick up their coffee cups and decamp to the glassy extension to complete their interrupted breakfast.

After all, it makes a bit of a change.

They find Elspeth gazing out onto the terrace, arms tightly folded, still looking very cross. She glances across the garden and notices some of those white hellebores that on other, happier occasions, she has quite enjoyed. She even smiles briefly to herself at the appropriateness of a Christmas rose for what she has in mind. In the distance, beside the greenhouse, she can see Stanley Grainger planting something. The bloody man gets everywhere.

To her surprise, it is Jacob Bloom who addresses her recent impassioned outburst.

"What else is there for us to live on, dear, if not the past?" he says sadly, even for him. "Except maybe beta blockers, levothyroxine, warfarin—"

Diana Appleyard interrupts the man, who is now counting on his fingers, as she knows that he has a longer prescription list than the local Boots. "Jacob is right, Elspeth. At our age, all we can have are our memories. Some of us not even that."

Rex Markham points a long, slightly nicotined finger up into the air. "Hear that sound, love?" Elspeth looks quizzically at it. "It's the sound of a phone not ringing. Gets louder every day."

Elspeth Quest pauses and looks around at the assembled company, although they haven't any of them been part of a company for so very long. When she speaks, it is in low tones and with a deliberately offhand casualness.

"Well, of course, I'm only a temporary resident, hardly here, then I'm gone."

She stops, aware, or at least hoping, that they aren't going to allow this thought, whatever it might be, to expire half expressed.

"Mm?" says Rex.

"No," continues Elspeth, shaking her head. "Forget it. I'm speaking out of turn."

"No script here, love," says Barry Prince, in his own voice, which shows he must be interested.

"Oh very well, then," sighs an arm-twisted Elspeth Quest. "I do have a proposition."

"Proposition, Elspeth?" says Gerard Bunting.

Elspeth brushes it off with a wave of her hand, as if in truth it is barely worth mentioning. "More of a notion, really. A conceit. An ill-considered trifle." She gives a little laugh, which could almost be interpreted as nervous. Except that it isn't. And neither is she. Or at least not as much as expected. She gazes around the ancient order of breakfasters in the conservatory, all of whom now appear to be listening as best they can. "Why not, well, why not put on something yourselves?"

They can hear resumed mutterings and clinking from the dining room. And the ageless and unperturbed rumblings of the sea beyond. The little group stare at her, some with more clarity than others.

Jacob Bloom adjusts his hearing aid. "Sorry, dear, didn't quite catch that."

"I *said*, PUT ON A FUCKING PERFORMANCE OF YOUR OWN!"

The dining room is suddenly silent, save for those who can't hear so well, but very soon they cease their talking because they can tell that nobody else is. And anyway, they're all too busy shuddering. Everyone is looking in the one direction now, including the serving-staff. The only sounds are those of the waves below.

Elspeth continues more quietly, although those indoors would have preferred her to continue shouting, as none of them has seen a live Elspeth Quest performance for ages and this has to be worth the price of a ticket.

"I'm not talking West End, for pity's sake! I'm not talking *RS bloody C*! I mean, here, in this godforsaken room behind us. No long runs, no out-of-town tryouts – one night only. For family, friends. Staff. Agents. Just to show them you're still alive. If indeed you are. And that you've still... got it in you!"

"Judy and Mickey," supplies Barry Prince, with some inevitability. "Let's do the show right here!"

"If you wish," concedes Elspeth. "And, naturally, with Christmas coming up, it's the perfect time."

A moan from Jacob Bloom causes them to turn. He appears to be clutching his chest. "Oy – just the thought of it! I get these palpitations."

"It's called adrenaline, dear," explains Elspeth. "Remember?"

Jacob nods, as if adrenaline is simply another of the many plagues with which he and his people have been afflicted.

Having made her point and wishing to leave them still wanting more, which is indeed her trademark and could well one day serve as her obituary, Elspeth Quest makes her exit out onto the broad terrace and down the steps leading to the garden.

She notices Stanley Grainger watching her from his admirably flexible, stooped-over position on a planting bed. He waves a mucky trowel to her, and she offers a very slight nod, which could be taken as reciprocation or simply the involuntary judder of an elderly head. She herself would be hard-pressed to decide categorically which.

Elspeth turns back to see her stunned little band of fellow residents almost rooted to the spot, as if in a tableau. Before she can even fully rejoin them, as she has no intention of wandering off, leaving the job half-done, that whatsername woman begins to berate her.

"Elspeth," insists the erstwhile understudy, "this is a retirement home, not a repertory company. We're past it, dear. That's one of the qualifications. Some of the residents here can't even put on a shoe, let alone a show."

Elspeth Quest shakes her head. No wonder this woman never took the leads. "Muscles only atrophy, Doreen, if they're not put to good use."

Rex Markham gives his classic buccaneer laugh. "I'll vouch for that, love."

81

Elspeth recalls now that this man was on the shortlist several decades ago to be the first big-screen James Bond. They went instead for an Edinburgh milkman. She has to remind herself that she too emerged from humble origins and didn't always sound as she does today. But she tries not to remind herself of this too often, as her world is all about illusion.

She is aware that more residents, despite the crisp November air and a nipping breeze from the sea, are venturing out onto the terrace to discover what all the fuss is about. And to reassure themselves that they hadn't really heard what they suspect they really might have.

"I am genuinely feeling rather ill," says Jacob Bloom. Whilst this might simply be construed as his catchphrase, some of the listeners reckon that this time, it is simply confirming their own deepest concerns and fears.

"Well, if you want my opinion, darling, I think it's sheer folly," says Rex, who has taken up the mantle of Dustingford's go-to voice of sanity. The universal nods around him act like a Greek chorus.

Elspeth Quest doesn't contradict the man nor does she acknowledge his doubts. She simply stares at him, as if she has already read the script and knows that this is his space to pause rather than her cue to speak.

"But let's say we did, oh, I don't know, consider a little, divertissement," he continues after the break, "just for the hell of it. Who on earth would we get to pull it all together, and why am I asking?"

He – and the others on the terrace – look towards Elspeth. With an interest, it has to be said, more dispassionate than avid.

Elspeth Quest appears quite shocked. How could they have so misunderstood her? "Oh, no, no," she protests with a trilling little laugh. "I'm so sorry. No, no, it was a vague thought, darling, from a mere someone in transit, not a-a job application! *Dear Lord!* Perhaps I shouldn't even have…" Now it is her turn to pause, as if waiting for latecomers to take their seats. When she proceeds, she appears almost to be talking to herself. "It would mean my lingering on here longer than I intended. Far longer. No, no. My lovely builders are practically on their final Hobnob. Rex, dearest, I really don't think so."

A few of the stragglers stare at her, then turn round and shuffle back towards the dining room, with mutters of 'then why the fuck did she bring it up?' and 'silly cow' being amongst the most restrained. Her immediate coterie begin to join them.

"Of course, I *REALISE* that in order for me to stay on…" she says, thoughtfully yet swiftly, and at greater volume, "I shall have to rearrange things, you understand, domestically."

"With your underpinning," says Rex.

"Indeed," agrees Elspeth with a little laugh. "Although you make it sound so vulgar. Yet hey ho, I suppose we all of us have to make sacrifices. Kensington will simply have to wait. But if anyone mentions the word 'festive' between now and then, I shall personally slit their throats with a holly wreath. Anyway, no rush. It's a quantum leap for everyone, I quite understand. Have a little mull."

With this, she strolls purposefully and alone down the stone steps and onto the still glistening lawn. Too stunned to talk, they hear her final words all too clearly, although her back is turned.

"The Green Room at 11.00! Everyone who wants to be involved. *Don't* be late."

Rex watches her in admiration and gives a smile that, despite the years and the filter tips, has retained much of its gleam. "Consummate," he opines.

"And I thought my parts had all dried up," says Barry Prince, as Frankie Howerd.

scene fifteen

"Well, I'm not going to beg, if that's what you were expecting."

Stanley Grainger is trimming back an unruly shock of leylandii, a hedge that offers much-needed privacy and security to Dustingford Hall but from time to time gives the impression of wanting to devour its residents. He has no idea whose insanity it was to plant it in the first place, but he actually finds this regular taming of it rather relaxing. Unless he is having conversations like the one right now.

"This isn't personal, Stanley," says Gavin Silk, aiming for some sort of professional intimacy, without having his eye gouged out by the older man's flashing shears.

"It bloody is to me," says Stanley, deliberately turning his head away from the person who has just invited him to retire.

"You're over *seventy*, man! Or very soon will be!" protests the director, who is already tiring of the professionally intimate stuff and has emails to send, which are really far more his thing.

"With the body of a sixty-six-year-old!" cries Stanley, resorting as he usually does to humour and, as he inevitably does with this particularly challenging audience, failing dismally. "That was an attempt to lighten the atmosphere," he explains. "Although God knows why."

"Because you've been here too long," retorts Silk, clearly

delighted to have been handed this feed-line on a plate. "You're getting like *them*."

"*Them?* They're people, Mr Silk."

For the first time in this conversation, not that he has been exactly face to face with his oppressor for most of it, Stanley Grainger notices Gavin Silk attempting one of his smiles. It reminds him of a creepy uncle at a children's party, with precious little humour or warmth involved.

"No, they're not, actually. They're not human, Stanley. They're... showbiz. Everything about them is a performance. You never know who they are from one moment to the next. And neither do they half the time. One of them has only to fall out of bed and he'll give you the dying speech from King Lear."

Despite the new and dire threat to his livelihood, Stanley listens to this monologue – or, more accurately, rant – with increasing fascination. Against all logic, he suddenly feels luckier than he has ever realised. Here he is, a man of a certain age, who dearly loves the job he is currently being asked to quit. Isn't this so much more fortunate than the situation in which the individual beside him finds himself? Someone who clearly detests his every working – if not waking – moment but most probably couldn't walk away if he tried.

"I've got a tubercular old man who struts around with a wooden owl on his arm; another who talks in everyone's voice but his own; a highly irritating and, to my mind, rather suspect little person who does nothing but scoot in and out all day on her flaming stick, getting everyone dangerously overexcited; and another ex-superstar who thinks she's our beloved Queen on her mobile throne, trying to lead my weak and impressionable young daughter right off the bloody rails!"

Stanley waits until he is reasonably certain that the apoplectic man is spent and the sudden redness has finally dimmed from his hollow cheeks. "Let me stay on just a bit longer, Mr Silk," he pleads, whilst trying to maintain the dignity that has slowly become more important to him, as he can sense certain other faculties starting to play out the little cruelties of age. "Say until the summer? Meantime, whoever you choose, I can train 'em up. How's that for a plan, eh?"

"Can't you just grow old gracefully?" sighs Gavin Silk.

"*No!*" insists the older man, without the requisite gracefulness. "No, Mr Silk, I can't. I need to be doing something." The director can take resistance in his stride, indeed he can barely walk into a public room in this place without encountering it, but he finds himself thrown jarringly off course by the sudden sadness that clouds his ageing employee's face. "I need the company," says Stanley.

Silk looks like a man who has just won an argument. "This is their retirement home, Stanley. *Not yours!*"

Stanley looks like a man who is about to kill the person to whom he has just lost an argument. The shears are starting their dangerous trajectory – then, Lisa arrives.

"Hi, you two," she says cheerily, although she can sense that the cheer is hers alone.

"Can't you see we're busy?" barks her father.

"Oh, sorry."

Lisa has no idea what manner of situation she has just stumbled into, but she is pretty certain that it isn't hedge-related or some other harmless horticultural chat. As she looks at Stanley, he slowly turns his face towards her. She is instantly shocked, in a way that she seldom is, as an emotion she has never witnessed, or even ascribed to the older man, appears to be writing itself onto his familiar features. It reminds her of some sort of earthquake or one of those old buildings you see on the news that is being deliberately collapsed to make way for new construction.

She tries to lighten the mood. "Well, you're probably not half so busy as that lot in there," she says, pointing back towards the house.

The men turn, following her arm, although there is nothing to see.

"We'll continue this talk later, Stanley," says the departing Silk. "But I've made up my mind. You can start teaching Jason the ropes now and leave *early* December."

Lisa appears shocked and helpless. She gives Stanley a slight, yet she hopes consoling, smile, then turns to follow her father. She doesn't think she could bear to see the older man cry.

scene sixteen

Unusually for him, the tap dancer is sitting down.

Jacob Bloom wonders if he is the only resident in the crowded Green Room to notice that the quiet man's feet won't, and perhaps can't, stop moving. If it weren't for the fact that he knows who the man is and that he has always, for some unexamined reason, been drawn to this performer's enviable magic, Jacob would be thinking restless leg syndrome or far worse. (Not that he doesn't think about far worse a great deal of the time anyway.)

Elspeth has not yet begun to address the residents.

This is due in part to the last curious stragglers still gamely shuffling in but also because Zelda Gatley (who, to her credit, has been corralling people with some vehemence) appears to be skittering rather anxiously around the room, conducting a very loud questionnaire as to what people think of the new proposal. One that, as yet, has barely even been proposed.

"May I start?" enquires Elspeth Quest of the room in general and of that irritatingly frenetic little person, Zelda Gatley, in particular.

Elspeth has sufficient trust in her own internal barometer, born of decades of stellar and occasionally less than stellar theatrical experience, to be aware, from the very faint buzz around the place, that – whilst there are as yet few, if any, hints of excitement – there is at least an acceptable modicum of curiosity, which, for this particular crowd, has to be some sort of result.

"*Speak the speech, I pray you, trippingly on the tongue,*" smiles Rex Markham.

"No!" yelps Zelda. "Not yet! Speak ye – don't."

"Why the fu- why ever not?" says Elspeth.

"Marguerite isn't here!"

The elderly gathering looks around and has to agree with Zelda for once, this being a matter of plain fact, not questionable artistic opinion.

"Well, this is no concern of mine," dismisses Elspeth Quest. "I'm sure her lackey is on her way up there right now. Singing her little lungs out. And please note that when I *say* 11.00…" She looks stern for a moment, then softens and offers a smile which is genuinely self-deprecating. She hopes. "Now naturally, the last thing I ever desired was to shoulder all the immense responsibility that such an endeavour quite naturally entails. However, as I believe I am the only one here with directorial experience—"

"I directed a panto in Skegness in 1978," interrupts Barry Prince as, for some obscure reason, Laurence Olivier.

"And I'm sure it was bracing. So, what I propose…" She pauses as she spots Stanley Grainger and his director entering through the open French windows.

"I'm sorry," says Gavin Silk, "but what *exactly* is going on here?"

"We're planning a coup, dear," confides Gerard Bunting. "First the old-age homes, then the Werther's Original factories."

Silk just looks at Stanley, thrilled to be nailing the veracity of his earlier rant right between the ageing handyman's eyes. But Stanley is staring directly at Elspeth Quest, who clearly holds the room.

"The residents have graciously invited me to stay and put

on an entertainment, Mr Silk," she explains. And she almost believes it, because the words are so clearly and effortlessly emanating from her own mouth. "For Christmas."

"An 'entertainment'," repeats Gavin Silk with a nod, fortunately ignoring the 'invited to stay' bit. "And might I enquire where this 'entertainment' is to occur? The Royal Opera House? The London Palladium? I believe Glyndebourne is not that far away."

"Please refrain from being facetious. It's not attractive. I'm talking dining room." She points to the adjoining wall in case the director has forgotten where he last located it. "I'm sure your people can erect a temporary stage and some curtains."

Stanley is in there immediately, exposing his credentials with the deft undoing of a jacket button. "His 'people' certainly can, Miss Quest," he says, hand on chisel. "Mr Silk knows what a wizard I am with curtains." He grins at Silk. "Christmas, you say?"

"*Hold on – hold on a minute!*" protests Gavin Silk, raising his voice to be heard above, well, above nothing. No one is talking. But the silence is hurting his ears. "With respect, you are all people of a certain age. Vulnerable people. And this is a rest home."

"Arrest us, then. I'll go quietly," says Mr Chips, who hasn't cracked one out this morning and feels it is time.

"And, anyway," continues Silk, "we always have the choir from St Luke's in the town. They very kindly come in to give us a lovely carol concert, with home-baked mince pies and alcohol-free mulled wine." He smiles and puts his hands together in a mime of communal clapping. "And, of course, there's lots of singing along."

"*Kumbaya*," chants Zelda Gatley gleefully, smacking her hands together, until several residents glare at her and she stops.

"Now, why don't you just forget all about this and carry on with whatever you were going to do this morning," says Gavin

Silk, offering up one of his most unctuous smiles. "You'll all have seen from today's notice that, even as we speak, Mrs Fanthorpe from the town is on her way here to give her very popular sign language class. You know I only have all your welfares at heart and it's really not good for any of you to become overexcited."

Elspeth gazes around at the assembled company, although company is hardly the mot juste to describe them right now. They certainly don't appear overexcited, a fervid mob just looking to the newest and most vocal arrival to lead them, armchair blankets unfurled and walking aids held high, out of the old world of torpor, nostalgia and ennui. But neither do they appear in states of uncontrollable ecstasy over the prospect of a return visit from St Luke's Choir or its ability to make one bleak mid-winter's eve at Dustingford Hall so very different to the next.

There is hope here, she senses, if she can only harness it.

If she can only persuade these – sorry, she has to say it or at least think it – these 'has-beens', for once in their rapidly shortening and seriously diminished lives, to look just slightly forwards instead of almost religiously back. Desperate as she is to maintain her own 'performance' – although she is well aware that desperation is the last vibe she should be giving off right now – Elspeth does not yet have the self-knowledge, and perhaps never will, to realise that she, grande not-quite-dame of the English stage, is very much in the same camp.

When reinforcement comes, it is from a source she would have least expected.

"*Think of the publicity, Mr S!*" says Stanley Grainger. "The Trust would go a bundle on a Dusty Panto!" Fortunately, he doesn't catch the swift but uncontainable wince of horror on Elspeth Quest's face. And by no means hers alone. "You could invite, I dunno, the mayor, your pals on the council, the big bods from the Trust—"

They haven't noticed Lisa at the doorway from the corridor,

until she adds to the roll call. "Your creepy pal from the Herald would wet himself," she says.

Elspeth watches the director's face, as every thought going through his brain appears telegraphed between his eyes and his chin with absolute clarity. *If this were a film*, she thinks, *the man would be shot for overacting.* And she instantly finds herself knowing exactly what he is about to say next.

"Who's going to be paying for it?"

Somebody once told Elspeth that when they start to talk about 'how the hell?' rather than 'what the fuck?', you know the first battle has been won. But, of course, it doesn't stop the war.

It is Rex who puts his hand up. Or rather theatrically raises a louche, Harris Tweedy arm. "Some of us, love, despite the gross unfairness, nay malice, of the English divorce system…" he pauses whilst everyone except him sneaks a swift look at his former spouses, "still have the odd groat or two."

Lisa has to smile because she knows just how much her father hates being addressed as 'love'. She finds herself praying for a 'darling' before this unusual morning is done.

"Yes, we're not all charity cases, Mr Silk," says Cyril Dodds.

Elspeth spins round to stare at the small ventriloquist, but he isn't looking at her. She has to assume his comment is totally innocent or at least unspecific. But she can't be sure that his owl isn't giving her a knowing stare.

"What sort of show are you intending to do, Miss Quest?" continues Mr Dodds.

"Nothing too energetic, dear. I'm only half the chap I was," adds Mr Chips.

"You and me both," says Jacob Bloom, who had a testicle removed at the age of thirty-eight and has felt lopsided ever since.

Elspeth is certainly not going to admit to these people, all of whose eyes are on her, that she has been so preoccupied with finding a cause to justify the extension of her 'temporary'

Dustingford status that she has afforded precious little time to the exact parameters of that justification.

"I am mulling very seriously over several options," she informs them, authoritatively. "But rest assured, it will have integrity and substance."

Elspeth Quest decides to ignore the communal groan this nailing of dignified colours to a mast receives and is almost grateful for an interruption by that understudy woman.

"Elspeth?"

"Yes, er-er—"

"*Diana*. What about Marguerite?"

Elspeth can see the crowd nodding. Let them nod.

"What about Marguerite?" she responds, as if it is a matter of little import.

"It's just, well, we can't have anything without her, can we, dear? She's our most famous resident." She suddenly catches herself and looks at Rex, almost apologetically, but he doesn't appear in the least put out. "Lady resident," she corrects herself, offering him a sweet smile, which he gently returns.

"*Was*," mutters Elspeth quietly, observing this exchange. "So, where is she, then? I don't see her rushing to join us." She turns round to stare pointedly at Lisa.

"She said she didn't want me to bring her down," says her unofficial helper.

"Well, there you are, then," replies Elspeth in hopeful conclusion.

"She wants you to go and ask her yourself. In person," says Lisa, smiling innocently at Elspeth.

"There is always one, *always*," sighs Elspeth, shaking her head dramatically, "who has to be a controlling prima donna. Alright – we meet back here after lunch. By which time I shall have decided on the date, the production, the rehearsal schedule and which leading role I shall play."

Having made her point, she sees no other option but to

sweep out past a rather stunned Gavin Silk, and barely less stunned residents, into the piercing coastal air.

Only Stanley Grainger catches what is barely a flicker – the surprising yet unmistakeable flicker – of undiluted terror on the face of the elderly actress. An actress he has never actually known in the past but senses that he will begin to know rather well, perhaps too well for his liking, in the immediate future.

"Just try not to 'corpse' in the process," says Gavin Silk to her departing form, before turning back to his already muttering charges. "Isn't that one of your little words?"

The remaining residents aren't listening to him.

Something just happened, something they sense could forever change Dustingford life as they know it. And quite possibly shorten their own lives if they let it. Aside from the odd 'Jesus Christ', 'what in hell's name?' and at least one 'oy vey', surprisingly few are talking.

They are each simply looking at their fellows, as if trying to gauge a communal reaction and see if this might just assist them in determining their own. For, in truth, they all feel more than a little overwhelmed. It is almost as if war has been declared or, even more cataclysmic, that they got that part they read for in a West End play.

Something has altered, a shift in the tectonic plates, and they appear unsettled. Massively apprehensive. But not necessarily unexcited.

Quite a few trembling hands reach into pockets or purses for quite a few little pills. Gavin Silk just looks royally pissed off as he snaps his fingers and sends his inappropriately grinning daughter back to work.

scene seventeen

Zelda Gatley is troubled.

So troubled that she has missed the start of lunch, something she has never done, even when she had that unsettling virus back in March. Her guiding philosophy would appear to be, according to those who observe her, 'feed a cold, feed a fever, feed a really bad case of gastro-enteritis'. The only way she doesn't need a pulley to hoist her in and out of chairs, again opined by Zelda-watchers, is that she must be both secretly and industrially bulimic.

Stanley is checking the equipment in his tool shed, in hopeful anticipation of his new supporting role in the field of entertainment, when he notices the little lady passing at some speed on her stick, her head almost buried in her insubstantial chest.

"Hello, Miss Gatley," he greets her, with some surprise. "Aren't you having lunch? Chef's done his salad bar. And some of it is even fresh."

"Er, no. Thank you, Mr Grainger. I'm not actually feeling very hungry."

"Really? Excited about the show, eh?"

"Yes, that must be it." She seems rather anxious to be moving on, but Stanley appears to be on a roll.

"Wonder what it's going to be, eh? *Aladdin*, *Babes in the Wood*, *Dick Whittington*."

"*I have no sodding idea!*" she responds crossly and walks away, smacking the head off one of his Algerian irises with her stick.

*

In the lobby, Gavin Silk pins a single, typed sheet of headed paper onto the central noticeboard.

These notices are usually comprised of a list of the day's activities, which are relatively few in number but may include the occasional visiting speaker, from a world his residents used to inhabit and like to think they still do, alongside menus for lunch and dinner. The chef doesn't offer a huge choice, but Gavin Silk has found that his old people prefer to be able to identify what they are eating and possibly prepare themselves beforehand.

Today's notice, however, is different. It reads, in a sufficiently large and bold font, '*Christmas tea dance. Imperial Hotel*', with date, time and room below for signatures.

Of course, Christmas is still a good few weeks away, but the hotel – the second best of a mediocre bunch in the local town – likes to offer this treat relatively early in the season in order that it doesn't interfere with their more lucrative and slightly livelier Yuletide business. Gavin Silk prefers it as they offer him a reduced rate and he happens to loathe Christmas.

The residents are aware that this is the season when, many years ago, the director's wife abandoned him and his young daughter, without even a forwarding address. Inspector Malhotra of the New Delhi Police is convinced that the missing spouse is dead and buried in these very grounds but, as Gavin Silk was not employed by Dustingford at the time (and, in the opinion of most who know him, she would be the one more likely driven to homicide), the theory holds little water. This does not, however, prevent the dogged detective from occasionally borrowing one of Stanley Grainger's best garden spades and digging up random patches of earth when he thinks no one is looking.

*

It is not, however, a body that the occasional Indian is seeking this morning when Jacob Bloom finds the 'detective inspector' scrabbling beneath a large laurel tree.

"I am looking, kind sir, for Elsie Turks' ball."

Jacob Bloom finds that he has no idea how to respond to this, before thankfully recalling that, of course, poor Elsie Turks was, in her day, a rather well-known juggler. Even latterly, the old lady was still to be observed throwing several items at a time right up in the air – items such as salt cellars and pepper grinders, desk bells or even umbrellas. And occasionally catching them. In fact, there were times when the poor woman couldn't actually stop juggling, her hands refusing to stay either still or empty, whether it was at the dining table, the Green Room or even in bed. It was rumoured that her final injuries were in fact caused by a lethal combination of diminished dexterity, excessively weighty props and an unforgiving gravity.

Inspector Malhotra of the New Delhi Police has other ideas. "It is my belief, Mr Bloom, that the juggling ball responsible for killing the late Mrs Turks was sprayed with a lethal yet quite undetectable snake venom that is seeping with ease into paper-thin and ageing skin."

Jacob Bloom is usually rather relieved to discover that the cause of death of a fellow Dustingford resident is sufficiently victim-specific to be a highly unlikely contributor to his own inevitable demise. Yet this notion of foul play is quite new to him and, to be honest, not one to which he is prepared to afford much credence.

"I really doubt that, Derek." He realises his error immediately, without even catching the glare from the other man's distinctly un-Indian eyes. "Derek-tive Inspector."

"Please be bearing with me," continues the smaller man, doggedly unperturbed. "The victim had a son, an only child, who stood to inherit all her worldly goods. I am having it on the best authority that she was about to meet with her solicitor and to alter her will, to the immense benefit of this very home. And shortly afterwards – in fact quite soon after her son's last visit – she is passing away. Coincidence, Mr Bloom? I do not think so."

"She was eighty-eight," protests Jacob Bloom.

"But still juggling."

In order for this indisputable fact to sink in, the diminutive, sometime-Indian detective stares up into Jacob Bloom's gaunt and perpetually haggard face. As the stare shows no sign of receding, its object decides to nod politely and move on.

"I must be talking to Mr Jackson," he says, falling into the other man's curious speech patterns with an actor's gift, as he gratefully spots the tap dancer swaying on his own in the centre of the lawn.

The doughty little detective simply nods and seeks out another likely shrub. He is well-accustomed to scepticism but has never yet failed to conclude a case outside the six-episode window delineated by his superiors.

Jacob Bloom has not conversed with Mr Jackson since the latter's relatively recent arrival at Dustingford, nor indeed did he have any such opportunities before this, in the wider world. He is only realising now how much he has wanted to. Yet he is not at all certain why. This would appear as good a time as any to find out.

The dancer doesn't curtail his routine when he spots the elderly white gentleman approaching, with a somewhat relieved look, from the shrubbery. Yet Jacob does notice that those affectionate smiles and glances to an invisible partner become slightly less frequent. In their place, the still supple Mr

Jackson offers friendly nods, and even the occasional grin, to the considerably less flexible figure who has taken time out to admire his footwork.

Jacob Bloom realises that he hasn't observed anyone actually chatting with the tap dancer, even at mealtimes, although he is pretty certain that the more kindly and sociable of his fellows must at least have tried.

"I remember the Jackson Brothers," he tells the dancing man, surprising himself with his intervention. "I saw you first in Glasgow. 1972. A weekday matinee at the Kings just off Sauchiehall Street. When I was doing a Rattigan at The Cits. But, of course, I've seen you since, many times. And on television."

The tap dancer simply nods once more, but this particular nod is one of pure delight, rich in gratitude. Jacob Bloom is always amazed at how much information can be conveyed by the facial muscles alone, although as an actor – especially one who has played so many small, but he hopes not insignificant, roles on TV and in film – he knows that he shouldn't really be so surprised.

"You must miss him a lot."

The surviving Jackson Brother executes a brief but eloquent sequence to show that where once there were two, there is now sadly one.

A notion occurs to Jacob, and it is so overwhelming that it roots him to the spot, at a time when the tenderly flowing movement beside him is filling the air with melancholy, as the last leaves falling slowly from a dying tree. It must be in the way the man is looking across at the empty space, in a manner Jacob Bloom would not immediately categorise as fraternal.

"We all have people we miss," says Jacob Bloom, then wonders if this is true. Perhaps he has simply taught himself to stop missing them because it only adds to the sorrow that already feels an integral part of his condition, like some sort of autoimmune disorder that will feed upon itself.

The tap dancer does something that jolts Jacob immediately out of his sadness.

This embodiment of perpetual motion suddenly points to the ground beside him, the other side to that on which his missing partner must still be doing his phantom dance. He is clearly asking Jacob to join him.

Jacob smiles and shakes his head. "With *my* heart and legs? I'd be dead before my feet hit the ground!" He moves away from the man, as if Terpsichore itself might be catching. Yet he finds himself curiously touched. "But I remember you, Mr Jackson. You were very special." Jacob points to the empty space. "And so was… he."

Their eyes meet for a final time as Jacob walks off. He nearly bumps into Zelda Gatley, who is still stomping around as if the world is ending. Which for once, isn't the way Jacob Bloom feels at all.

Provided he doesn't have to be in Elspeth Quest's bloody show.

scene eighteen

The prime mover and sole producer of her bloody show is gazing in some puzzlement at the wall shelf in her room.

This narrow shelf now boasts, somewhat precariously, a selection of the precious, fraying books that she has finally liberated from one of her suitcases. Nestled alongside these weighty volumes is a small, framed photograph of a young boy. He is staring apprehensively into the camera, as if it is about to shoot an apple off his head.

Elspeth Quest selects one of the books and blows off some dust that isn't actually there. Taking a deep breath, she walks out of the room.

Her journey takes her no further than what has to be an irritatingly larger bedroom adjoining her own. Looking around, as if she might be caught in an act that would be the mainstay of tonight's dinner-table conversation, she knocks sharply on the door.

It is some seconds before the invitation to enter is given. Elspeth knows that it hasn't taken this long for the knocking to resonate. This is all about power and she must concede that she is now in the hands of one of its most consummate wielders.

"Ah," says Marguerite, as Elspeth obeys the summons. The visitor is not quite certain whether the older woman's exhalation is one of genuine surprise or realised expectation. But she has her ideas.

This visitor finds herself unable to gaze directly at the wheel-chaired figure dominating the room's centre-ground. Instead, she begins to examine the playbills swamping the otherwise bland, rest home walls.

"I'm not going to beg, Marguerite," says Elspeth Quest.

"I expect you at least to ask," chides the ageing star.

"Why don't I just call your agent? Check your availability."

"You still hate me so much," says Marguerite, with a touch more fascination than regret.

"I barely think of you," replies Elspeth, which is true. But yes, of course, when her thoughts do happen to turn towards Marguerite, they are at least a little hate propelled. She continues to scour the room, almost offhandedly, as if searching for something she really doesn't want to find.

"Yes. It's there," points the room owner, saving her guest the trouble.

And there indeed it is.

"*Dreamtime*," reads Elspeth, moving closer to the wall. "Starring 'Marguerite'. Who else? And oh yes, there, in infinitely smaller type, 'Elspeth Quest.'"

"I did you a favour, you know," says the name above the title. Elspeth can detect no obvious cruelty in the voice but a truckload of self-delusion.

"By getting me sacked just before opening night? I only wish I'd been able to return the compliment."

Marguerite smiles wryly as she shakes her head. "If I hadn't told them your singin' was weak, you'd have been playin' tiny parts in a dozen identical and equally silly shows and endin' up a sad little hausfrau in Sevenoaks at thirty."

Elspeth opens her mouth to argue, even about the unlikelihood of hausfraus in that part of Kent, but swiftly realises that there is little point. Especially as the older woman may well be right. Yet she knows all too well that altruism played barely a walk-on role in that particular production. And that, to this day, the older woman has never mentioned the acting or – let's call a spade a spade – the star quality.

"Well, I was never one to be petty," admits Elspeth. "So, if you wish to be in our little production, Marguerite, then naturally you are most welcome."

"Thank you, Elspeth. Of course, it all depends, doesn't it, on exactly what type of production you are contemplatin'."

Elspeth offers up one of her kindliest smiles and hands the old lady the large volume she has brought in, allowing it to fall open at a particular page. Marguerite looks at it for a few moments, adjusting her silver-framed glasses, then glares up at the offerer.

"I thought *The Dream* seemed appropriate," explains Elspeth Quest. "Oh sorry, Marguerite, it's what we actors call *A Midsummer Night's Dream*, you know." She taps the open book with a percussive finger. "See if there might be anything in it that's you, dear."

With that, she turns and leaves, wishing that she could offer up one final dramatic swivel and see the look on Marguerite's face.

scene nineteen

"*A Midsummer Night's Fucking Dream? For Christmas!*"

The residents now assembled in The Green Room are restless. Those whose restrictions of movement limit their restlessness are at least able to be disgruntled. The staff who are setting out coffee and biscuits for everyone appear the most restless and disgruntled of them all, as they can see that whatever is occurring will undoubtedly mean a load more work and an excess of aggravation. These are not uncaring people, but they regard themselves as seriously underpaid and they have just heard mutterings about the oldies putting on some sort of show. (As if they aren't always!) It doesn't sound like any sort of show they'd want to watch in a hurry, unless of course it means paid overtime, in which case they will clap and whoop for Britain.

Cyril Dodds is on a roll. "Where's the vent in *A Midsummer Nights Dream*?"

Barry Prince gives his most guttural Satchmo. "Or the impressionist? Oh yeahhhh!"

Two of the nursing staff, who are always at hand but who have never heard of Satchmo, (or Louis Armstrong) worry that the bouffant-haired codger is either choking or practising his death rattle. They rush over to him with all their skills and a glass of water, which he readily accepts, although he does feel a sudden need for something far stronger. Fortunately, there is more than one such item in his room.

Jacob is indicating the single remaining Jackson's ever-tapping feet. "*Or?*" he says, pointedly. And this is a man who knows his Shakespeare.

Rex Markham just smiles admiringly at Elspeth, who stands facing the throng, with her back to the ever-intrusive television that she has just moments ago switched to standby.

The would-be producer appears frustrated. "*The Dream* is universal!" she protests. "Magical! And don't we all need some magic in our lives? Especially as the days grow short."

"*As we reach September…*" sings someone in the throng.

She attempts a placatory smile. "Indeed. Anyway, I'm fairly certain that most of the people in this room *live* on dreams. Midsummer nights or, more likely, bleak mid-winters."

The solid sound of two hands clapping ripples the utter silence that Elspeth's call to arms has provoked.

"Bravo, Elspeth. Elegantly put," says Rex. "And who, dare I ask, from amongst this multi-talented company, will be giving her Titania? *Tarry, rash wanton: am not I thy lord?*"

Elspeth can't quite believe that she still remembers. It has been a while. Yet the actress finds herself word-perfect, even though she feels a few divots more of this mortal earth than at that earlier triumph.

"*Then I must be thy lady: but I know*
When thou hast stolen away from fairy land,
And in the shape of Corin sat all day,
Playing on pipes of corn and versing love
To amorous Phillida. Why art thou here,
Come from the farthest Steppe of India?"

She shakes her head, self-deprecatingly. Enough already, as her one-time American colleagues were wont to say. And now she waits. And waits. Until, finally, the majority of those listening and watching supply her with the requisite applause.

Diana Appleyard can feel her eyes zipping, like a spectator at Wimbledon, between the two of them, Rex and this strikingly imperious woman who never quite became an ex. It is self-evident to her, and most probably not just to her, that there is still chemistry here between these two leading actors of their day. She gives a quiet sigh, which even she might find hard to explain. Rex's Exes rise up from their usual chairs and decide to take separate walks around the garden.

Elspeth appears a touch more satisfied than when she had first confronted the residents with her inspired, if stunning, announcement. Despite the grumbles, this has gone better than she had anticipated. At least they didn't hurl their walking appliances at her.

"Interviews tomorrow morning immediately after breakfast. Please have something suitable prepared. Needn't be from *The Dream* itself, but my advice – think lofty. There are, I believe, books and tapes on the shelves and in the library."

She stares around the room. At those performers whom once she knew, those she has grown quite swiftly to sort of know and those she doesn't really care much whether she knows or not but with whom she assumes she will in time have some passing acquaintance. For a moment, she wonders where that annoying little starstruck woman might be, but then she simply assumes that she has fallen off her stick or died or something and gives the matter no more thought.

Turning to Diana – or perhaps not quite to Diana, as if full Quest gaze might be too overpowering for the elderly understudy – she announces, "You can be my assistant, er…" She struggles for the woman's bloody name but decides it isn't a necessity. "It'll be just like old times, won't it?" she smiles encouragingly, as a producer is supposed to do.

Diana has her doubts and for a moment appears to be on the

verge of polite disagreement but instead just nods resignedly.

"This is all too much," protests Jacob Bloom. "I need my afternoon nap already."

"I've a feeling the next time we sleep, it'll be in our graves," mutters Gerard Bunting, returning to the crossword that, until relatively recently, was his safe haven.

Everybody nods at these sentiments.

The elderly people in the room, who had assumed that they were happily retired, or at least retired, look less as if their dreams are about to come true than that their worst nightmares are on the cusp of being realised. In fact, each resident in that crowded space knows that if there is one image that still wakes them up sweating during the long, dark nights, it is that of appearing onstage in front of a packed house with absolutely nothing prepared because you've either (a) memorised the wrong play (b) pitched up at the wrong theatre or (c) forgotten everything in the world you ever knew, including putting your clothes on, before you step out into the light (unless, of course, you're in *Hair* or *Oh Calcutta*).

Yet, even whilst picking up on this genuine fear in their failing eyes and knotted brows, watching already well-worn faces take on stretcher-case pallidness, Elspeth knows – or thinks she knows – that somewhere deep inside them, they want this. More than that, they need this. Despite themselves and all the touchpoints of reality, they genuinely *yearn* for this. Well, at least some of them do. Not all by any means. But enough of them, hopefully, to form a cast, a troupe, a company.

After all, she's only holding a play text to their heads, not a loaded revolver.

All she needs, reckons Elspeth Quest, is a sufficient number of players with the requisite skills to keep her in business. To render her sufficiently and purposefully occupied on a venture that explains to one and all a necessarily elongated Dustingford stay and justifies not returning any time soon to her Kensington flat. A flat that wasn't hers in the first place and to which she no longer even has keys.

Once Christmas is done, she'll think of something else.

scene twenty

"*Shakespeare!*" comes the echo from the terrace.

Stanley is sitting on a low brick wall with Jason and a couple of the junior gardeners/handymen, all enjoying their mid-morning tea and watching their breath rise into the chill coastal air, alongside the steam from their mugs and the smoke from their frowned-upon fags. It is Jason who shakes his head with almost theatrical vigour. This is apparently at the notion of very old people attempting to put on a performance when, from his youthful perspective, they can hardly put on their own underpants.

"*Shakespeare?*" he repeats, which not only nails the lunacy of the entire project but also intimates to his colleagues that he knows whereof he speaks.

"Ours not to reason why," adjudges Stanley, who reckons that this phrase has to be Shakespearean if anything is. Funny how it can almost sound like English at times. "Ours – according to Lady Muck of number sixteen – is to stack and unstack the tables every day; build a ruddy stage with curtains 'n' all; rig-up some lights that aren't too cruel; paint a few pretty trees onto some cheap wood I've probably got lying around from bed boards; and make sure none of the old folk trip over and break their bloody legs. I'm not shooting another one!"

"Isn't that what they say?" says Jason.

"Isn't that what who say?" asks one of the lads.

"*Break a leg.* It's what they say."

"Break a leg? Who bloody says that – the Mafia?" says Stanley.

"Actors. My mum does amateur dramatics down the Scout Hall and they're always saying that to each other."

"What – break your bloody leg?"

Jason nods authoritatively. All four of them shake their heads in unison.

"Actors!" they intone like a Greek chorus.

*

By eleven o'clock, almost all the tables and chairs in the dining room have been carefully stacked, courtesy of a whistling Stanley and his grumbling stagehands.

At the sole unstacked table sits Elspeth Quest, glasses tilted on her small nose, a nose just a degree too asymmetrical to have made her a great screen beauty but which has served her well enough onstage and in those TV dramas where 'interesting' had its place. She fiddles with an elegantly slim, silver propelling pencil. This was once a prop in one of those dramas, something that she knew they would never really miss. Or, if they did, that she would be the last person they would ever suspect. She was, in fact, mistaken in both suppositions and it was only her slightly failing hearing that prevented her from catching the senior props man mutter, on one of her latter productions, 'here she comes, lads, get the superglue out'.

Diana Appleyard is struggling to extricate one of the chairs from the pile. She can hear Elspeth Quest sigh, as if the clattering is being done simply to annoy her. So, the lady clatters just a tiny bit more, simply to annoy Elspeth Quest.

"Send the first person in, would you, dear?" says Elspeth,

who can't understand how anyone can make such a business over finding a chair. But, of course, this is what she is most probably going to have to put up with over the next few weeks and it is indeed fortunate that she has the patience and understanding of a saint. "Oh, for pity's sake, woman!" she says, by way of encouragement.

Diana plonks her chair down and shouts towards the door. "*Dame* Judi Dench! Could you come in please and why not drag along *Dame* Maggie—"

"I'm really not in the mood for humour."

"I thought we were doing *Midsummer Night's Dream*."

"I can find other assistants, you know."

For the life of her, Elspeth Quest can't understand what this woman's grouse could be. If it's the fact that Elspeth never took a day off for sickness, bereavement or a better job interview, well pardon her, but surely this was something to be applauded. She will have to watch this one – she could be lethal.

"Can we have the first person in please?" calls Diana Appleyard, politely.

When no one turns up after a decent interval, Elspeth instructs her minion, with a brisk wave of her hand, to go to the door and drag someone – anyone – from the lobby into the dining room. Or rehearsal space as it has now become and so will remain right up until the week before Christmas, even if it means Stanley and co stacking and unstacking until their muscles and patience give way.

Cyril Dodds – who always appears to Elspeth to be in the vanguard of any situation, whether it's a welcoming committee or a chorus of disapproval – enters with his owl. The latter is scouring the huge and now almost empty chamber, as if searching for mice.

Diana returns to her seat next to Elspeth and opens a bound and flowery notebook she has brought with her from her room. This pretty object had been intended to contain a handwritten memoir to leave to her great nieces and nephews, but every time she sat at her small dressing table, poised to write, she found herself staring blankly into her mirror, convinced that she really wasn't particularly interesting. At least now the hitherto pristine stationery won't remain quite so virginal.

"Good morning, Cyril," says Elspeth with a welcoming smile. She feels a sudden nudge from beside her. "And, of course, Mr Chips." She tries and fails to keep the sigh silent. "So, what are you going to do for us this morning?"

"We thought something from *Hamlet*," says the ageing ventriloquist.

Elspeth Quest can't pretend not to be a little surprised, but she does her best. "Very well, then." She finds herself skimming briskly through the play in her head. Obviously, the part most suitable for every single male resident – in fact, the only suitable part – would be the elderly Polonius, father and chief counsellor. So, she prepares herself for his advice to his son Laertes – *neither a borrower nor a lender be...*

Cyril Dodds gives a little cough and turns to his partner. But not before smiling warmly at the two ladies, who are kindly offering him this special opportunity. One that, he would have to admit, he had initially met with reluctance, before telling himself that the chance might never come again and that he owes it to his fellow residents, to the dear family who will undoubtedly be driving down to see him and to his public, however diminished they might be. He just hopes that he and Mr Chips can meet the challenge, but of course he doesn't have far to go to touch wood.

"Ready, Mr Chips?" he says to his trusty owl.

The bird starts to wriggle around almost uncontrollably. Elspeth sighs once more, realising with some regret that even on so brief an acquaintance with the little man, she has already anticipated a wisecrack about woodworm and will just have to grin and bear it.

"What are you doing?" asks a genuinely puzzled Cyril Dodd.

"Adjusting my codpiece," comes the reply. "It's still sitting on my stomach from supper."

No, I wasn't expecting that, thinks Elspeth, although it doesn't diminish her irritation. Nor do the giggles coming from the woman beside her. "Please don't encourage him," she whispers, which even Diana Appleyard thinks is not exactly a company-spirited note.

Both women, however, are rather taken aback by what their first interviewee does next. With one firm jerk of the wrist, Cyril Dodds removes the dummy's head completely from its body and holds it almost at eye-level with himself. Thanks to its intricate mechanics, the owl's face and eyes can still move and the bird does indeed appear as alarmed as his observers by this sudden and unprovoked severance.

"*Alas, poor Yorick!*" intones Cyril Dodds in classic, if possibly slightly outmoded, Shakespearean tones. "*I knew him, Horatio. A fellow of infinite jest, of most excellent fancy. He hath borne me on his back a thousand times; and now how abhorrent in my imagination is it.*"

The owl's face turns slowly and meaningfully towards the elderly Hamlet. The outrage is palpable. "You didn't tell me I'd be playing a dead person!"

"It's an old age home, Chips. It's what we do best."

With this, Cyril Dodds looks to his producer/director, whose bemusement appears to echo around the cavernous hall.

"Hotcha!" concludes Cyril Dodds, with a touch less verve. His smile only returns when he hears some kindly and not unappreciative applause from the producer's assistant.

"Thank you, Cyril. That was quite lovely. Don't you think, Elspeth?" She believes she can hear a muted grunt from nearby. "Could you send in the next person please, Mr Chips?"

Cyril Dodds restores Mr Chips's still animated head to its rightful position. "Just supply my agents with the dates, if you please," says the owl, "and she'll confirm my availability... nights are better for me."

The two women behind the table just nod and await the next interviewee. They know now that they should be fully braced to expect the unexpected and, to this extent, they are not disappointed.

*

During the course of this first morning, they hear the Bard rendered exquisitely; hesitantly; croakily yet word-perfect; croakily with book in hand; audibly but with unmerited confidence; and, towards lunchtime, delivered exactly as Laurence Olivier might do it were he equipped with a jet black bouffant wig and an irrepressible desire to step once more into the breach as Joan Crawford.

Occasionally, the proceedings are interrupted by those ruder mechanicals who really can't be arsed to walk right around the entire building just to arrive at the central staircase.

The young men would also admit, perhaps a fraction reluctantly, to finding themselves fascinated by the entire process. The residents have usually been only too happy to fill in any passing member of staff on past triumphs and have often done so interminably, with visual evidence to back them up. So, it is almost refreshing for these young people, and indeed for some of the kitchen staff and carers, to watch their charges actually strutting their celebrated stuff, although 'strutting' may be a fanciful acceleration of what is actually taking place.

After Barry Prince's onstage lingering for several superfluous minutes with his singular and impossibly deformed Richard the Third, which makes Elspeth wish that the long hook on a pole was not merely the stuff of legend, Diana finally manages to take the man's newly withered arm gently, but with surprising firmness, and lead him towards the door.

"I had a winter of discontent once. Went down to the paper shop – it had blown away."

"Ken Dodd!" laughs Diana, in pure delight.

"Tommy Cooper!" corrects the peeved impressionist, as he leaves the room. "But I'm easy. Ooh, Madam!"

The producers find themselves so relieved when Rex Markham finally walks in that they just want to hug him and offer him any part he chooses, including Hermia. Even they are surprised, however, when they find him carrying a battered old sword.

"I still have my weapon from the RSC," the star explains.

"I remember it well," says Elspeth. The tiny Appleyard moan is buried beneath Rex's next double entendre.

"At my age, I think I'm allowed a little 'Lear', don't you?" Before they can acknowledge this, not that it begs acknowledgment, the man is off. "*And my poor fool is hang'd! No, no, no life! Why should a dog, a horse, a rat, have life, and thou no breath at all? Thou'lt come no more, never, never, never, never, never!*"

His eyes meet Elspeth's. The famed actor is still good and both parties are fully aware of this. It is as if Diana Appleyard has left the room. Sometimes, she wonders if she actually has. Yet she knows that she hasn't because then her eyes wouldn't be so fully focused on the stars that are in them.

"Why did you let the big screen seduce you, Rex?" asks Elspeth, to which the man shrugs, with what appears a genuine regret.

Yet this actor has also learnt, over the years and despite his stardom, not to hog the limelight. So, with a polite nod, he exits, weapon in hand, and allows his successor to take centre stage.

Diana notices but keeps to herself the fact that – whilst clearly there are more female residents at Dusty Hall, as she imagines there must be at the majority of such establishments – it is the men who make most of the running this morning. She wonders if this is less a matter of talent, for surely this is evenly spread, and more about actual desire and yearning. And also, that these men, as patently evidenced by their longevity, have some sort of life force within them, enviably potent and perhaps more suited to this particular endeavour. Some of the female residents have in fact told Diana that whilst they might be happy to carry a spear (or a walking stick), they have no intention of parading their goods in front of bossy newcomer Elspeth Quest.

The remaining Jackson has been happily so parading for years and, despite everything, has no intention of quitting now. As he taps swiftly in towards them from the doorway – wearing worn but shiny shoes, which he has clearly cherished and kept in peak condition – he appears delighted to be able to hear his acknowledged mastery echoing back to himself, and to everyone concerned, from the old floorboards, as it obviously cannot on carpet or the grass outside.

He arrives in front of them neither empty-footed nor empty-handed. The performer holds a small and rather old-fashioned tape cassette player, gripped tightly in a strong left fist. Elspeth had noticed such an appliance in the library, alongside cassettes that must have been in Dustingford for years. She assumes that music of all kinds, bar the most contemporary, would be there to enjoy and fully expects to hear a backing track reflective of an era when tap was at its zenith. Which, so far as the production team are aware, was not the sixteenth century.

John Gielgud's matchless rendition of *All the World's a Stage* comes as rather a surprise to them. Yet, as the remaining Jackson tailors his intricate tap routine to the melancholy trawl of Shakespeare's Jacques through the seven ages or, more aptly, stages of man, they start to realise how ingenious this riff on *As You Like It's* greatest hit really is. Indeed, they begin to see the aged hoofer in a different light as he segues, with a deftness belying his age, from infant and whining schoolboy, through lover, soldier and corpulent justice, to culminate in shrunken pantaloon and second childishness, a genuine tap dance of death.

They can only applaud as the sombre man returns to silence.

"That was extraordinary," pronounces an enchanted Diana Appleyard.

"Indeed," confirms Elspeth Quest. "Totally useless for what I had in mind, but I do applaud your taste and ingenuity, Mr er…"

"Jackson," supplies Diana. "Of the Jackson Brothers."

Elspeth, who has never heard of them, merely nods. They could have been a male, black version of The Rockettes for all she knew.

Yet one person who knows exactly who they were, and finds himself overwhelmed, has been watching through the slightly open doorway. Which makes his own entrance – once Mr Jackson has elegantly sidestepped out, with an acknowledging smile – appear all the more poignant.

"I am a Jew," announces Jacob Bloom, before he has even reached the table.

"Yes, we know that, Mr Bloom," says Elspeth, wearily. "Have you prepared a piece for us?"

"I believe this *is* his piece, Elspeth," whispers a slightly embarrassed Diana Appleyard.

"*Hath not a Jew eyes?*" continues Jacob, before a formal discussion of his heritage can set in. "*Hath not a Jew hands, organs, dimensions, senses, affections, passions? Fed with the same food, hurt with the same weapons, subject to the same diseases, healed by the same means, warmed and cooled by the same winter and summer, as a Christian is? If you prick us, do we not bleed? If you tickle us, do we not laugh? If you poison us, do we not die?*"

The pain on Jacob Bloom's pallid face is almost unbearable and the two women appear genuinely moved.

"I do comedy, too," says the aged actor, which they find slightly less convincing.

Over the years Jacob has learned the invaluable skill of not overstaying one's welcome. So, without any encouragement, he gives the ladies a polite nod, receives an equally courteous thank you, then turns and heads for the door.

Opening it, he makes way for a slightly grumpy Gerard Bunting, who is clearly not thrilled to be here but is determined not to let the side or his fellow residents down. Or indeed himself. And, despite a natural and possibly career-limiting humility, he knows that he is amongst the best of the bunch.

Without waiting to be greeted, the actor sets out his stall.

"Thought as we were doing the bloody *Dream*, I'd give something from the bloody *Dream*. As you doubtless recall, I've played Bottom many, many times. At the Vic, of course, when it was home to the National, and in-in, well, in several other places." He taps his head. "It's all still up here."

"Then, do please proceed, Gerald," says Elspeth. "Forgive me. Gerard."

The rotund, red-faced man gives a rather chesty cough, then commences the speech with a confidence both women recognise as the mark of a seasoned and well-respected professional.

"*That will ask some tears in the true performing of it: if I do it, let the audience look to their eyes; I will move storms, I will condole in some measure.*

To the rest: yet my chief humour is for a tyrant: I could play Ercles rarely, or a part to tear a cat in, to make all split.

The raging rocks... the raging rocks..."

Gerard pauses. This is not where one might expect a pause, but the listeners give him the benefit of the doubt. It is only when the pause moves beyond the acceptably meaningful that they begin to show concern. A concern they find echoed in the face of the elderly actor, which appears to be growing considerably more red.

"The raging rocks... yes? *And shivering shocks!* Yes! *Shall break the locks...* the locks... the er... I've known this since forever. It was often my audition piece. How silly of me."

"Oh, Gerard," says Diana Appleyard, gently. "It's alright. It's fine. How can anyone be expected to remember after—"

"I am *not* anyone, Diana! *Of prison gates.* You see! *And Phoebus' car*, yes, fucking Phoebus' car... *Shall shine from far and make and mar the foolish Fates. This was lofty! Now name...* now name... er... and I think that's quite enough, don't you? Bottom... Gerard Bunting. Join the bloody dots, as they say these days!"

On this, he spins round and shuffles disgruntledly off towards the door. It is pushed open an instant before he arrives by an elderly, but clearly still remarkably supple, contortionist, who is managing to get her right knee respectably close to her head, whilst propelling herself with both hands and an impressively slim backside towards the table.

"Shall we have lunch now?" says Elspeth, beginning to stand.

Before Diana can encourage her to allow the contorted interviewee a sighting, the same door slams open and Marguerite steams in from the hallway, wheeling her chair with her own still powerful arms.

"I don't *do* auditions," she informs them.

And out she goes, propelling the hitherto flawless contortionist into an inelegant heap on the floor.

"*Lunch!*" announces Elspeth Quest once more, as there is nothing left to say.

*

It is Zelda Gatley who kicks off what is often referred to as the 'graveyard slot', when bellies are full and bodies weary. Diana Appleyard finds herself hoping, as Elspeth clocks who is coming in next, that she doesn't choose to make mention of this.

"Ah hello – Zelda, isn't it?" says Elspeth. "Poor you, getting the graveyard slot."

Diana Appleyard's despairing sigh is muffled by the practically catatonic little interviewee's infinitely more despairing whimper.

"Hello, Miss Quest. Hello, Diana," murmurs Zelda, her

visible lack of enthusiasm in stark contrast to the usual climactic reactions to anything remotely starry.

"You can call me Elspeth," says the magnanimous producer.

Despite her crippling stage fright, Zelda Gatley is beside herself. "Ooh. Can I-can I really? *Thank you.* Thank you so much, Miss... Elspeth." She looks even more sheepish and apologetic, which onlookers might have assumed well-nigh impossible. "I... haven't actually memorised a piece of Shakespeare... Elspeth."

"You must remember *something*, dear. From drama school."

"Oh, yes. Yes, of course. Yes. But nothing... suitable... for a seventy-eight-year-old."

"Nothing in *The Dream* is suitable for a seventy-eight-year-old. Except perhaps Titania." She allows herself a small, and she hopes reasonably modest, smile at this. "But the play is, after all, about imagination."

The three women are so involved in this process that it is only after Diana looks up and notices Gavin Silk lurking in the doorway that they begin to wonder how long he might have been watching. His eyes, if this is possible, appear even colder and more reptilian than usual.

The producers are rather taken aback by the effect this person's presence is having on their current interviewee. She has begun to shake alarmingly. The stick, which has hitherto been employed solely for propulsion, seems now to be the only thing preventing her from keeling over.

Finally, she manages to regain a tiny sliver of control. "Would you mind awfully if I had a bit more time, Miss Quest – Elspeth? Diana?"

"Oh, very well," allows Elspeth. "It has already been a very long day."

Overwhelmed with gratitude, or at least with relief, the tiny woman scuttles away, her trusty stick reverting gamely to its default function. Zelda pointedly avoids any visual contact with

Gavin Silk, whose pitiless eyes she can feel burning into her face, like tiny spotlights too close to the stage.

"I think we're done with this, aren't we? At least for now," says Elspeth to her subordinate. "Can't think why that dull little woman even wants a part in the first place." They are both ignoring Gavin Silk, who eventually retreats across the corridor to his office, looking no happier than when he turned up.

A gentle voice stops the producer as she is gathering up her belongings.

"Er, what about me, Elspeth?"

Elspeth turns with some genuine surprise to the woman still sitting in the chair beside her.

"*You?* Oh. Well, I thought you'd understudy me." She smiles into the kindly, open face of the other actress. "Nobody did it like you, Diana."

"Oh. Oh – thank you," says the newly appointed (or reappointed) understudy, not certain whether to be flattered or tearful. "Yes. Alright." She changes the subject to one more buoyant. "I think it's all going rather well, don't you?"

Elspeth Quest just stares at the woman, then stomps out.

She notices Gavin Silk standing in the lobby, outside his office, clearly waiting for her. Ignoring him, she climbs the stairs to her room.

scene twenty-one

It is during the lazy time of the afternoon, when the majority of residents are enjoying a little restorative nap, that Stanley Grainger finds himself at his most productive. And, of course, at his least pestered. This particular afternoon, Lisa Silk catches him happily hard at work, repairing a metal handrail on the grand staircase.

Despite his being on 'borrowed time', the ageing handyman is diligent in his maintenance, perhaps even over-diligent, but just one skittering resident is, in his opinion, one too many. Stories of the great Dustingford Stairwell Disaster of 1989 abound and by now, it has taken on the proportions of the Bethnal Green Tube Station catastrophe of 1943. Which some of the oldest residents still vaguely recall.

Stanley Grainger pauses, as he unfailingly will, for a chat and a brief gossip with his special friend. But right now, the young woman doesn't appear in a particularly chatty or gossipy mood. The older man immediately notices the unusual panic on her face.

"Have you seen Miss Quest?" she blurts.

"I haven't, pet," says Stanley. "Not that I've been particularly looking for her. Why?"

"She hasn't come down for her tea and she's not in her room.

I've been in the Green Room. The toilets. She's not anywhere."

"Did you check the register?"

"Nothing. She's not in the garden either. I know what'll happen. My dad'll blame me, you'll see."

"You can't be watching every resident," says Stanley, dialling his voice down to ultra-calm, in the hope it will reduce the frantic young woman's panic levels. He has to admit to some surprise, as Lisa Silk doesn't usually appear so easily ruffled. He wonders what has happened and whether it has anything to do with her father's stupid scoresheet. The man has seemed even more officious since the news of the Christmas panto.

"Have none of the others seen her?"

"No. And after all the goings-on, you know, with her Shakespeare thingy, it doesn't look like they particularly want to. They all seem knackered."

"So, what do you—"

"That nice Miss Appleyard," continues Lisa, "she says Miss Quest just sort of stormed off. Wasn't looking any too happy, apparently."

"You know actors, petal. They go through as many moods in a day as we go through breaths." Lisa keeps staring at him. He sets his screwdriver back into its pouch. "Come on, I'll help you look. Before it gets dark."

As they move down into the lobby, Stanley spots the Christmas tea dance notice pinned to the board. He points it out to Lisa. "I see nobody's signed up yet."

"Can't think why," says Lisa Silk.

*

Elspeth has always loved the sea.

As a child, her parents would very occasionally take her to Scarborough. Whilst they seemed excessively preoccupied with the potted shrimps and the pink rock that said the name of the town all the way through it, in case you needed reminding where the teeth-rotting set in, little Elspeth only wanted to rip off her second-hand Start-Rite shoes and tiny white socks and go for a paddle along the shore.

She would have loved a sister, or even a brother, to share the sand and starfish, but in later life, observing the relationships most of her acquaintances had with their siblings, she has felt that being an 'only' is, on balance, the better of all possible worlds. Even though her father had often, and quite publicly, expressed the desire for a son to make him proud. *Well, screw you,* she thinks – *look at your little girl now*. But then she looks at his little girl now and thinks that perhaps she won't go there. Anyway, she has plenty of new concerns to bother her. The main one being this bloody play.

The sea is acting up a bit today, which is exactly as she would wish. If you can't find drama on the English coastline… and how better, cinematically, to reflect the inner turmoil of her character? Or, perhaps, the desperate and unrelenting isolation, which is another issue best shelved for a better time.

She really has to admire her ability to compartmentalise. It has served her well over the decades and will hopefully do so now. Yes, of course, it will. No hopefully about it. And as for that prize diva, Marguerite…

Still mulling on this, she turns into the wind and walks barefoot towards the waves, holding her sensible shoes in her hand. The cold spray on her face and the tiny stones beneath her feet begin to make her feel alive again, in a way that she truly hasn't since—

"*Miss Quest! Miss Quest!*"

She can hear the panic in the man's voice, ramping up the Geordie accent as he yells. "Oh Lord," she says to herself, "the bugger thinks I'm about to do a Virginia Woolf." She notices that she uses the word 'bugger', which certainly isn't her vocabulary but would undoubtedly be a mainstay of his. *How clever*, she thinks, *to appropriate another person's dialect in extremis.* Yet even this self-admiration doesn't mitigate her fury at being interrupted.

She turns to see not just Stanley Grainger but also that irritating little Goth girl clambering frantically down the steep cliff path towards her, repeating her name over and over, even though she has patently heard and recognised them.

"Dear God, can't a woman even take a quiet walk?" she says, although she is not projecting as yet.

"*You didn't sign the book!*" chides Lisa, arriving just inches away from her runaway.

"She's been looking everywhere," adds Stanley. "And it'll be dark any minute."

"Oh, for pity's sake, it's not boarding school. Did I miss lights out? Are the prefects furious?"

"There are still rules, pet," says Stanley.

"Please don't 'pet' me, Mr Grainger."

"I wouldn't dream of it, Miss Quest. Lisa, you run back now, or your dad'll play steam. I'll see Miss Quest home."

"I don't need 'seeing home'. And why was the girl looking for me so urgently?"

To the older woman's surprise, Lisa Silk doesn't respond. It is almost as if she has become painfully shy, although reticence and a respectful reserve were hardly foremost amongst the qualities Elspeth has observed in her.

Stanley takes on the oft overlooked role of prompter. "It was something about the show, wasn't it, Lisa?"

"It's not a 'show', Mr Grainger," corrects Elspeth Quest, although she is not surprised. "Shakespeare didn't write 'shows'. *Or* pantos."

Elspeth is slightly wrong-footed when the young woman becomes suddenly mouthy. It is as if Lisa Silk has summoned up all her available courage and released it in one firm blast. "You shouldn't be doing a Shakespeare! Not at Dusty Hall."

"Shouldn't I? Then what, pray, should I be doing, dear? Arthur Miller? Strindberg? Ooh, I know – David Mamet! Cut out the 'motherfuckers' and we can all be in bed by eight."

"Something that gets everyone involved!" insists Lisa. "It's Christmas, for heaven's sake! Something that's fun."

"Instead of that grim Shakespearean tragedy, *A Midsummer Night's Dream*." Elspeth Quest stares out into the sea, which is currently looking far more tempest-tossed than fairy-friendly. And then she smiles, as what should have been only too obvious lands like a sudden wave lashing a defiant rock. "Something no doubt that you can warble in," she suggests, without looking back at the young woman.

"That wasn't why—"

"Oh, please," says Elspeth. "I've never been one to discourage self-promotion. But neither am I inclined to give a person false hope."

Elspeth begins to walk away along the shore, her bare and increasingly sensitive feet registering every rock and pebble with more discomfort than she can ever recall.

"You haven't even *heard* her, Miss Quest," calls Stanley. He follows the recklessly shoeless woman, easily catching her up. "She's very good."

"For the end of the pier, possibly. Whatever one might say about the residents, Mr Grainger, they *were* professionals. They spent years learning their craft."

"She's trying to learn. Miss Marguerite's teaching her."

"Ah yes, Marguerite. Encourager of young talent." Elspeth turns to find Lisa within shouting distance. "Be wary of that lady, dear. I know her of old."

"Yeah. She knows you too," mutters Lisa. She is not sure whether Elspeth heard nor if she really wanted her to. Elspeth simply walks on.

"Off you go, love," says Stanley gently, smiling at the lost-looking girl. Eventually, Lisa nods and walks back over the beach to the cliff path. He reckons that if her spiky head were to hang any lower it would be banging into her regulation Dustingford belt.

Stanley catches up with Elspeth.

"Why do you act so unpleasant?" he asks her. "Or are you not acting?"

Elspeth's first instinct is to berate the man, a fairly lowly employee, for his insolence to a respected, and in some circles still revered, Dustingford guest. But as she looks at him, his eyes wincing and crinkling up even more in the damp winterish wind, she finds such anger strangely impossible. "Because I tried not to give a young woman unreal expectations?"

"I'm talking about the way you treat people. Like they don't matter."

"Perhaps they don't."

"Or perhaps you haven't found the right people."

She turns to Stanley, with a genuine interest that even she finds disconcerting. "Did *you* find the right people, Mr Grainger?"

The sadness that comes so swiftly over his usually cheerful face reminds Elspeth of Melpomene and Thalia, those exaggeratedly tragic and comic masks of Ancient Greece and myriad amateur dramatic society logos. "I did, Miss Quest. For too short a while." In an instant, the smiling mask is back, although to be fair, this would suggest a certain artifice, a façade, something of which she would be genuinely loathe to accuse him. "Why are you doing all this play stuff, pet?" he asks gently, or as gently as he can and still be heard above the waves. "Don't you want to just relax… for the short time you're here?"

"Mr Grainger," explains the lady with a sigh, "I'm an actress. It's not what I *do*; it is who I *am*."

"So, who are you this time round?"

"Titania – Queen of the Fairies."

Stanley opens his mouth to respond, but then realises that

he has absolutely nothing useful to say. Elspeth Quest knows that she has absolutely nothing more to add.

And so, she walks regally – if just a bit gingerly – off towards the winding cliff path.

Stanley spends a few wistful seconds watching the waves wear away at the stones. For some reason, he thinks of Whitley Bay and his childhood, although the beaches were so much better, even if the weather demanded a stoical northern soul.

After a suitable interval, he follows on.

scene twenty-two

You could cut the tension in the Green Room with a safely blunted knife.

The staff can sense it as they clear up the residents' afternoon tea and biscuits. They don't say anything, it's not their place, but even what they might call the geography gives it away.

There are two distinct clumps of Dusties, huddled in their armchairs, with a gaping hole between them that you could drive a tea trolley through. The staff are no experts on life in the performing arts, but when they retreat with some relief to the kitchen, Nancy Fowler is able to hazard a guess as to what is going on.

"On the window side, those are your actors. Straight actors I think they call them, although not all of them are. Straight, I mean, but live and let live, I say."

The others nod, then one of them, who thought the whole ruddy shower were actors, enquires as to who that lot on the other side are then, those ones with their backs to the lobby.

"Variety," says Nancy Fowler with some authority. "You know, like poor old Elsie, the one who just died. The juggler."

They nod. They all remember poor Elsie. The one who couldn't stop chucking things skywards at dinner, stuff that they often had to scramble on all fours just to retrieve and then set down again well away from her. The one who left nasty great dents in her bedroom walls when one – in fact most – of her more ambitious stunts went pear-shaped. But word has it she was a very wealthy lady thanks to a good marriage, with pots to leave, which was why the usually irascible Mr Silk was rather too indulgent.

"That little feller who thinks he's a Pakistani or an Indian says her son went and murdered her," chimes in one of the younger staff.

"I don't want to hear no more of that talk, Kylie Morton," chides Nancy. "That poor woman died a natural death a good few days after her son's last visit. Everyone knows that. And you don't want to start listening to men who think they're Indian. No good will come of it. Now, you go into the dining room and help Lisa set up for dinner. God knows what the old folk'll do with their seating arrangements tonight. We'll be the ones bloody juggling!"

*

Gavin Silk takes one look at the opposing forces facing each other across the red carpet of the Green Room and prudently decides to stride briskly through the febrile gap without favouring either side.

He does notice that Marguerite is, as ever, conspicuous by her absence, so at least that's one less contraption around which to manoeuvre.

There are the occasional muttered greetings, but he chooses to ignore them, as they would only lure him inextricably into arcane theatrical conversations, none of which would improve his day. A day through which he would prefer to navigate unmolested until he can reach the safe harbours of 23 Blomfontein Terrace, where the makings of an eighteenth century Retourship Batavia and a large glass bottle await his unexpectedly tender ministrations. He has a feeling that a slightly less empty bottle may also be laying claim to some of that precious time this evening.

Silk finds Lisa in the deserted dining room, carefully laying out place settings on one of the hall's long tables.

"What the HELL is going on?"

Lisa drops a clutch of cutlery and turns round in shock. She hates it when her father does this – surely, he could signal his presence less alarmingly. And now, of course, he becomes irritated by her understandable surprise and the whole thing escalates. Tosser!

"They're a bit upset," she says, unhelpfully.

"I can see that! Any particular reason or are they just being actors?"

"It's old Miss Quest's show thing. The theatre lot want to put on a play. Obviously. But the other lot want more of a… I dunno. Show. Concert. Whatever. With little acts and stuff. They had a bit of a row; a buttered scone was thrown and now they're not talking to each other."

"And all thanks to our celebrated grande dame!"

Lisa starts to clatter the crockery with more force than the task demands.

"What's up with you?" asks her father.

"Isn't it weird? You'd probably like the whole world to work in a care home. That lot just want to put everybody else off doing what they do."

Gavin Silk just stares at his daughter.

He notices the sadness in her face and the darkness around her eyes, which he doesn't believe is entirely due to that curiously morbid make-up she puts on. Chosen, he can only assume, to match the stark blackness of her weird standing-up hair, not unlike her mother's, and to contrast with the paleness of her skin, which could also be make-up but might possibly just be her. He is aware that he can't venture much beyond this, towards questioning or even understanding. Perhaps because this is too painful or more probably because these simply don't figure amongst his many skills.

"I have no idea what you're talking about," is what he says.

Which sort of ends this discussion.

When she spots the lady-in-question entering through the French windows, Lisa slips away. The table settings are unfinished, but sod it. The oldies will probably only use them to attack each other, anyway.

Elspeth has every intention of entirely bypassing the annoying director, but she discovers her path blocked. To angle her way round would afford this person a power that right now she is in no mood to concede.

"Miss Quest, a word please. If you are not too busy." He realises that this is a phrase he often employs somewhat sardonically with his residents but that this time the irony is rather misplaced, as busy is exactly how the old woman looks. "Until a couple of days ago, this was an orderly – dare I say contented – retirement home. Now, we appear to have The War of the Roses."

The genuine confusion aroused by this observation warns Gavin Silk that the addressee has absolutely no idea what he is talking about. A bony finger pointing back towards the Green Room doesn't aid her one jot.

"Would you mind?" he continues, nodding in the direction of his finger.

Casting him one final, then-get-out-of-my-bloody-way look, she strides on feet that are still bruised and sore from the shoreline towards the indicated battleground.

Gavin Silk continues on his own trajectory towards the kitchen. Elspeth catches his petulant barking as they each move towards their respective sphere of operations.

"Those tables won't lay themselves, you know!"

The moment she enters the Green Room, Elspeth Quest understands exactly what this afternoon's drama is all about.

She would have to admit that in life she does prefer such immediate comprehension, as indeed she would were she reading or watching a play. She has an aversion, even an impatience, with mystery and obscurity; texture and subtlety excite her but the fashionably oblique or trendily impenetrable leave her cold.

Breaking the angry silence with a brusque clap of her hands, she addresses both factions. "Ladies and gentlemen, if I might interrupt for a moment." The residents turn to her with a collective and distinctly belligerent sigh. "Thank you all so much for auditioning yesterday. I have to say, I was… impressed."

Rex Markham sits with Gerard Bunting and Diana Appleyard. "We *are* rather good at what we do, Elspeth," says Rex, glancing down at a recent copy of *The Stage*, which rests on his lap. "Even if, for some of us, it's barely worth doing."

"You are awful, but I like you," says Barry Prince, as an epicene Dick Emery, whom only a few remember and which doesn't ease the atmosphere one bit.

"Listen, heart," explains Cyril Dodds, amiably, from the other side of the grand divide, "if we put on a play about young lovers lost in the woods…" At this, he pauses, which Elspeth somehow knew he would.

"Bottom won't be the only one making a bloody silly ass of himself. Hotcha!" completes Mr Chips.

Gerard Bunting responds with a weary sigh that lingers in the toxic air. "It's called make-believe, darling. Like we believe Mr Chips isn't just a bit of four-by-two from B&Q."

At this, Cyril puts his hands protectively over poor Mr Chips's ears. Meantime, the tap-dancing Johnson is displaying his anger via his perpetually mobile feet. For reasons best known to himself, this causes the never-less-than-versatile Barry Prince to segue into Ethel Merman as Annie Oakley with 'There's No Business Like Show Business'.

"Well, I for one am not doing a song and dance in my condition," says Jacob Bloom, switching his mournful gaze from Elspeth to the variety club just a few yards and several chocolate digestive crumbs away. "Or sticking my toe in my ear," he adds, a trifle obscurely.

Diana looks helplessly to Elspeth, with some genuine sadness. "Perhaps – I'm wondering, dear – well, perhaps a performance wasn't such a good idea after all."

The softly spoken lady expects a glare of such incandescence from the fiery actress that it will singe off what are left of her eyebrows. Instead, and to her surprise, Diana Appleyard is picking up what looks a good deal like panic.

"People – *please!*" placates Elspeth Quest, in barely modulated desperation, as she glances from one simmering camp to the other. "I do assure you that I had absolutely no intention of… doing a Montagues and Capulets. Quite the reverse."

"Capsulets and Montagues?" hazards Zelda Gatley, who patently hasn't heard of either but doesn't want to be left out.

Curiously, Elspeth doesn't appear to be disconcerted by this interruption. It is as if the odd little woman has given her a few precious moments to collect her thoughts. "Perhaps-perhaps we might do an evening that – and, of course, I'm thinking out loud here – that can incorporate the best of *all* our worlds. Everything from well, ventriloquism to tap-dancing to twisting your body into unnecessary postures to," and here, she manages to catch Rex's quizzical eye, "to The Bard himself."

"Forsooth!" laughs Rex, in admiration.

To Elspeth's surprise, it is her faithful understudy who appears less than impressed. "Oh Elspeth, you can't just mix—"

A thought occurs to Elspeth, although she can't quite recall its origin. "The two muses, dear, remember? Melpomene and

Thalia." She raises two hands towards her cheeks and instantly, employing the bare minimum of carefully chosen facial movements, creates the opposing, or perhaps complementary, masks of the theatre with something approaching magic. "The-The Dustingford Follies will have both."

The two opposing forces in the Green Room are immediately as one, at least vocally, as they slowly repeat, with a healthy tinge of scepticism, what this daunting but infuriatingly seductive woman has just said.

"*The Dustingford Follies?*"

"Of 1923," adds Barry Prince.

"Why not just call it 'Dust to Dust'?" suggests Jacob Bloom.

"No. Now, does anyone play the piano?" asks Elspeth, continuing with something approaching enthusiasm, without ever quite leaving desperation. Rex's Exes both shoot up their hands and then glare at each other.

"Magic fingers, both of them," says Rex Markham, nostalgically.

Elspeth, who hasn't spent this long at her craft without knowing when to quit once ahead, snaps her own magic fingers at Diana Appleyard. "Davina, come. We have a programme to plan."

The two ladies move off, one determined but fearful, the other just fearful, to find a quiet space. They don't notice, although they can probably hear the scraping of chairs and the creaking of limbs, that the two warring factions are very gradually and tentatively coalescing once more. White Kleenex are being waved, newspapers and caramels exchanged, photographs of grandchildren shared.

Peace has broken out once more.

Now, all they have to think about is whether this final performance of their lives will end up being the death of them.

act two

December 2019

act two

scene one

The smokers huddle together on the chilly, windswept terrace, looking out onto the winter garden. Lunch is over and Lisa Silk can tell that they have much to discuss.

She is walking briskly past them, pushing Marguerite in her wheelchair. The elderly lady nods at the small gathering, who nod respectfully back. She also chooses to cough, although Lisa has ensured that the smoke is not in coughing distance of those famous and still powerful lungs, but Miss Marguerite feels that she has to keep making the point. The smokers acknowledge her point by rolling their eyes.

When Lisa is confident that the other residents are unable to hear her, the wheelchair and its celebrated occupant being by now well onto the ocean end of the garden, she decides to broach the one subject that has been on her mind for the past forty-eight hours. (Still pushing all the while so that she at least can get some exercise.) But first, she ensures that her charge is sufficiently warm and blanketed to be able to respond in any meaningful way.

"Miss Marguerite, I was wondering…"

"Something by Noel Coward. *Yes!*" says the elderly lady.

She moves her swaddled head slowly in both directions to admire the garden, savouring what winter has to offer and mulling over how the word now denotes far more than just a passing season.

"Him again," says Lisa, who has heard the name mentioned more than once. "Well, I suppose I could download it and have a go. How do you spell—"

"What are you talking about, child?" interrupts Marguerite, craning her neck to glare at the young woman.

"Learning the song. You know. By this Coward bloke you keep banging on about."

Marguerite thumps her wheelchair angrily with both powerful arms. "Not you, girl – *me!*"

Lisa pauses her pushing.

"Did I say stop?" says Miss Marguerite, crossly. "Push. *Push!* Yes, I shall do my Coward medley. I knew the Master, you know – he used to call me M."

"I thought you said you weren't going to be in 'that woman's show'?" says a puzzled Lisa.

"I said I wasn't going to audition." She turns to face her carer. "I won't be *in* her show, Lisa Silk – I shall *be* her show. Star billing. As always. 'For one night only. Marguerite and-and company. In The Dustingford Christmas Follies."

"Dunno what Miss Quest is gonna say about that," says Lisa Silk, pushing the old star with increased vigour farther down the garden path.

*

"*Over her dead fucking body!*"

Is what Elspeth Quest unsurprisingly says, although this is not an expression much encouraged in such establishments.

She and her loyal assistant Diana Appleyard are in a quiet room off the main lobby, deftly claimed before a possible interloper from the town could commandeer it for some worthy but futile arts or crafts endeavour. They sit at a small collapsible table, surrounded by notes and papers. Lisa stands beside them, having brought them the good news. She finds herself rather relishing the malign old drama queen's displeasure.

"She says unless she's top of the bill – *and* it's in writing – she's not doing it," explains Lisa, although the 'in writing' codicil is her own invention.

"What the audience don't see, they won't miss," responds Elspeth, who hates ultimatums, unless they originate with her.

"Oh, I think they will, Elspeth," says Diana but receives only a chilling glare for her disloyalty.

"Why's it such a big deal, anyway?" asks Lisa.

Elspeth responds with a weary sigh. "My name, Miss Silk, was up there in the brightest of lights for nearly half a century. It is most certainly not going to be relegated to second fiddle in a paltry little concert party, in a sorry little home for sad old has-beens. Especially not to a woman who hasn't sung in public for well over twenty years and whose once admittedly fine voice has no doubt followed the downwards path of the rest of her."

"Don't think much of yourself, do you?" says Lisa.

Before Elspeth can form a response, which Diana fears may arrive in the form of a threat or a curse, the understudy attempts kindly – and for her own sanity – to ease the tension.

"So, how's the singing going, Lisa?" To which Lisa simply – and perhaps sensibly – just shrugs. "I'm sure Miss Quest would love to hear you, wouldn't you, Elspeth?" persists the tender-hearted woman.

"Not especially," says Elspeth. "Now, please tell Miss Marguerite that this is *my* production, and I am not taking orders from her or from anyone."

"Elspeth—"

"Top of the bill," insists Lisa, rather enjoying herself. "And that's our final offer." On this, the self-appointed 'manager and agent' strides defiantly out.

"I do think you could at least have heard her," says Diana

Appleyard when the young woman has made her exit.

"Let one amateur in, dear, next thing you know you'll have her appalling father entering stage left in a fez, doing the Egyptian sand dance and that Stanley fellow playing the spoons as he sings 'Billy Boy.'" She puts on her glasses and picks up her purloined propelling pencil. "Show me that bloody list. Now that my *Dream* is unrealised, I have a show to devise. God help me."

scene two

"*Where have ye been all the day, Billy Boy, Billy Boy,
Where have ye been all the day, me Billy Boy...*"

Stanley is walking along the first-floor corridor, carrying a clutch of energy-saving light bulbs, which he clicks together as he sings. It startles him when the song is picked up just along the corridor.

"*I've been walking all the day, with me charming Nancy Grey...*"

The handyman turns with a beam to greet Rex Markham, who is sauntering slowly towards him. The older man, whom Stanley rather likes and even half recognises from long-gone trips to his local Odeon, is looking quite dapper in a smart blue blazer and old college bow tie.

"Hello, Mr Markham," smiles Stanley. "Dressed for dinner already?"

"Dressed for something, Stanley," replies the actor, giving his tie the tiniest twirl. To Stanley's surprise, the man, usually so brimming with confidence (alongside that other, far rarer quality, which Stanley might join the rest of humanity in being unable quite to define but you kind of know it when you see it), appears a tiny bit apprehensive. "'Twixt you and me," the star confides quietly, yet in a voice that could still cross corridors and indeed continents. "I've come to plight my troth."

"Have you?" says Stanley. "Well, whatever that means, I hope it doesn't spoil your appetite."

"At my age, Stanley," says the debonair old gent as he passes by, "whatever doesn't kill you, makes you whole."

Not for the first time, Stanley Grainger realises how little of what these usually rather sweet, albeit occasionally tricky, old people tend to say makes any sense to him whatsoever. Yet what surprises him even more is that Rex Markham has paused outside room sixteen and is giving gentle knocks on the door.

Sensing that he might be an intrusion, even though the electrical problem of the moment glares at him – or rather doesn't – from right outside this same room, Stanley decides to move on and find some other home for his energy-savers.

As he slips discreetly past the actor, he hears the current resident of room sixteen calling, "It's open."

Stanley Grainger finds himself taken by how pleasant a voice this irascible, opinionated old lady has, when she is not being abrasive. (Which would appear to be most of the time, as this has to be why he hasn't noticed the pleasantness up until now.)

Moving on, he vaguely wonders why he should be the least bit interested in what a couple of old Dusties get up to. It has never concerned him before.

He gives a brief glance behind him and just catches Rex Markham disappearing rather tentatively inside.

Elspeth is at her dressing table, busily scribbling indecipherable notes on several small sheets of cut-up paper. Her unexpected visitor looks around the poky room, feeling slightly saddened by the austere, almost spartan quality the place gives off. He has to remind himself that she is, of course, here only temporarily. Unlike Rex, the Exes and most of the other residents, Elspeth Quest has no intention of putting down roots. Or putting up playbills.

"Am I disturbing you, darling?"

"Yes," she replies, not lifting her head from her paperwork. "Rehearsals start tomorrow."

"Mm. About that. I was just wondering whether you and I could, you know, do something together?" He can't help thinking that she appears quite stressed.

Elspeth turns round to look at him. To her surprise, he is standing rather close to her, clearly attempting without his glasses to read her notes.

"What did you have in mind?" she asks, a little throatily, sliding the notes away.

"Oh, I don't know," he smiles. "Perhaps some little thing we've performed before?"

As she catches his drift, or believes she does, Elspeth ponders for a moment on whether she might have inadvertently wandered into a drawing room comedy of the sort they did in rep way back when such things existed, then reassures herself that these days she would be playing the dotty granny or the ingenue's eccentric great-aunt.

"You're talking about something we haven't done for over fifty years," she continues, picking up the thread. Elspeth appears reasonably content with the diversion, as these hours of planning and paperwork have rather worn her out.

Rex moves even closer and rests a comforting, still carefully manicured hand on her shoulder. "The basic thrust hasn't changed, I gather. And, like fine claret, a certain maturity makes up for that much overrated, juvenile pep."

"Is this a serious proposition, Rex?"

"Oh yes."

The warmth of his hand, which in truth she has rather liked, is suddenly gone. Following its journey, she finds the owner, to her astonishment and she has to admit terror, leaping away from her and up onto her small, single bed.

That same hand is now raised aloft, as if brandishing an invisible sword in victory towards the heavens. For one stirring moment, she enjoys a glimpse of the dashing action hero this man once was. Even as she ponders whether this particular battlement, despite its recently enhanced fortification, will bear the heroic weight.

"*She speaks.*

O, speak again, bright angel! For thou art
As glorious to this night, being o'er my head,
As is a wingèd messenger of heaven
Unto the white, upturnèd, wondering eyes
Of mortals that fall back to gaze on him
When he bestrides the lazy-puffing clouds
And sails upon the bosom of the air."

For a second or two, there is only silence.

"It's you, love," prompts the hero.

"I know!" snaps Elspeth Quest. "*Jesus!*" She then continues with a not very maidenly sigh.

"*Oh Romeo, Romeo! Wherefore art thou Romeo?*
Deny thy father and refuse thy name.
Or, if thou wilt not, be but sworn my love,
And I'll no longer be a Capulet."

She shakes her head and tries not to consider her ravaged face in the small, uncharitable mirror in front of her. "Oh, this is ridiculous!"

"You're still that young girl, fresh from RADA, setting the Stratford stage ablaze."

"No, I'm not," insists Elspeth, sadly. "I'm an arthritic old woman, Rex, careering rather creakily towards her eighties, temporarily beached on a very foreign shore. Viola in *Twelfth Night*. A very mature Viola. *What country friends is this?*"

"Listen, dearest," says Rex, leaping without incident off the bed to smile into her unforgiving looking glass. (Although, she still feels that this man is rather more forgiven than most.) He watches their two faces, not unlike those old masks she talked about. "We have some time before dinner, which they will insist on serving even before the cocktail hour…"

Elspeth watches her own countenance with interest, as her eyes tilt slightly towards his, opening wider with genuine and registrable surprise.

"You're not seriously asking me to…"

Rex Markham smiles rakishly at her. But then, to her genuine dismay, his still beautiful face slowly begins to crumple.

"Oh, Rex," she says, gently.

"Age cannot wither me but intensive radiotherapy can."

"Why don't you just sit there, on the edge of the bed you very nearly ruptured, and help me with my running order?"

He sinks down tiredly, splaying his long, once-buccaneering legs out in front of him. "Where did the time go, lovey?" he asks, not expecting a reply. He smiles in resignation towards her mirror. "You can always tell an old thesp – he's still counting his lines."

Through the thin walls, they hear a shaky yet distinctive and still rather beautiful voice.

"*I'll see you again …*"

"Put the radio on, darling," says Elspeth Quest.

*

Stanley is walking in the other direction along the corridor, this time carrying a broken chair, when he almost bumps into Rex Markham leaving the bedroom of Elspeth Quest.

Ever one for his audience, Rex 'straightens' his already immaculate bow tie and flashes his famous smile. "Well, I'm ready for my dinner now, Stanley," he beams.

To the natty resident's surprise, and indeed to Stanley's own, the handyman ignores the elderly matinee idol and stomps crossly away down the corridor, banging the already fractured furniture into the home's drab green walls.

scene three

Once breakfast is over and the residents have departed, the entire complement of young men who work at Dustingford Hall are immediately taken off their maintenance, gardening and catering duties by Stanley Grainger, in order to transport the large trestle tables and most of the collapsible chairs from the dining room and stack them temporarily on the terrace. Which right now is fortuitously rain-free.

Gavin Silk can only nod to them as he passes by on his daily rounds.

Having given tacit assent to the proceedings – seduced by the notion that it might actually reflect well on him, without hopefully terminating too many of those in his care – he feels, with some admitted displeasure, that there is not actually a great deal more he can do, other than watch and wait. The man is, however, experiencing a genuine dose of his own first-night nerves. Shot through, in his case, with a suppressed but permanently bubbling anger that he no longer truly questions and has learned to accept as part of his make-up.

He barely notices that the young men appear to be carrying out Stanley's instructions with little grace and a good deal of mystification.

"We put the sodding tables out; we stack the sodding tables

up; we bring the sodding whatsits back in again. We're not maintenance or kitchen staff anymore; we're sodding scene-shifters," alliterates one of the younger men.

"Wait until they really get into it," warns Jason. "We'll be doing a shitload more shifting than this, darling."

The young man eyes Jason with suspicion. "What's with the 'darling'?"

"It's what actors call each other," explains Jason, who has served such people at rest and at, well, mostly at rest. "'Darling.'"

"Are they all, you know?"

"Most of 'em. Not the ladies, I don't think."

"Been there, have you?" asks another, which causes his fellow shifters to gag and stick several fingers down their throats.

Stanley walks past his crew, carrying a large plank of wood. "Step up, darlings," he exhorts. "Rehearsals starting any minute."

The young stagehands just look at each other.

*

The entire 'cast', save for the estimable Marguerite, stand around in the newly depleted dining room, silently and rather anxiously awaiting the arrival of Elspeth Quest, who will hopefully update them as to the exact manner of beast in which they have been summarily selected to appear.

One rather frail, elderly Chinese lady leans resolutely on her Zimmer frame, clearly determined to play her part in whatever show is about to go on.

The loudest noise in the room is that of the ever-industrious Stanley Grainger, piling heavy planks of wood as far away as he can from the assembled residents. If even one old person brains themselves in a timber-related incident, Stanley knows that it will be his head on the block.

"Where's Elspeth – I didn't see her at breakfast?" says Jacob Bloom, worriedly. "I do hope she hasn't passed away in the night."

"Oh, Jacob," says Rex, with a sigh. Slinging a comradely arm around the doleful man, he points the other arm dramatically out into the emptiness. "But talking of 'dying', loves, gaze out there."

Like meerkats responding to the lookout's cry, all the performers – straight theatre, variety and those with a well-worn foot in both camps – stare out into the newly stripped, intimidatingly stark dining room. They no longer take notice of Stanley. He is surplus to their imagination and their fears.

"Where?" says Zelda Gatley, who is not entirely sure what all her fellows are staring at.

"*There*, Zelda," says Rex, helpfully. "See the audience? All one hundred and fifty of them. Sweeties rustling, phlegm gurgling, mobile phones buzzing. Expensive teeth glinting in the darkness."

Zelda nods, trying so hard to see what this wonderful, beautiful man is seeing. The others have no such trouble.

Slowly but inexorably, the lighting in the room, usually so bright and clinical, transforms and dims for them, until they can see through their imaginations exactly what is going on out there. The audience fades to a darkened blur, the only illumination being that which is so familiar yet still so merciless, starkly pinpointing their nervous, expectant and swiftly ageing faces. Now, they can truly hear the timeless buzz as the curtains open. The shuffling and coughing, the muttering and settling.

As one, they all of them look excited. Energised. And totally petrified. Especially Zelda Gatley and Gerard Bunting.

"Full house tonight. All dolled-up," continues Rex, slowly but mercilessly building the scene and the terror. "All replete with fine suppers, large G & Ts and unrealistic expectations."

Without even realising it, the cast of – they know not what – form a straggly line.

"There'll be patrons of the Trust there," says Gerard Bunting, helplessly fuelling his own trepidation. "Household names. Powerful people."

"Agents. Producers. Directors," adds Jacob Bloom, dolefully.

"Family, friends, local press," says Diana Appleyard, who won't of course be in it but is fearful for all of them.

"My relatives," says Cyril Dodds.

"My relatives," says Mr Chips.

"Got your relatives here," mutters Stanley Grainger to himself, hefting a plank.

"Knock 'em dead, kid," says Barry Prince, as somebody or other.

"I think I need to sit down," says Jacob Bloom, wiping his forehead with a handkerchief.

"So do I," says Zelda Gatley.

"Me too," murmurs Gerard Bunting.

The imaginary lights go up, the audience fades away. Very slowly and shakily, already thoroughly exhausted, they retreat to the few remaining chairs, which Stanley and crew have considerately left unstacked.

About ten seconds later, a businesslike Elspeth Quest strides in, notebook and pencil in hand, and takes in the scene. Or doesn't. She turns to Stanley, who is crouched beside the door.

"Mr Grainger – might I have a table please?"

With a grumpy yet resigned sigh, Stanley gets up and starts to make for the terrace.

"Not too 'tired', are you?" he asks meaningfully, as he sets off.

Elspeth, who clearly has no idea what meaning he is full of but isn't over-inclined to think about how tired she does actually feel these days, says, "No, I'm fine, thank you. Why do you ask?"

"No reason."

She watches him trudge away, then shakes her head and returns to the job in hand.

"Er... alright. So, ladies and gentlemen, now that our *Dream* is dead but newly arisen, I'd like to commence by asking you all just to introduce yourselves." Elspeth smiles, in what she considers a suitably motivating way. "Not that any of you *need* much introduction," she lies. "But, of course, you must in the process tell us *exactly* what you have decided – perhaps misguidedly – to perform for our audience in just a few short weeks' time. And then we can take this event you've kindly implored me to stay on for, against perhaps my better judgment, and magically transform it from a dog's breakfast into a meal fit for kings." The cast stare at her, not quite knowing whether to be insulted or inspired. "Mr… Jackson? Why don't we commence with you?"

The tap dancer leaps up from his chair with a lithe and enviable grace. He nods respectfully to Elspeth and Diana, glides forwards to the very centre of the room, as if endowed with a mechanism superior to that of ordinary mortals, and eases seamlessly into a spirited and highly professional, albeit unaccompanied, routine. The sound of his worn but loyal tap shoes resounds like a fusillade around the newly stripped, high-ceilinged room. One can fully appreciate how fine this performer once was, whilst being just as roundly impressed by what he still is. All eyes are on him but none more so than those of Jacob Bloom.

"Absolutely delightful," pronounces Elspeth, with an encouraging smile. "I'm sure we can think of something better than that." She looks up at Diana Appleyard, who immediately grabs the flowery notebook from her handbag. "To be discussed… Diana. Alright. Moving on. Mr Dodds?"

"I've been working on some new material, Dame Elspeth." Elspeth Quest just sighs. "Nothing Shakespearean, thank God. Contemporary stuff."

"Contemporary to what?" pipes in his wooden friend. "The Wall Street Crash?"

"I shall ignore that, Mr Chips. I know you haven't been well." With this, the ventriloquist turns to address his fellows. "That was our catchphrase: 'I haven't been well.'" The others simply nod. Elspeth wants to say that it can't have been much of a catchphrase if you have to remind people but shows what she considers admirable restraint.

"I'll outlive you, Dodds," says Mr Chips. "I saw your last CAT scan."

Cyril appears rattled by this, which Elspeth considers just weird. But he soon rallies.

"I'd rather be given a scan by a cat," he retorts, "than be mistaken for a tree by a dog. Hotcha!"

"Mr Dodds," says Elspeth, in what she decides is the kind but firm voice she will be needing to employ on a regular if not interminable basis, "people will be coming here at Christmas to have a good time. Not that I intend giving them anything remotely Christmassy. But they really don't want to keep being reminded of—"

"Dying?" interposes Jacob Bloom. "It's our speciality. It's what we're heavy-pencilled for. Or perhaps I should say, *heavenly*-pencilled." He almost smiles to himself at this rare foray into gallows humour. Which leaves his fellows equally nonplussed.

"We are all Bloomed!" laughs Rex Markham, attempting with that sonorous voice alone to elevate proceedings from the graveside. "So, Elspeth, dear, are we giving our *Romeo and Juliet* or are you in your Titania mode?"

They are suddenly disturbed by a loud, angry banging from behind. Elspeth turns to see Stanley hammering something unnecessary into a plank.

"What the... *Mr Grainger!*" The banging continues. "*Mr Grainger!*"

"*What?*" calls Stanley, without turning round.

"We are trying to rehearse."

"Then you need a ruddy stage, don't you?"

Diana Appleyard realises that yet again she must step into the role of peacemaker. She really should have joined the United

Nations. "Could you possibly do it in the afternoon, Stanley? We have our doze in the afternoon."

"Not anymore you don't," says Elspeth Quest.

The cast look at her askance, as if she has just suggested they conclude the evening's entertainment with the finale from Stomp.

"I'm seventy-eight!" protests Zelda Gatley. To which she receives nods and grunts of assent.

Elspeth says nothing. She just sets her cardiganed arms to akimbo and casts her glare on each would-be performing resident in turn. "Are you professionals or what?" she challenges.

"Nobody's paying us, heart," says Gerard Bunting.

"Nor would they," counters the producer/director/star, "if you're going to doze off every five bloody minutes." Elspeth sighs, as if old people have been the bane of her life forever, and tries to erase from her memory the little afternoon snoozes to which she herself has been partial for several years. "Alright – take your naps when you're not rehearsing. Diana, make a note. And a rota. Now, we desperately need a stage manager, someone who isn't going to fall asleep on us." As the PA scribbles, Elspeth turns back to her cast. "And we can rehearse the grand finale in the mornings, when you're at your freshest."

The grand finale? They stare at her in total dread.

"It's not easy to do that 'eleven o'clock number'," says WC Fields (resurrected), "when you're usually in bed by 9.30."

"Very good, Barry," says Elspeth, "whoever you were. Now, is anyone here a choreographer?"

The elderly Chinese lady with the Zimmer frame raises it up to be counted. "Agnes Wu," she announces, to which those around her nod, as the lady is far from unknown.

"Oh yes. Indeed. A pleasure, Agnes and an honour," says Elspeth to the respected dancer-turned-choreographer. "Well, that *is* good news. Even if… well, just leave your name and contact details with Diana." Elspeth ignores the stare from her understudy/PA and turns her head round towards the door. "Stanley, dear, could you have the piano moved in here from the Green Room, please? By tomorrow."

The handyman touches his forelock, but the gesture is wasted as Elspeth has already spun back.

"Let's break for coffee. Back in fifteen."

The hammering resumes with a vengeance.

scene four

Elspeth Quest strides down the corridor towards her room and walks straight past it.

Were such an action to be observed by a member of staff, it might well result in her being taken gently by the arm and guided back to where she rightly belongs. Fortunately, there is no one around and the lady knows exactly where she is going.

She knocks on the door of number eighteen and already has it some way open by the time she receives permission to enter.

Elspeth is gratified to find Lisa Silk in here with Marguerite, although she can't imagine that this is the most appropriate use of time for the young employee.

"So, finally," says Miss Marguerite. Elspeth remains silent. "I know it must be hard for you, Elspeth. But you're bein' gracious and it is not unappreciated."

"Good," says a gracious and appreciated Elspeth.

"I shall be givin' my Noel Coward medley," continues the star. "As the closin' item of the programme. Which, by the way, will have my name—"

"Yes, yes, very interesting. I didn't come here to horse-trade, Marguerite. I came here for Miss Silk."

"What?" The elderly lady swivels her chair to face the young woman accusingly, as if this is some sort of malign plot.

"*Me?*" says the mystified young woman.

"We are in dire need of a stage manager, if you even know what that is. I don't suppose you have any experience?"

"I have, actually. *Rocky Horror Show* at school. We got full houses and the English teacher fired."

"Well, Rocky and Horror could apply equally to this production. It will be your job to ensure the cast turns up each day on time and in one piece. *Especially* on opening night." Elspeth Quest continues at some speed, offering the older woman minimal eye contact and precious little chance to interrupt. "Over the coming week, we shall finalise what each member of the company is actually doing as their 'act'; try to make it so that the whole enterprise is less of a godawful mish-mosh, more a structured and life-enhancing potpourri; and then begin proper and rigorous rehearsals as soon as humanly possible. My task will make cleaning the Augean stables seem like a little dusting behind the skirting boards."

"Yeah, okay," says Lisa Silk, who has barely understood a word of this. She awaits Elspeth's nod and half turn back towards the door. "On one condition."

Elspeth spins round. "You're giving *me* conditions?"

Lisa glances at Elspeth but then shifts her gaze towards Marguerite, whom she has observed quietly fuming during the monologue. The gaze remains until the young woman is certain Miss Elspeth Quest understands.

"*Fine!*" says the beaten producer, with a long-suffering exhalation. "Marguerite, you will close the show. No special billing. Neither for you nor for myself. It is to be a team effort. Just make sure your voice is 'strong enough'," she adds pointedly. "Suck a Zube."

This time, she leaves the room without turning back.

Lisa grins at Marguerite, then leans down to offer her a high five. The elderly diva stares at the approaching hand in total confusion but does produce a moderately satisfied smile.

scene five

A week may be a long time in politics, thinks Elspeth Quest, as she mulls over events since that first introductory session in the dining hall, *but it feels like bloody seconds when you have a show to put on!*

After five solid days of rehearsals, or as solid as they can be when the average age of your cast is eighty-one and standing up is considered choreography, she sits at her dressing table/desk, trying not to look at herself in the mirror and attempting even harder not to ponder on what she has become.

The surface of the charmless unit is now littered with scraps of paper, each one a performer, as she works out some sort of notional running order that will afford the evening its essential light and shade. Unlike previous events, when she has presented inspired selections of scenes and readings from the classics, performed by esteemed colleagues in appropriate venues to well-chosen guests, she can see a fair amount of shade on the schedule but precious little light.

She looks up into the mirror and tells herself that this glass-half-emptiness might perhaps just be her, signifying little, as it has been a seriously trying week and she feels wearier than she recalls having ever been. She tells herself this, but she doesn't believe it for a moment.

Finally, she gives in and takes to her bed.

She even *thinks* these words in her head as she flops down, recalling that this is how her father would describe her mother, when the woman would disappear somewhat mysteriously into her room at any hour of the day. Elspeth believes that this would have been categorised, in a more enlightened era, as manic depression and now, most probably, as bipolar. But in her day, it was just our mother 'taking to her bed', leaving our Elspeth to play her pretend games on her own in her forever chilly and very cramped room.

Elspeth sometimes wishes she were just that bit more famous, had been offered a couple more juicily pivotal film roles, then somebody might have wanted to collaborate with her on her life story. And she could have damned her limited and insensitive bloody parents for all time but courageously.

As she lies on the bed – trying very hard not to make herself even more cross over the fact that this brand-new mattress, lugged in by that unfathomable and suddenly petulant handyman, is in fact just a tad too firm for her small frame – a song careers through her head. What is it the Germans call it? An *ohrwurm*. Well, this bloody *ohrwurm* is still burrowing its relentless way into her skull, like an irritating and invasive musical accompaniment to the sorry events of the week.

It had begun with one of Rex's Exes, she can't recall which and sees no particular need to, bringing in a song that the woman herself had performed privately over the years, with and for a few friends. The old actress still had the sheet music in her room, in that worn and dusty suitcase of memories that is wedged into every resident's small wardrobe (and most of their hearts) and had managed to collar Lisa to make a photocopy for each member of the cast.

Elspeth hadn't disliked the piece, a Broadway show song from some decades earlier, and it did appear as if it might offer an appropriate theme to the evening, one slightly more uplifting than 'aren't we great for our age?', 'catch us before the Grim Reaper does' or possibly even 'bet on us lasting the evening'.

She had decided to commence the entire rehearsal process with an attempt at this song, however ragged and basically awful it inevitably would be, as it would involve every member of the company, bonding them hopefully as a troupe, in ways that a simple succession of single or even double acts might not.

Whilst not totally averse to the idea – they had been through enough rehearsals and run-throughs over the years – the cast's enthusiasm had not yet achieved that state Elspeth might truthfully term boundless. In fact, it hadn't even reached a level anyone would call enthusiasm. They had stood on the makeshift platform that Stanley and his young men had swiftly yet carefully constructed, holding their song sheets in trembling hands and wondering, often quite vocally, what the hell they had allowed themselves to be cajoled and bullied into.

The ancient choreographer, despite the toll visibly inflicted on her crumbling frame by years of merciless dance, had managed to arrange them into some semblance of a line. Or rather two lines, as the stage wasn't quite broad enough for all of them, especially as many were leaning on an assortment of hand-carved or collapsible walking sticks that obviously demanded their own safe space. Agnes Wu had seen no shame in using her Zimmer frame to direct the movement, where words and even expletives weren't quite sufficient. In fact, her sense of balance was praised on several occasions.

Happily, for all concerned, Lisa Silk was there to help out.

Her father had reluctantly permitted his daughter to be seconded to 'that Quest woman' for the duration of the show (in addition, of course, to the fulfilment of her regular duties), having been persuaded that it would probably reflect better on him and the home if Dustingford Follies of 2019 wasn't total shit.

The young stage manager has been doing all that might be

asked of her with remarkable good grace and humour, retrieving dropped song sheets, preventing performers from falling off the stage and gently turning others in the right direction. "Don't worry," she had said at one point, "I was epic at 'pick-up-sticks' as a kid," which had made the ones who heard it, and even her producer, smile.

Now, as Elspeth attempts to doze off in her room, every word of the bloody song appears to type itself noisily across the screen behind her eyes.

No one starts at the top and a lot of us drop, before we can reach the heights,

But with a gallon of pluck and a barrel of luck, we can see our name up there in lights…

Punctuating the routine in her swirling, sleep-deprived brain, a routine which – despite a full week of rehearsal – has yet to progress from the embarrassingly awful to the merely mortifying, are the individual acts that she is attempting to drill into shape and mould into some sort of cohesive, or at least vaguely presentable, whole.

She had selected Gerard each day to be her first solo performer, which Elspeth felt was only respectful to the elderly actor, as she genuinely admires his craft and his commitment. Whilst some of his fellows would take time out to watch and enjoy, others would seize the opportunity to practise their own routines or, more often than not, have a little nap.

Even on day five, however, Gerard was still reading from his own volume of collected works.

"*This royal throne of kings, this sceptred isle…*"

"Gerard, dear," Elspeth had finally interrupted. "You *have* played John of Gaunt, haven't you?"

"Er… yes, darling. Several times. I recall once in—"

"Well then—"

Diana had attempted quietly to intervene. "Elspeth—"

Elspeth had heard the woman but waved her off like an

annoying bluebottle. "Then do you think you might try to do it without the book?" Elspeth had felt that all her trademark understanding was wrapped up in gracious omission. She had never once said 'fucking book'.

"Er, yes. Yes, of course, Elspeth," he nods. "Just not quite yet. Say, Monday?"

"It's okay, Gerard," said Diana with a kind smile, adding to Elspeth, "It's okay."

It was far from okay, but Elspeth wasn't going to make a big thing of it. Yet.

The work may be hard and the way may be rough
But whatever it takes we can take it,
We know at the end that the journey's our friend
And we are the kids that will make it.

She had thought that the still wordless tap dancer, whatever his name was – Johnson, no Jackson – whilst actually surprisingly adequate in his interview, had been looking rather forlorn during the week.

"It's first class, Mr… Jackson. First class. Needs something more. Can't think what right now. I'll get back to you."

For some mysterious reason, the tap dancer had pointed rather sadly to an empty space beside him. Elspeth had noticed Jacob Bloom, who had been watching the man intensely, suddenly heave a massive sigh, which was equally baffling. Although she has long suspected that the gloomy man has a bottomless well of sighs, all strengths and dimensions, from which he might draw whenever the appropriately miserable circumstances demand.

For every end there's a beginning,
To make the finish you just need that start
After the rain you'll find the rainbow
You just have to hold hope in your heart…

Or some such crap.

And as if these spiralling memories aren't torment enough, thinks Elspeth Quest alone and squirming on her rigid bed, *here comes Barry bloody Prince*, reminding her (but only vaguely) of Harold Macmillan. "Let us be absolutely frank about it – most of our people have never had it so good. Me – I haven't had it since 1949." And then he would, of course, check his watch. "Mind you, it's only 19:58 now."

"Barry, I'm not saying that isn't amusing… but do you really think anyone will remember Harold Macmillan?"

Mr Versatile had responded by segueing immediately into a relatively identifiable, but possibly quite un-PC, Al Jolson. "*Climb upon my knee, sonny boy* – you never heard of a black Jewish Santa Claus before?" He had stared down at Elspeth and Diana. "I've got hundreds of them."

"I don't doubt it," Elspeth had muttered, a touch despondently.

It was Diana Appleyard who finally came up with the idea. Elspeth had been obliged to admit, albeit quietly, that it was rather a sound one, perhaps even inspired, although she would have preferred that her PA/understudy had broached it with her in private before announcing it to the world.

"*I know!*" the understudy had chipped in, rather too excitedly. "What if we split them up, Barry – these impressions, I mean – and you be our compere for the evening?"

"I think we've got ourselves one helluva deal," responded the delighted impressionist instantly. To be met with puzzled looks all round. "Er, no, loves – that was me."

For every triumph you brave a few disasters
The curves they throw you that drive you round the bend,
Every journey starts with one small footstep
So let's step up – we're at the winning end!

Just on the cusp of finally nodding off, Elspeth recalls, with a familiar yet unwelcome palpitation, the least life-enhancing moment of them all.

"We're waiting, Miss Gatley… Zelda," said Diana Appleyard.

"I'm not," muttered Elspeth, who had already expressed more than once, in a *voce* not that *sotto*, her profound bewilderment that this curious person should be volunteering so earnestly to participate in something for which Elspeth is rapidly suspecting she has little or no aptitude whatsoever.

The small woman had stood there, staring at them with bulging eyes, like an escaping and very old POW caught in a searchlight. But then her petrified glance had suddenly shot beyond them, causing both seated women to spin round and notice a creepily silent Gavin Silk watching once again from a doorway. Which had petrified the woman even more and totally puzzled her onlookers.

"Er, yes. Yes, sorry, I know," Zelda had said, finally. "I-I haven't quite decided… on my piece yet."

"Oh, for fuck's sake," said Elspeth, throwing her silver pencil onto the ground. "You must have dozens. Call yourself an actress!" Lisa had steamed over to pick it up. "*Leave it!*"

"Do you need any help, Zelda?" Diana Appleyard had offered, kindly.

"No. No, thank you, Diana." The woman had stood there for some further crippling seconds, before walking dazedly off towards the terrace, diligently avoiding Silk and all her unimpressed fellows. "I'll be fine."

"It's the beginning of the end," sighs Elspeth, as blessed sleep finally overtakes her. Which aren't the words to any song at all.

scene six

After a day of rest, during which most of the cast did much the same as Elspeth recalls her mother having done so regularly (although the discovery of lithium would not have made a miraculous difference here), everyone is returned to the dining room.

Breakfast has been cleared, along with the furniture designed to accommodate it. And a put-upon Stanley is beginning to feel that retirement might not be such an unappealing prospect.

Elspeth has decided over the break that rather than commence the proceedings once again with 'that sodding song', which she knows will only depress her and everyone else, she and Rex will give their much-cherished-to-this-day *Romeo and Juliet*. Or at least a potent extract.

Even if she says it herself, which she does more than once, the effect is inspiring. She would go so far as to suggest galvanising. Or – yes, okay – little short of mesmeric.

Whilst the celebrated lovers are clearly no longer in that first romantic blush of youth, a situation which no amount of make-up or sympathetic lighting will transform, the passion of the words and the sincerity of their delivery are reckoned by those in attendance to sustain the illusion and carry them rapturously through.

Dustingford's silvery Juliet is poetically oblivious to the tiny waves of sadness that lap the still soft and gentle face of understudy Diana Appleyard, although even Elspeth can't quite fail to notice Romeo's previous inamoratas leaving abruptly through two separate exits.

Genuine applause from admiring onlookers elicits an almost embarrassed smile from at least one of the Verona-based duo.

"Ah, the magic of make-believe," whispers Rex.

"Sometimes, it's the only thing that's real," says Elspeth Quest, enigmatically, to which Rex Markham can only nod, as he is not quite certain what it means. Although it does admittedly sound rather good, as brittle dialogue so often can.

Neither of them notices Stanley, balanced on his tall stepladder at a deserted edge of the spacious room as he attaches a new light. But he watches them with an interest not quite that of the avid theatregoer.

Quite a few of them notice him a tiny bit more when Cyril Dodds rushes into the room in a panic and nearly topples the distracted handyman from his eyrie.

"*I've lost Mr Chips!*" comes the anguished cry. "Anyone here seen him?"

"What's he look like?" says Barry Prince, which only amuses Barry Prince. Yet this is often sufficient.

"Well…" begins the ventriloquist and then sighs helplessly.

Before anyone can hazard a suggestion, Lisa comes in, happily holding the lifeless owl by a wooden ear.

"You left him in the bathroom," says Lisa, without a hint of reprimand. She hands the grateful man a downcast-looking dummy.

"I was in a bit of a hurry," says Cyril Dodds, apologetically.

"You and me both," pipes up an instantly revitalised Mr Chips. "Mind you, my grandfather *was* a stool."

"Well, that's certainly not going in my show," declares

Elspeth, somewhat proprietorially, before diplomatically correcting herself. "*Our* show."

Before her or anyone else's show can proceed to whatever could possibly follow the Quest/Markham tour de force, they hear the pound of approaching footsteps on the wooden floor. This deliberate vigour suggests to Elspeth a younger, fitter person, and indeed she is confirmed in her assessment when she hears Gavin Silk's angry voice.

"I'm afraid I have to interrupt," he announces, with no attempt at apology. "Lisa, enough of this nonsense. I know I have granted you some space for this… rigmarole, but you do have other duties, you know. Have you forgotten it's Family And Friends Tea Afternoon today?"

"Er, no. I didn't forget 'FAFTA', actually," says Lisa, instantly reverting to what her aged onlookers recognise only too well as sullen teenage mode. "That's why I'm working overtime – for nothing. *Actually*. That's why I'm still here after you've gone home every night. *Actu—*"

"Miss Quest," continues the director, ignoring the youngest person there. "I am not wholly against your little concert, and I am sure you mean well, but it does appear to be taking up rather a lot of valuable staff time." He points behind him towards Stanley, as if to nail his point even more firmly. Stanley wonders for a moment if it is he or simply the time that is valuable.

"A production does demand a stage manager, Mr Silk," explains Elspeth. "And besides, it's good experience for a young woman. If she wants to work her way up in the business."

She doesn't notice the young woman squirm at this. But Stanley can feel himself squirm with her.

"My daughter does *not* want to work her way anywhere in your business. Up, down or sideways. She's had quite enough of your sort of… lifestyle."

"Dad—"

"Fortunately, she is now in a business that best suits her… abilities. *Lisa!*"

"Ten minutes!" pleads an embarrassed stage manager.

"*Now!*"

He turns and goes, ignoring a downwards glare from the stepladder. Lisa looks round at the cast, who simply feel old and helpless. Or even older and more helpless. With just the tiniest of apologetic shrugs, the young woman turns and follows her father out. She hears Stanley whisper her name but ignores it.

"Why does she let him do this?" asks a sympathetic Diana Appleyard. "She's not a child. It's like he's got some strange hold over her."

"We don't need pop psychology," says Elspeth. "We need a stage manager. That man is a complete philistine."

"I thought that was my job," says Stanley Grainger, who Elspeth hadn't realised was still there. She can see no overwhelming reason why he still is.

"And we don't need a bloody Family And Friends Tea," continues Elspeth "Today of all days. Alright then, who's next?" She scans her cast list, clearly unimpressed with any of the available options. A raising of the eyes to scan her actual cast, who stand, or more often sit, around awaiting her call, only diminishes her confidence even further. "Barry Prince," she sighs, "I suppose we had better start with you."

"*I don't believe it!*" says Barry Prince, channelling Victor Meldrew from the hugely popular nineties situation comedy *One Foot in the Grave*.

"Why not?" asks a bemused Elspeth Quest.

*

By the time Elspeth is able to slip down to the shore once more and regain her sense of composure, or simply just some sense, the tide is coming in.

To someone well-versed in metaphor, this feels vaguely appropriate as, only a couple of hundred yards away, a tide of humanity is flooding into Dustingford to visit their nearest and dearest or perhaps just their oldest. None of which, save for the irritating disruption to her already perilously tight schedule, is any concern of hers.

She slips off her shoes. Not because they're too precious to soil or she needs to be at one with nature or any of that nonsense, but rather that the extreme pain of sea-sharpened shards of shingle cutting into her ageing and brittle feet feels a suitable penance for what she is doing. Or failing to do. Yet in another, equally potent way, it reminds her that she is still alive and to some extent functioning, not simply a decaying bag of bones and butterscotch, waiting resignedly to be carted off down that bumpy tree-lined drive in the opposite direction, without even a cab window out of which despondently to gaze.

Elspeth is aware that she tends to mutter to herself as she walks, especially in times of stress, and has in the past attempted to control it. Right now, she simply couldn't give a flying—

"*Miss Quest… Miss Quest!*"

"*Jesus H Christ!*" says Elspeth Quest. "Not again, Mr Grainger," she sighs, without turning round. "I signed out, didn't I? Don't tell me – I forgot to put my electronic tag on!"

By the time Stanley Grainger reaches her, he is quite out of breath. Which rather surprises him as he has always considered himself reasonably fit, especially for a man of his age. But it is a nippy day, at the start of December, and he is feeling unusually exercised.

"It's not that, Miss Quest." She can hear the irritation in his voice, along with a genuine concern but is in no mood for either.

"Well, if you've come to rally me with more perky Northern philosophy, please don't. The show is a shambles and, by the looks of it, shambles will be its high point. There's a reason why we're all of us 'resting'. It was just a very stupid idea and I totally blame myself for everyone else's shortcomings."

"It's early days yet, woman!"

"I bow to your greater experience at the altar of Thespis."

"I have no idea what you're talking about," says Stanley, as if this is not a new phenomenon. "But it's probably condescending."

Elspeth nods, as she can hardly argue with this. When she finally does look round, the man is almost completely bent over and appears to be finding it hard to catch his breath.

"I just – sorry – I just," he pants, "just came to tell you… that you've got a visitor."

Elspeth actually laughs at this. The man watches her breathe in the salty air, as it mingles with his own. "Oh, please. Don't be ridiculous, Mr Grainger. Nobody even knows I'm here. *Temporarily*. Who on earth is going to visit me?"

"Your son?" suggests Stanley Grainger.

scene seven

The Green Room is crowded and buzzing as residents and visitors savour their monthly (pre-paid) Family And Friends Afternoon Tea. With Cake.

Near and dear ones can, of course, visit their particular resident at other times, in fact seven days a week, but Gavin Silk feels that something communal, a nurturing, nourishing get-together for which people pay substantially through the nose, has its own indefinable charm.

Small children are enjoying Zimmer frame races around the armchairs, seriously rattling the cheap crockery as well the overworked staff, whilst slightly older ones are being allowed to trounce their grandparents at chess or Scrabble. The few teenagers who have deigned or been frogmarched to attend are silently wishing everyone would hurry up and die so they could go home and play on screens with their mates.

Barry Prince and Gerard Bunting, both widowers, are amongst that number contentedly bouncing small grandchildren on arthritic knees, bravely keeping the pain to themselves. Rex's Exes entertain offspring who have nothing to do with Rex, whilst the great man is happily charming a daughter and son-in-law who have nothing to do with any former wife currently in the room.

Only three of the Follies' cast are quite alone.

Zelda, Jacob and the remaining Jackson quite naturally gravitate to one another, although the dancer's companions notice that the man's constantly moving lower limbs are proving a source of total fascination to some of the afternoon's younger guests.

"Still nothing, Jacob?" asks Zelda, sympathetically.

The elderly man offers his most stoical shrug. "My family didn't approve when I joined the business, why should they approve now? I was expected to be a rabbi, like my brother." He gives her one of his rare smiles. "Is that a job for a Jewish boy?"

"I would have thought so, Jacob," she says, seriously. "Did you marry an actress, then?"

"I never married, Zelda," he informs her, adding sadly if a little obscurely, "or... anything."

"Oh?" says Zelda Gatley, who finds any little nugget a resident might tell her absolutely fascinating, even if it is what might be regarded by others as negative information. Yet, as ever, something even more enthralling suddenly appears on her horizon and she swiftly swivels round to offer this her fullest attention.

A young man – or, at least, far younger than any of the residents – is sitting patiently on a wrought-iron memorial bench in the garden. Despite the chill, he wears only what Zelda would estimate is a rather thin, though clearly smart and expensive, jacket. He appears to her to be a person attempting to look calm and relaxed rather than someone for whom this is currently their authentic state. Sometimes, Zelda amazes herself with her perception. What might she have been in another life? Anyway, she reckons that this semblance of the placid could very soon be rippled by what – or rather, who – is tentatively making their approach along the path that leads up from the sea.

The almost painfully enthralled woman can't help noticing, even from a distance, that this seated man – with his muscular build and abundant, rather windswept head of auburn hair, glinting in what little winter sunlight there is – appears rather handsome. In a Heathcliff, Mr Rochester, early Rex Markham kind of way. She wonders if he is also an actor. Far too young to become a resident here in her lifetime, sadly.

Zelda only wishes that she could overhear the conversation. One that she senses, from the body language of the as yet unobserved woman, whose motion has suddenly slowed almost to a crawl, will very soon be taking place. She doubts that the ensuing talk will be any less uncomfortable and stilted than the walk that precedes it.

"*She's back!*" she informs the room.

To her surprise and perhaps disappointment, no one appears particularly interested. And perhaps it is better that others (*especially* Zelda Gatley) remain out of range of this particular conversation, the one between a well turned-out if rather stiff man in his early forties and a windswept elderly lady, whose feet and heart are quite probably killing her.

"Oberon?"

To the majority of residents on this Family And Friends Tea Afternoon, should they be the least bit bothered to eavesdrop, this greeting would more than likely summon up sweet memories of theatrical visits long gone. To Zelda Gatley, it might simply come across as a peculiar name to call a child. To the curiously named child in question, it is something of a shock, as he had been preparing himself for it to land on him from another, more tranquil direction.

"Hello, Mother," he says, putting the brakes on an actual turn-around until he can fully accommodate the encounter.

Neither person would appear to know the appropriate protocol that might allow them to proceed. So, at first, they simply remain in first position, as if frozen in time and space. Then, after a few moments of awkward shuffling, they jointly decide to peck cheeks, like two friends or acquaintances meeting in their seats just as a play is about to start. Yet these particular cheeks are cold, and this is not entirely due to December.

"You're the last person I expected to see here," says Elspeth.

"You too," he says, although she is not quite certain what he means. "I do have a sense of duty, you know. You taught me that. Except yours was usually to your audience."

"You look well," says Elspeth, ignoring this first early salvo. "Estate agency suits you." She tries really hard not to make it sound like money laundering or male prostitution.

The man smiles wryly. "Chartered surveying, actually. I'm probably the only chartered surveyor in the world called Oberon."

"You could have changed it. You changed everything else."

He shrugs, then looks up at her. His mother is shivering. "Would you prefer to go inside?" he asks. "It's getting quite cold."

Elspeth shakes her head. Wrapping her old raincoat tightly around herself, although it does little to quell the tremors, she sits down on the bench. She takes care not to brush up against him. Discovering that she can't think of anything else to say, which even she knows is unusual for her, Elspeth wonders if there is actually somewhere way beyond that place in which time is the supposed healer and it becomes merely time.

"It seems like a very nice home," says Oberon, finally.

He realises that his mother looks better than he had expected. Not younger, she does indeed look her age, but perhaps not quite as ravaged as he had imagined. Or possibly hoped. Hoped because he finds himself wishing that she did bear more of life's burdens on her person, some visible scars, as if this might signal and bear witness to what's hopefully going on inside. Especially about him.

Elspeth Quest doesn't respond but simply shrugs. She realises that at this moment, she has no feelings one way or the other about her new residence, or about much of anything else, and marvels how swiftly all that passion and fire she used to have – for work, for life, for her art – can suddenly vanish.

"Have you met some old friends?" he asks.

"Do you see any other kind?"

At least she smiles as she says this, giving the man permission of sorts to proceed.

"So, what do you do with yourself all day?"

"We sleep, we talk, we eat – we rage against the dying of the light. And we're putting on a show. Of sorts."

"*You are not!* A show. Whose mad idea was that? And why am I asking?"

She looks at him. The little smile that tips up his sweet, full-lipped mouth in one direction, as if attached to his eye by an invisible string, this hasn't changed. "What do you find so amusing?"

"The only time I ever saw you was onstage. I come here and find you're going to be onstage again."

"I had to support you, Oberon. We had to live."

"Please don't tell me that I'm the reason you went to work each day. I'm probably more why you didn't always come home each night."

They sit in an uneasy silence.

Elspeth Quest knows that she should feel a crippling sadness and, of course, its usual fellow-traveller, guilt. About the son she had so late, possibly never really wanted and so often never saw. The son she certainly doesn't see now, yet surely this is more of his own volition than hers. She has *tried* to reach out, at least she believes she has, although perhaps not for some while. But hasn't the man always made it so clear that any such reunion or, let's say, rapprochement, might not contribute hugely to the sum of his human happiness or even his wellbeing? Especially as some years ago, his father, with his new family, came back into the picture, wishing to redeem himself and by and large succeeding.

Yet curiously, despite all these things that she tells herself, she wonders whether in fact she is genuinely feeling what somebody in her exact position would feel. Maybe she has been simulating emotions for too many decades to be able to recognise or acknowledge the true ones when they actually decide to sneak through.

Maybe.

Or perhaps, she has to concede, she is a sorry specimen physically incapable of the genuine article and only as good as her last performance.

She wonders also, as she has been since she was first informed of his arrival, how on earth her son had known that she was here. And why the hell he would turn up now.

She doesn't wonder for long.

"*Oberon!*"

Diana Appleyard is walking across the lawn, arm in arm with an attractive and considerably taller young woman, whom Elspeth would assess as being in her early thirties. Elspeth has often noticed women walking arm in arm, as an expression of friendship, and has occasionally mused on what this might be like.

Oberon doesn't appear nearly as surprised to see the elderly actress as his mother might have expected.

"Hi, Diana!"

Diana breaks away gently from her young companion and rushes to embrace the man.

"Obie!" says Diana Appleyard, staring into the younger man's open and instantly beaming face. All Elspeth can do is watch. "It's so lovely of you to come."

His glance crosses that of Elspeth, as it makes its way to the gently warm smile of the more established resident.

"Oh, sorry. Oberon and Elspeth," says Diana, "this is my youngest niece, Laura." She moves to grip the young woman once more so that they can both gaze up at Oberon. "I used to look after this young man when..." The elderly lady stops, suddenly embarrassed.

"When I was onstage," completes Elspeth. "And he sat in your dressing room."

"Yes. Of course," stammers the understudy. "But I always took him into the wings so that he could see you."

"One day she'll buy me a proper seat!" laughs Oberon, immediately easing the tension, if only a fraction.

"Oh – well, I'm sure she'll buy you one for *The Dustingford Follies,*" says Diana. "*Of 2019!* I was telling Laura all about—"

"I don't think I'm around that evening," says Oberon, swiftly.

Elspeth has no intention of demeaning herself in front of others by remarking that she hasn't as yet informed her son of the event's exact date. So, she simply watches as Oberon hugs her 'surrogate' once more.

"I'm actually on my way somewhere. A work thing. But I couldn't very well come so close by without dropping in on FAFTA!" He shakes his head with what appears genuine regret. "Although I'm afraid that it's a bit of a flying visit this time. It was lovely seeing you again, Diana. And looking so well. I so cherish the lovely times I shared with you and your dear Andrew. Nice to meet you, Laura." He pecks Elspeth's cheek. "Bye, Mother. It's good to know you're in safe hands."

Elspeth suddenly reaches out to him and grips both his cheeks. Just as swiftly, she lets him go and steps away, as she feels every muscle in his face stiffen against her dampening palms.

"I hope you enjoy your... swan song," he says as he edges away, trying and failing to lighten the mood.

Oberon Quest walks back into the house, without turning round.

Elspeth watches him until he disappears, then returns her gaze to the aunt and niece with a strained smile. She catches them staring back at her, with such an obvious show of sympathy that she feels she should retrace her steps to the far less painful shingle.

"I told him you were here, Elspeth!" blurts Diana Appleyard, in a sudden rush. She trembles slightly. "I hope you don't mind. You see, he very kindly writes to me from time to time to see how I am. And sometimes – not too often! – he pops in for a chat. But he made me promise not to tell you that-that he might visit today. He thought you may not turn up. To be honest, I wasn't sure that *he* would… and then you would be so disappointed."

Elspeth disconcerts the anguished woman even further by saying nothing and seeming utterly blank. Watching the tall girl as she softly strokes her aunt's back, she tells herself that she would quite like one of those niece things, too.

"He has kept in touch over all the years," says Diana, uncomfortably, thinking that perhaps she ought simply to stop but not quite knowing how. To her chagrin she wonders if she is actually enjoying this, just a little. She hopes not. "Very sweet of him. Don't you think he's grown into a lovely young man?"

To her former understudy's relief, Elspeth simply smiles and walks away, certain neither of direction nor destination. Moments later, she finds Stanley watching her from the door of his greenhouse.

"Wrong number," she says and makes her way round the windswept garden and back towards her room.

scene eight

She has no idea how anyone could expect her to concentrate on Christmas frippery.

It would be – she tells herself, as she tries to avoid her mirror – like tagging Bottom's dream onto the final wrenching scenes of The Scottish Play, in the hope that it might just lighten the mood.

Elspeth Quest is, however, a professional.

And even though she has to accommodate herself to dealing with those who, resignedly or not, have reverted to amateur status, and a few whose professionalism would always have been in serious doubt, she must fulfil those duties she has been assigned. Okay, duties she has willingly assigned herself, not out of any genuine or deep-seated enthusiasm, it has to be said, but rather to disguise the true and shameful reasons for her permanent residence here at Dustingford, a charity case after decades of dutiful service and public acclaim. But she doesn't think she'll go there right now, thank you very much.

Yet, to her surprise and even alarm, something definitely feels as if it has changed, something in its own small way rather momentous. And she can't quite bring herself to acknowledge the unexpected catalyst, this recent deus ex machina on the memorial lawn.

How can a deeply unsatisfying encounter with an estranged and, if she's being totally honest, very marginally neglected child contribute in any way towards an intensifying of determination and even enthusiasm? Towards, of all things, the salvaging of a tatty end-of-the-pier concert party, one that right now is looking as if it is about to capsize straight into the English Channel.

To Elspeth Quest, it makes absolutely no sense at all.

Unless…

Might it be as simple as that she desperately needs, at this very moment, one final thing in her long, distinguished but now tailing-off life to offer some vague semblance of success? Or, if success is too lofty a word, at least accomplishment? (Avoidance of unmitigated total catastrophe would work for her, too.) And that the cavernous and occasionally stripped-bare room downstairs in Dustington Hall is, for Elspeth Quest MBE, the salon of last chance?

She wonders why lovely Alec Guinness and his bridge over that muddy river keep popping into her head.

The tentative knocking on her door jolts her, as does the idea that an interruption at this point feels not entirely unwelcome. She determines, however, not to give the visitor any benefit of the doubt.

"Oh, who is it?" she sighs, loudly.

Stanley opens the door and pops just his head and torso in, as if a mere half body is somehow less of an intrusion, even though it is generally recognised as the more talkative end.

"Come to gloat, Mr Grainger?" she says.

"Gloat? Course not, pet." He shakes his head. "Kids, eh? They're never gonna love us as much as we love them. Way of the world."

Elspeth looks at the handyman, solid and decent in every way, platitudinous in some, and her face softens for an instant. But she really can't be doing with any face-softening, or indeed any other sort of softening, right now. Not if she wants to maintain a respectable level of equilibrium and not fall completely apart.

"And a rolling stone gathers no moss. I'm really very busy, Mr Grainger. Is there anything else I can help you with?"

"No," he says, then pauses, thoughtfully. "Well, not me, exactly. But it does involve a member of your – what d'you call it – your cast."

She stares at him in the mirror, as he ventures further and unbidden into her small, still un-personalised room.

He notices index cards scattered across the bedspread, each scrawled with the name of a performing resident. He can hardly fail to notice the one which bears Zelda Gatley's name, scrawled as it is in glaring red felt tip. Especially as this particular name has next to it, in a larger and perhaps even angrier scrawl, three huge red question marks. Elspeth watches the man as he picks it up. The card seems tiny in his large, strong fingers.

"Do you know," she says, "sometimes I don't believe the bloody woman ever acted at all."

Stanley looks at her, without saying anything. Elspeth wonders why the man doesn't respond, something that he does to virtually everything else she says, usually with some fatuous Northern wisdom that drives her insane.

It takes a few seconds before she fathoms exactly what his silence means. And why he has chosen to come upstairs and bother her in the first place.

*

The last guests are gone. All familial duties accomplished.

Elspeth finds Zelda Gatley slumped in an armchair, beside the thankfully silent Green Room piano, sobbing loudly into her tiny, trembling hands. Diana Appleyard is crouched uncomfortably beside her, attempting to offer some comfort, which looks to Elspeth like a most futile endeavour. The odd little woman appears quite inconsolable.

Other residents are trying really hard not to stare. They appear to be seriously embarrassed and would rather find themselves somewhere – anywhere – else. She can tell that several have already retired to their rooms, at least until the dinner bell.

"Not your day for sorting out other people's dilemmas, is it, Diana?" says Elspeth, uncharitably, as she draws up a chair to sit herself in Zelda's eyeline, should those eyes ever be uncovered.

"*Zelda!*" she begins, firmly but not unkindly. "What is it, dear? Now, no one can possibly help you, can they, if you're just going to sit there and sob." The sobbing continues. "Oh, for fuck's sake, woman!"

Very slowly, the hands move away, revealing a face riven with despair and showing more genuine emotion than Elspeth might have considered available.

"I just wanted to be here with all of you," she bawls. "I always wanted to be an actress. I just never – ."

"Had the talent?" suggests Rex Markham from behind his Stage.

"I was going to say 'opportunity'."

"But to forge a review, love?" says Gerard Bunting.

"It's only what they would have said," she protests, "if I'd actually been in it."

They can almost feel the wake of Mr Chips as he flops backwards over Cyril Dodd's arm. Now he has heard everything.

"Were you ever *in* Australia, Zelda?" asks Diana, gently.

"Oh yes, Diana. That bit was absolutely true. I worked in a theatrical costumier. I met ever so many famous people."

"Places here are like gold, sweetheart," says Barry Prince as Walter Huston in *The Treasure of Sierra Madre*. This one totally baffles the usually rather good Nancy Fowler, who is still there collecting teacups from the afternoon sitting. She shakes her bemused head as she returns to the kitchen to help prepare for the residents' imminent supper.

"Old actors are dying to get into Dustingford," explains Jacob Bloom. "And out."

"I never thought Mr Silk would check," moans the little impostor. "He never has before. He's got a very suspicious nature, that man. It's why he *insisted* that I be in your lovely show, Miss Quest. So that he could see me for himself – not acting." Elspeth and Diana exchange a look, as one puzzle appears to have been solved. "Where will I go?" she asks, then rather mysteriously adds a 'whither?'. Finally, she looks up at Elspeth. "Miss Quest, could you talk to him?"

"*Me?* Oh, I really don't think... why me?"

"Because it must have been the show, *your* show – you know – that made him think of it. As a way to... flush me out. And you used to be big."

Without turning to face what she senses has now become her audience, or heaven forbid announce that she *is* big, it's just the rest homes that got small, Elspeth Quest hurls a question into the fuggy, overheated air. "Well, what does everybody else feel?"

She doesn't need to look around to know that everybody else feels that life is too short, that they shouldn't be interfering and that they'd be better off upstairs, like those more sensible others, dressing for dinner.

Finally, Rex offers a few brief words in Zelda Gatley's defence. "I suppose she has *acted* the part of an actress."

"Wasn't very good, though," adjudges Gerard Bunting.

*

Gavin Silk is fitting his latest miniature frigate into an impossibly small bottle as she enters the dimly lit office. An LED desk lamp illuminates the tiny shipyard.

Elspeth Quest follows the intricate and still fully collapsed model (looking to her like nothing more than a lump of painted sticks) as it is very slowly and carefully inserted, centimetre after centimetre, by bony but unwavering fingers, through the gleaming glass neck into its transparently safe and final harbour. She realises that this is clearly an incredibly skilled, complex and undoubtedly pivotal manoeuvre. And can only assume that it will immediately be followed by the launch itself, as the tiny strings attached to the ship are magically and triumphantly pulled and the craft achieves its miraculous transformation. The (literally) fitting climax to however many nights' painstaking and, to her mind, futile work.

She has no idea why the man has decided to execute this final, momentous stage of the operation within the grim walls of his poky office, other than as a defiant screw-you to the higher echelons or perhaps simply to attain some arcane form of bragging rights in the regional ship-in-a-bottle society. Whatever the reason, Elspeth knows that right now would be the very worst time to interrupt him.

She really can't explain why she does so.

"Can you spare a couple of minutes, Mr Silk?"

If Elspeth Quest has been expecting a tempest to surge or a ship to founder, she must now be feeling justifiably disappointed. Reluctantly, she is bound to acknowledge that this is a very cool customer indeed. Her initial assessment of the director as reptilian has not yet been proven inaccurate.

"If you're wanting Lisa back, Miss Quest, the answer is still the same," he says, his eyes never moving from the task in hand. "To paraphrase that song, she has no business in show business."

Elspeth can tell that he is rather pleased with this.

"It's not about your daughter," she corrects him, "although she has to come back to work, or the ensuing disaster will be in your court entirely." She allows this to sink in, before continuing. "The residents are very upset about Miss Gatley."

"And I'm very upset that a resident should lie to me, Miss

Quest. The Trust has a very strict constitution. It is how we – and indeed I – maintain a reputation." His eyes meet hers and then return to his task. Only a slight breathlessness betrays the tension in his body. But Elspeth is not as yet certain whether this is about Zelda or his bloody boat. "Sometimes, my dear Miss Quest, the pieces just don't fit."

Ignoring the metaphor, Elspeth sits down on the uncomfortable chair opposite him, although she hasn't been invited. But her legs still ache from her walk, and she wants to be in the man's eyeline. "I have known Zelda Gatley for over fifty years."

"Oh, please. I know you people like to stick together. But truly, she isn't one of your kind at all, is she? The woman is not, nor has she ever been, an actress."

"No. You're right, Mr Silk."

She watches his pale hands pause for a moment. He nods, clearly assuming this is the end of the conversation. And of Zelda Gatley.

Instead of which, Elspeth Quest leans over the desk until her soft breath gently clouds a surface of the soon-to-be-filled bottle. "Zelda Gatley is – or was – what we in our business would call a 'supporting artiste'." She registers his quizzical look but assumes it is not about the term itself. "Indeed, she was one of the unsung heroes of our profession."

"An 'extra'," says Gavin Silk, with an unbecoming disdain.

"If you will. But hardly superfluous. Whenever a director of film or television wanted someone totally insignificant, Zelda Gatley always failed to stand out from the crowd."

To Elspeth's surprise, Gavin Silk begins to smile. Whilst far from attractive, it is at least hopeful. "Alright, Miss Quest. I'm not a cruel man. So, I'm going to make you a proposition."

"A proposition?"

"If your Miss Gatley passes muster in your little show, she can stay."

Elspeth looks horrified. "Passes? And who on earth is going to be the judge of that?"

An almost mischievous look from across the desk tells her all she needs to know. She sighs, not quite certain whether she has won or lost.

"Moving on," continues the director briskly. The as yet still furled frigate sits comfortably in the bottle's neck. "As you may know, we occasionally have outings for our residents. I have arranged one such for Wednesday. A Christmas tea dance at a very fine hotel in the town. The notice has been sitting out there on the board for weeks, in full view, but sadly precious few of you have as yet signed up."

"*A Christmas tea dance!* Dear God! We're rehearsing. We really don't have time for—"

"We are all guests in this town, Miss Quest. Sometimes, we have need of positive local support. And a healthy relationship with the council and the press."

"To make you look good."

"You might find it conducive to have me on your side. Stanley will drive the Hall coach. It can accommodate twenty. Please be ready with your entire cast at 3.00 sharp. All of you." He smiles that lizard smile again. "And bring your dancing shoes."

Elspeth shrugs and begins painfully to stand.

"If we do this for you, I want Lisa back on board. Now! That's *my* 'proposition.'"

The man doesn't answer. But, as someone accustomed to pulling strings, he leaves her with the glory of another successful launch.

"Bravo," she says. And, to her surprise, finds that she means it. There is something quite wondrous in watching that little heap of matchwood flower into an object of some skill and beauty.

As Elspeth opens the door, it occurs to her why Gavin Silk had chosen to perform this singular and perhaps more usually private act right here in his office. He needed to prove that, in an edifice overflowing with talent, he wasn't without gifts of his own.

This is probably why she turns one final time, to catch him beaming. It is almost as if he is taking a bow.

"Tosser," she says. But wisely, only to herself.

scene nine

"*I'll see you again..*"

Marguerite is in full, albeit hyper-vibrato voice, notable especially for being offered so unashamedly to the world, first thing in the morning.

Lisa Silk isn't really listening.

It could be because they are in Stanley's greenhouse rather than a private bedroom and she has an aversion to being watched. Not perhaps the best quality for someone with her heart set on a career in performance, but she decides that this is purely because of the circumstances in which she has found herself and the secrecy with which she is obliged to refine and indeed practise her craft.

Yet the main reason for her attention not being fully devoted to the elderly songstress right now is that she had understood the agenda of this morning's rendezvous to be her usual clandestine tutorial, rather than 'an audience with Marguerite'. She is not the woman's personal servant, however much the imperious woman may choose to disagree.

"I still have it, don't I, dear?" decides the singer, with a satisfied, crimson-lipped smile. Lisa would have to agree that she still does. The old lady is a marvel, as the old lady would be the first to admit.

"Yeah. Still do. I'd best be getting back, Miss M, or my dad will—"

"Will what?" says the woman angrily, tucking her thick tartan blanket more tightly around her impeded frame. "Admonish you? Stop your pocket money? How old are you, girl?"

"You know how old – nearly twenty-two."

Marguerite laughs, revealing that some of her bright magenta lipstick has found its way onto her still impressive – though not entirely her own – front teeth. Which Lisa finds both poignant and strangely satisfying.

"When I was twenty-two, sweetheart, I'd already run away from home, slept on floors and doorways, almost starved but was in the chorus of a West End show. One of the first black girls to make it. Hmm?"

Lisa says nothing but grips the back of the wheelchair with both hands and starts to push her charge none too carefully out of the greenhouse. Before they reach the door, she suddenly stops and shuffles round the narrow, fern-ridden corridor to face the elderly legend.

"When I was seventeen, Miss Marguerite, I was in intensive care at the local hospital from a drug overdose. Ah, golden days in the theatre. But at least it stopped me getting the old dancing blade out. For a while." She rolls up the sleeves of her Dustingford blouse to reveal a network of bulging scars. "I'll show you my cuttings if you show me yours. And here's another one for the old scrapbook. 2007 – my mum pissed off to Canada with the bloke who fitted our double glazing and left me and my dad to look after each other. In a house that still let the draughts in. And between you and me, knowing my dad, I can't altogether blame her. Oh, and on a clear day you can see the three local schools that politely asked me to leave. Ah, that old school song – *We'll not fuckin' see you again.*"

The old lady doesn't raise her head to look at her, but Lisa knows that she is listening. Perhaps with her famed attunement to the human voice, she can even pick up that her dutiful carer is trying really hard not to cry. Or to scream in her face.

"So, you know what, maybe it's only right that I should be working my tits off to get onto that Care Management course at the town college, so I can be doing whatever the hell it is my dad does. Because apparently, I screwed up big time, and I'm nearly out of second chances. He may be a total wanker, but right now, he's the only wanker I've got. And as for my singing, well it looks like I'm just going to be sodding listening to you for a while, doesn't it?"

Lisa moves away to resume her position at the back of the wheelchair. With a modicum of shuffling, Marguerite manages to turn round and look up at the young woman's almost ghostly white face.

"Are you finished, dear?"

Lisa nods. Utterly spent.

"Then just stay there for a while and hear my Cole Porter. We open in ten days."

*

Elspeth Quest believes that she now has some semblance of a running order.

Yet, having observed rehearsals in the few hours spared to her this morning, before they were obliged to truncate everything and prepare to board the Dustingford bloody charabanc, she still regards it as more of a death march than a run.

Barry Prince had immediately set the tone for the day's proceedings by entering the room in blackface, to afford his Al Jolson an authenticity he was sensing that voice alone, however uncanny, might not fully convey. They had all wondered on his absence from breakfast this morning and now they knew. If the remaining Jackson was looking sad before, Jacob Bloom reckoned he must be on the cusp of suicide now.

Gerard Bunting is still not 'off the book' and Elspeth wonders whether the man, who veers from abject and painful contrition to red-faced fury, might never be and that they'll just have to think of something. Mr Chips had entered, coughing violently, with Cyril Dodds worriedly checking the owl's head for fever and talking about a science-baffling combination of avian flu and Dutch elm disease.

To Elspeth's particular chagrin, it was left to Marguerite to add the first smidgeon of true professionalism to the proceedings. Wheeled in by a grumpy-looking Lisa, newly reinstated as stage manager but looking none too grateful, the legendary singer offered up one beautifully rendered song, acknowledged the expected applause, then snapped her fingers at her girl and left.

Not to be outdone, Elspeth had asked Rex to step up for their scene.

They had each decided that nothing else would do bar the piece that had made both their names as youngsters in Stratford. She would have to admit that the crowd was rapt once again, caught up in the passion of a performance that almost defied the years. Elspeth had caught her old understudy watching with more than a touch of sadness and wished to herself that the silly cow could just get over it. She didn't even notice Stanley Grainger attending to an errant window latch and grumpily shaking his head.

This impressive brace of examples should, in some small but hopeful way, have reassured the producer and the remaining members of the cast that flair might still rule at Dustingford and that something resembling a show must and would go on. Yet the morning appeared to have had quite the opposite effect, in that it highlighted even more starkly the contrasts inherent in the project, exposing how dusty, rusty and singularly ill-prepared the majority of the cast really were. It wasn't just the production people who were looking despondent. This was the one thing they could all manage as a team.

And then, just to add to the almost terminal bleakness, Zelda Gatley had shuffled dolefully in, on her no longer magical walking stick, escorted by a rather smug-looking Gavin Silk.

The terrified woman was gripping a single sheet of paper, clearly a photocopy of some immortal text she was about to ruin. Elspeth followed her pitiful progress as the pretender made her way towards the stage, like a felon to the scaffold. When this latest sorry act of the morning had finally arrived before her, shaking visibly, Elspeth had immediately elevated her stern gaze to take in the cast and even Mr Silk.

"Sorry, people," she had announced. "Dear me, we've quite run out of time if we all want to dress up smartly and get to Mr Silk's lovely tea dance this afternoon. Rehearsals commence again tomorrow at 10.00 sharp."

A furious Gavin Silk had squeezed his thin moustache like a third-rate Grand Guignol villain and stomped out of the makeshift hall.

scene ten

The cast of the far-too-rapidly-impending Dustingford Follies, all wrapped-up and somewhere to go, shuffle with walking aids and heavy hearts onto the home's twenty-seater minibus, a gift from The Variety Club of Great Britain. Their lack of enthusiasm couldn't be more marked if Stanley Grainger, waiting patiently in the driver's seat, were the ferryman Charon himself and all their benighted souls were about to be transported across the River Styx.

The atmosphere isn't lightened by Gavin Silk standing on the steps with his patently relieved staff, primed to wave off the little group as if forever.

"*Have a wonderful time!*" he calls to them with a smile, but it still comes out as more of an instruction. Fortunately, he doesn't hear Jason whisper to Lisa, as they walk towards the coach, "Bet he's laughing all the way to the bank." The young employee, one of this afternoon's assigned helpers, accompanies this with the customary rubbing together of thumb and index finger. Lisa finds herself nodding in agreement, her sense of filial loyalty a trifle shaky these days.

The young members of staff nod to Stanley as they climb the retractable ramp, having been requested quite forcefully by the driver to help him out with any heavy lifting on the day.

As Elspeth Quest, director/producer/martinet, has not as yet joined the party, although party hardly describes the mood of desolation inside the vehicle, the reluctant tea dancers feel free to express their innermost gripes about the larger situation. (Stanley Grainger, who is tinkering with something mechanical in his cockpit, sensibly contributes nothing but hears every word.)

"Would they put an eighty-two-year-old away for murder?" says Gerard Bunting, setting the wrecking ball rolling.

"Not a jury in the land would convict you," reassures Jacob Bloom, who didn't even have his turn at bat this morning but can pick up a mood the way others catch flu.

Barry Prince seizes the opportunity to give his Poirot, although he hasn't quite decided whether it is Finney, Ustinov or Suchet. "They all had ze motive. They all knew how to wield ze machete."

Diana Appleyard, who many would agree has as much right as anyone to cast the first stone, selflessly attempts to placate the insurgents. "Well, I do think you're being a wee bit harsh on Elspeth. The poor girl just wants to put on a decent show. She's even stayed on especially to do so. And none of you had to say yes, did you? Dear Lord, you weren't *dragooned* into it."

They all pause their grumbling for a moment, as the softly spoken lady isn't wrong. She can almost hear the cogs and tumblers in their brains attempting to unlock that elusive combination of reasons for their answering Elspeth Quest's call so readily.

"It's alright for you, love," says Rex Markham, finally. "You don't have a spot."

This somehow fails to cheer Diana up.

"I'd swap with you, Diana," moans Zelda Gatley, seated way at the rear of the coach. "I feel like I'm on trial for murder as it is."

"Much worse, Zelda," suggests Cyril Dodds, swiftly adding, "but you're doing very well, dear."

"I hope your fingers were crossed when you said that," says Mr Chips. The owl proceeds to wriggle uncomfortably. "Ooh – in fact, I'm bloody sure they were!"

The grumbling stops again, this time even more abruptly. Stanley, registering the silence, turns to see Elspeth Quest herself come striding in. She stomps up the ramp – in her sturdy outdoor clothing, walking stick retracted – and stands at the front of the bus, next to Stanley. The seated driver, who is now all belted up, appears good to go.

"*I know what the problem is!*" she announces, without the least preamble.

"We're geriatrics and you're hastening our end?" suggests Jacob Bloom.

"You're not working as a team," continues Elspeth. "It's been so long since you were part of a company, any sort of company, you've all of you – and I shan't refrain from including myself here – you've forgotten what it's like."

"I don't see there's much we can do about that now, dear," says Gerard Bunting.

"Of course, there is, Gerald," insists Elspeth.

"It's Gerard," whispers Diana seated nearby in one of the front seats, but her producer is on a roll.

"If we are going to save this show from utter disaster – or worse, amateur hour – we have to go right back to first principles. Tomorrow we do *only* exercises. Bonding exercises. Remember those? As a group. And we keep on doing them until we all meld and gel as one."

They all gawp at her.

"I'd rather go to a fucking tea dance," comes a voice from the centre of the bus. Which would appear to crystallise the views of the entire company. *At least they're bonded over that*, thinks Stanley Grainger.

The ensuing uncomfortable, not to say resentful, silence, which hits Elspeth Quest like a smack in the face, is broken by a person she hadn't even noticed, or taken much account of, because he isn't in her show and therefore has precious little relevance.

"I have an announcement to make," says Detective Inspector Malhotra of the New Delhi Police, in an accent that might shame Barry Prince with its accuracy but without the dark make-up that the impressionist has spent most of his lunchtime removing.

The entire coach stares at the elderly radio actor, which he takes as granting him full permission to proceed. Not that a man of his distinction would need such an indulgence.

"The late Mrs Elsie Turks is not in fact being murdered by her only son, even though she is expressing the clear intention of changing her will and leaving everything to Dustingford Hall. Nor indeed, is the poor lady being murdered at all."

They all nod, without any sign that this news is even remotely a revelation. No one had believed for a moment that the recently deceased juggler had died of anything other than natural causes. Which was momentous in itself, considering how much potentially lethal material she had hurled up in the air over the past few years and failed to collect on its way down.

The Detective Inspector, however, has not finished.

"I am, however, still investigating a far from unconnected crime of the utmost callousness and depravity. I shall be revealing all on the night of your little show."

"Well, thank you very much, Inspector," says Elspeth. "I'm sure we shall all look forward to that, our breaths truly baited." She manages to whisper to Diana, "See to it that no one lets him in on the night... now, as I was saying—"

Elspeth is suddenly jolted as the bus begins to move.

"Take your seats, gents *and* ladies," announces the driver, pointedly. "Stanley's magical mystery tour is about to begin."

"It doesn't feel that magical," grumbles Zelda Gatley, who in better days might have enjoyed a decent tea dance.

"You wait, love," says Stanley Grainger, with a grin none of them can see. "You just wait."

*

"*Kumbaya my Lord, Kumbaya...*" sings Mr Chips as the coach, which, like its passengers, is not exactly in the first flush of youth, rattles along the pitted, tree-lined drive. Only the odd clump of parasitical mistletoe contributes anything vaguely festive to the landscape. "*Kumbaya my Lord, Kumbaya...*" No one is quite certain whether the owl is being comradely or ironic. "*I'll go shoot myself... Kumbaya.*"

They feel a bit more certain now.

After this, the coach is unusually silent, save for the engine, which Stanley would agree still needs some work. But give a man a break – he can't be set-builder, carpenter, scene-painter, maintenance man, gardener *and* coach mechanic all at one and the same time. At least, not when he's also desperately attempting to head off forced and unnecessary retirement, because the thought of being without work and not seeing these old folk – or indeed, young folk – again is just too crushing to bear.

In a matter of minutes, they arrive in the small, seaside town.

The grandly named Imperial Hotel, second-best hotel on the seafront, is beckoning them with a large Day-Glo banner that reads, 'CHRISTMAS TEA DANCE. 3.30 TODAY!', even though Christmas itself is still some way off. *Perhaps*, think those Imperial staff who await them in relative warmth just behind the revolving doors, *this is because a few of the old dears might not make it through the brisk pre-Christmas season.*

Standing alongside the staff are their manager, who looks like Gavin Silk's even smarmier young brother, a local reporter and a photographer. Dustingford Hall, with its selection of once famous and still not totally forgotten faces, is big news in this slightly faded southern backwater and a spasmodic but welcome source of revenue to the town. The hotel manager has of course been briefed on the upcoming, once-in-a-lifetime gala concert and those important overnight guests that the truly momentous event has already begun to entice.

And so, this influential local gentleman and his entourage are rather surprised, as they move down the steps and into the cold to greet the arriving coach, to find it picking up speed just as it hits the hotel forecourt and practically zooming off down the deserted front towards God knows where. A few did notice that the driver himself looked rather old and his passengers extremely bewildered.

Inside the runaway bus, these same passengers are too confused to speak.

Perhaps that wasn't the right hotel. Maybe the car park is round the back. Possibly, the driver has had a brainstorm and they are being held hostage. It is left to their producer to act as spokesperson.

"What exactly do you think you're doing, Mr Grainger?"

Stanley just smiles and puts his foot down harder.

"My dad is so going to kill you," says Lisa Silk.

*

The historic amusement park sits on the crest of a hill, overlooking the promenade.

Anyone daring to ride the massive, old-fashioned roller coaster has the enticing twin prospects of flying off into the sea or crash-landing onto a line of small establishments selling freshly fried fish 'n' chips or rock with the name of the town going right through it.

Fortunately, the proprietors of this particular haven have taken their lead from the famed Tivoli in Copenhagen and reopened for the season, decking the halls with Christmas tat and jollity, selling hot fruit punch and allowing happy, if shivering, customers to crunch through fake snow and real sludge to enjoy rides, stalls and an array of seasonal shops.

The coach drives straight through the gates into the car park.

"I dare to repeat the question," says Elspeth Quest, as the rumblings within the coach rise to a level that might soon compete with the rattling and full-bodied screams resonating just beyond its doors. She appears as infuriated at not having been permitted into the loop as she is by the apparent change of plan.

"Think of it as an 'exercise', Miss Quest," explains Stanley Grainger, parking his vehicle. "It's how I bond with *my* family."

Elspeth Quest just gawps at the beaming man, too stunned to speak.

"*But it's December!*" protests Jacob Bloom. "We'll all get hypothermia." He mutters something about a place like this being liable to finish him off even in summer, but his companions aren't really listening.

Lisa Silk, sitting in the centre of the coach, looks around at the old people she knows so well. Some of whom, in her own way and despite her best instincts, she thinks she rather loves. At first glance, their faces all appear to be wearing the same totally understandable expression. That of absolute shock. Then, to her surprise and indeed relief, they all begin to smile. Not just smile but laugh. Some of the laughs turn into hacking coughs and runny noses, but none of the owners appear to mind. Small prices to pay for an afternoon that looks like turning out a damn sight better than it started.

Jason nudges the young woman. He doesn't appear to know whether to look tickled or terrified. "Think we should call your dad?" he whispers.

"He's gonna know soon enough, babe," says Lisa.

As Stanley opens the doors, they hear the strains of an old-fashioned carousel playing Jingle Bells.

"Well, anything's better than a sodding tea dance," mutters

Gerard Bunting, which, whilst perhaps contrasting with certain earlier sentiments expressed on the coach, now appears to sum up the general feeling of the group.

"Everybody out!" says Stanley Grainger.

scene eleven

Fortunately, as it is a weekday and the schools have yet to break up for Christmas, the amusement park is not overcrowded.

The only youngsters in sight are wide-eyed toddlers with their parents or smoking truants who may soon be hearing from their parents but really don't much care. Otherwise, the happily diverted Dustingford group mix mostly with locals doing some Christmas shopping; a scattering of pensioners like themselves, only less bewildered, who are enjoying a welcome change of scene; or the unemployed, attempting to stave off the creeping paralysis of boredom in a fading seaside town.

Stanley Grainger glances back at the faces of his charges as he leads them slowly but determinedly through the artificial snow and fake holly. He can't help smiling, not simply at their growing delight in bunking off and, in their own eyes, flouting authority, but also at how brazenly they still attempt to catch the eyes of other visitors, in the vain hope that at least one or two of these might still recognise them.

Rex Markham's scorecard is the highest, which is hardly surprising. He appears to accept the quite audible mutterings of his name with some polite gratification, a courteous nod perhaps, or a trademark smile. Commendably, his demeanour does not alter too visibly when this recognition is almost inevitably concluded with comments such as 'hasn't he got old?' or 'I think I'll just remember him as he was'.

Cyril Dodds comes a close second, but it really isn't that easy to ignore a small, elderly man with his hand up the rectum of a goggling wooden owl. Especially when the latter is decked in glinting red tinsel that has somehow become entangled on his splintery head.

Barry Prince, Gerard Bunting and Jacob Bloom pick up the rather more quizzical 'don't I know you?' looks, as if you could be off the telly but more likely just an occasional visitor to The Grapes on the High Street or the local friendship club. Of course, Diana Appleyard and Zelda Gatley don't even attract this. And the remaining Jackson Brother is mainly of interest because it is a relatively white town, in which a precious few of its octogenarians tap-dance.

As one might expect, Elspeth Quest – despite her understandable astonishment and vague unease at even being here – walks through this alien environment with a stateliness and dignity that announces to the world: yes, I am indeed somebody and if you're sufficiently lacking in taste and discernment not to recognise this, then such deficiency is patently yours alone.

She does feel, however, that she should be addressing this whole off-piste issue with the person responsible before they become too ensconced in whatever the hell this godforsaken place is.

After a convoluted tour involving tired kiddie roundabouts, bulging Christmas gift stalls, seedy amusement arcades and plastic-duck-hooking enterprises, the two obvious – although perhaps competing – pack leaders catch up at the famous Leviathan. This somewhat ancient – but, one prays, not lethally so – roller coaster is the undisputed main attraction of the small town's currently glittering but still faded fun park.

The swiftly ageing cast stare up at it in abject terror.

Yet even Lisa and Jason, who in different circumstances

would be fighting each other to leap on board, can detect the emotions warring within their charges' not altogether hardy frames.

"You're the director," says Stanley Grainger, nodding upwards then sideways then finally down to the careering chain of carriages as it completes its last, heart-stopping loop. The odd scream can still be heard echoing around the park.

"Is this some kind of life insurance scam or are you just homicidal?"

Before he can respond, it is Diana Appleyard who unexpectedly moves things forwards. "Oh, do let's go on, Elspeth. You only live once."

"Once is enough," mutters Jacob Bloom. But he can hear the tap-dancing very close beside him, growing more agitated by the second, and very soon responds instinctively. "Well, alright then. Just this once."

"Just teach us how to say Kaddish," says Barry Prince, as Topol from *Fiddler on the Roof*, which is just about acceptable, at least in comparison to his burnt cork Al Jolson or his oft employed Fagin from the David Lean version of *Oliver Twist*.

As soon as the vintage roller coaster has stopped to disgorge its pallid but proud complement of passengers, the group move towards the ride, which now looks deceptively harmless. They try not to look at their wobbly predecessors.

Elspeth finds herself seated next to Stanley.

She is not sure whether this is by accident or design. Nor, curiously, is she even certain whether she heartily approves of this whole subversive enterprise or is doing it entirely under sufferance. For a person so rarely in doubt about her actions or emotions, so confident in her thought processes, even when they are totally misguided – witness her string of financial disasters – this is quite disconcerting.

Lisa and Jason each sit themselves beside one of Rex's Exes, who appear quite nervous, but admirably don't want to let the side, or indeed each other, down. Whilst, directly in front of them sits Rex Markham, with, on this occasion, Diana Appleyard, who seems to her fellow performers to be looking rather pleased with herself.

A bit of a squabble is going on at the ticket counter between Cyril Dodds and the booking clerk, as regards Mr Chips. The problem doesn't appear so much that he is inanimate and wooden but that he doesn't quite meet the legal height requirement. A compromise is happily reached when Mr Chips himself explains that he is well into his forties, will remain firmly behind the protective steel bar and that his companion's hand will never leave his arsehole.

"Did you ever see *One Flew Over the Cuckoo's Nest*?" asks Elspeth of her fellow passenger, as she wonders what on earth has possessed the man to risk not only the fragile lives of his charges but also his own reputation and livelihood.

"Never heard of it," says the man, predictably.

"They were all lunatics," explains Elspeth Quest, "so comparisons may be drawn."

For the next three minutes – which to some feels a lifetime and to others a near-death experience – there is no more talking. There is, however, a lot of screaming, oy-ing and ah-ing, taking of pulses, praying, clutching at chests and each other, swallowing of bile and pills, with, of course, the requisite amount of terror and panic.

Yet, as Elspeth sits there, devoid for once of all power and authority, resisting an odd temptation to grip the manly arm just inches away from her own, she can't help feeling a certain pride. Not purely for herself this time but for all the other old troupers whirling and pivoting behind, in front, above and below her. Not one of whom had refused to take part, despite their fears and infirmities, which has to say something, hasn't it?

Yet, as her stomach leaps out of her throat and back again, and she prays that her prescribed hypertension tablets actually function, it dawns on Elspeth Quest – although this should hardly come as such a revelation – that each and every one of these people, regardless of their skills or status, success or talent, has been taking risks all of their working lives.

That's what the job, the profession, the industry – their world – is all about. The highs and the lows, laboured ascents and sudden plummeting. Fate and fortune. What is that expression she has kept hearing over recent years – something about feeling the fear and just bloody doing it? Even poor, pathetic Zelda Gatley is of that ilk. Hasn't she been living every fragile moment of every Dustingford day with the stomach-churning terror of discovery and isn't she very shortly to take the crucial, most decisive test?

What's a sodding roller coaster ride compared to all that?

"You okay, Miss Quest?" enquires Stanley, in one of their less frenzied moments.

"I'm fine, thank you, Mr Grainger."

"I prefer it when you call me Stanley," he says, as their carriage grinds upwards to the final summit.

"Alright," says the elderly lady, with a drawn-out sigh, "and I suppose you might as well call me Elspeth." She offers him one brief but not too haughty smile. "And now, I imagine it's downhill all the way."

*

The entire cast of the looming Dustingford Follies of 2019 sit on cold metal benches at a hot punch stall, huddled in their winter coats and hoping that death, if it has to come, makes it swift and pain-free. Yet, despite the Hamlet's dad-like complexions and dangerously racing hearts, the overwhelming impression, as Lisa and Jason 'professionally' assess them (alongside their own chances of avoiding prosecution), is one of supreme satisfaction and even joy.

Notwithstanding their collective age closing in on two thousand, they look like nothing so much as naughty schoolchildren, who have disobeyed their teachers and are giving two fingers to the hard time they know is inevitably coming their way.

"Okay, so what next?" chirps Mr Chips, who is unique in maintaining the colour he came in with. "The Waltzer? Helterskelter? Wall of Death?"

"Will no one rid me of this meddlesome owl?" intones Barry Prince. "Peter O'Toole, loves. As Henry Two. In *Becket.*"

"Was it a real owl, Barry?" asks Zelda Gatley, then judges from the silence that it might have been wiser not to ask.

Diana Appleyard's reaction is more decisive. She knocks the dummy's head off with her stick.

"Does anyone want to go back now?" asks Stanley, looking up and down the line of exhausted but engaged faces. "Maybe catch the end of the tea dance?"

"*NO!*" comes the unanimous response.

"Could we perhaps try something less energetic, Stanley?" implores Jacob, as if it behoves their driver alone to decide on the afternoon's schedule.

"I'll give you a fiver each," he laughs. "But there's no more where that came from and only one candy floss per person, do you hear?"

"Yes, Grandpa," laughs Rex Markham, tossing his paper cup into a nearby basket and slowly rising.

The others take their cue and, at their own speed, join him.

Some are clearly keen to take a ride on the far less intimidating carousel, whilst others are content simply to peruse the stalls and tiny shops. Lisa and Jason split up, a mite reluctantly, so that each can take charge of a different group.

Lisa can feel the mobile phone in her shoulder bag vibrating like a ticking bomb but decides that it certainly isn't going to help matters, or indeed her precarious sanity, to respond. What's done is done and, as she keeps telling herself, it's her father's own fault. It was Gavin Silk who was railroading them all to go somewhere he knew perfectly well from Christmases past that the wrinklies hate and where they would be patronised and made to feel their age, all for the sake of a sadistic thrill and a few more quid in his pocket. And anyway, it wasn't her that drove the runaway bus, was it?

She is gently shepherding her more uncertain charges down a narrow Yuletide alleyway when two young men in tightly zipped hoodies approach her. They smile in recognition, eyebrows raised derisively, but she doesn't smile back. Yet she remains there, as if gripped, staring at them. The men say nothing, not even her name, but their eyes might as well be projecting shopping lists onto a nearby wall.

"You alright, Lisa?" comes a familiar voice from behind her.

She nods to Stanley, without turning round. But the spell is broken, and she safely guides her ageing flock away from the intrusion, which most of them have hardly noticed, being enraptured with the sparkle or still punch-drunk but not from the punch. Lisa Silk is not going to dwell on how close to the edge of not being alright she is forever in danger of coming. She takes hold of the arm of the nearest resident, who happens to be famed Detective Inspector Malhotra of the New Delhi Police.

"Enjoying yourself, Derek?"

"I am not Derek, young lady, and this arm, whilst not particularly long, is belonging to the law."

Lisa Silk finds it rather assuring that whilst things can move at breakneck speed all around her, there are some which thankfully don't ever change.

*

Elspeth Quest has never once tested her skills at a shooting gallery.

She has had sufficient targets to hit in her life, thank you, without looking for them in places such as this. So, she is quite surprised to find herself handing over what appears an extortionate amount of money to a large and extensively tattooed lady, in exchange for a rather unwieldy rifle.

Unaccustomed to failing, save perhaps as a wife, mother, provider and friend, Elspeth is unduly disconcerted to watch pellets land at every place other than where she is aiming them. She has heard that establishments such as these are known to file the rifle sights at odd angles in order to evade handing out the prizes that Annie Oakleys such as herself would otherwise be bound to win. Yes, this must be the reason. There is no other plausible explanation.

She is on her third and, as she has resolutely decided, final round, when she finds her arm being lightly held and gently raised both upwards and to the side. She recognises the broad, strong fingers and decides, just this once, not to offer too much resistance.

"I was ten years in the army," arrives the explanation.

She shoots and the pellets penetrate the bullseye. Unfortunately, not that of the target for which she was aiming.

"Signals," he continues.

But Stanley hasn't taken his arm away. The elderly actress turns to look at the younger – yet truly not that much younger – man for a moment, then abruptly recalibrates her gaze into the distance. As if she is looking out for her lost troupe. They appear to have coalesced into a single entity. She smiles as she notices where Lisa and Jason are leading them.

"Time for reflection, Mr Grainger?" she says, as she points towards a large and garish wooden structure straight ahead.

By the time Elspeth and Stanley arrive at the Hall of Mirrors, her fellow performers, hardly unaccustomed to looking at themselves, are just beginning to laugh at the silliness of it all. Not merely at the grotesque transformations occurring right before their eyes, immeasurably altering with just the slightest movement, but also the sheer, unsullied daftness of the entire afternoon.

Within what must only be moments, the entire cast of Dustingford Follies, plus a couple of others (including, despite his better instincts, Detective Inspector Malhotra of the New Delhi police), are laughing to the point of tears. The remaining Jackson's feet are observed to be doing things that no limbs, not even those attached to the youngest and most double-jointed, could possibly do. Even Zelda Gatley, whose mirror experience has hitherto been less intense and whose days in the fading limelight may well be numbered, is finding herself in serious, mirth-induced pain. Tear ducts and bladders are taking some heavy punishment.

"How's this for bonding?" says Stanley Grainger.

"The name's Bond. James Bond," responds Barry Prince as, almost recognisably, Sean Connery.

Rex Markham watches, with some interest, as Elspeth and Stanley, standing very close together in front of a mirror, laugh at themselves and each other.

"Oh, do shut the fuck up, Barry," he says.

A young mum with a small boy, who has just entered, immediately turns and drags the confused little chap smartly out again. Because you never know with old people. They're likely to fly off and do simply anything and not a person dares to stop them.

scene twelve

The atmosphere at dinner this evening is quite different.

Even the staff notice it, although they can't work out exactly why this might be. It certainly isn't the food.

Elspeth understands.

For the first time since she arrived at Dustingford, in a state of such hopeless despondency, the conversations she overhears and those to which she readily contributes, are rooted not in some long gone glory days but in the immediate present. And also, to her quiet satisfaction, in the none-too-distant future.

Her company, for this is what she can now begin to term them (although still with some apprehension as to their individual abilities – one roller coaster ride doesn't turn you into a Vegas headliner or a candidate for the Olivier shortlist) – are just beginning to gel and come together. Bonding, she tells herself again, to use that awful yet not inappropriate term.

There is a raucousness to the chatter, a nervous excitement, the way there can be when a group has been through something momentous, verging on the dramatic or even downright dangerous, and has emerged on the other side relatively unscathed. (Save, perhaps, for some residual flatulence, a few unsightly bruises and a hopefully temporary increase in palpitations.)

"Finally, after all these wilderness years, I can add a brand-new skill to my Spotlight entry," announces Rex Markham. "Right next to fencing and horse riding."

"Vomiting?" suggests Gerard Bunting.

"I was thinking dodgem-car racing," laughs Rex. "But yes, that too."

"This has taken decades off my life," moans the almost-octogenarian Jacob Bloom.

The remaining Jackson, who has switched tables to sit beside him, touches Jacob's hand comfortingly. Surprised by this, but not displeased, the elderly actor smiles gently to himself.

"Hang on in there a few more days, Jacob, please," encourages Elspeth. "Just until opening night."

The tables sense the approach of Gavin Silk, as a gust of cold winter air from a window neglectfully left open, threatening a chill or worse. Laughter stops far more brusquely than it began.

"A word, please, Miss Quest," he snaps. "*Now!*"

She knew this was coming. They all did. The silence from management since they returned from their little escapade has felt almost tangible, like that unnatural calm some recall before the unprecedented fury of the great storm of 1987. No birds were singing, not a rustle in the trees. So, the great actress turned producer simply rises, with all the dignity she can muster, and follows the rigid back of the director towards his office and her doom.

"*Tis a far far better thing I do now…*" quotes a solemn Rex Markham, who memorably starred in the remake.

*

Gavin Silk is spitting blood.

Not literally, although Elspeth would not be so surprised, considering the redness of the man's face as he leans across his ship-free desk towards her. He is certainly spitting something.

211

"I'm afraid we have an issue, Miss Quest."

"An issue," she responds, somewhat disingenuously.

"With health and safety."

Elspeth looks at the man. "We went to an amusement park, Mr Silk. Not to a leper colony." The director says nothing, which she finds rather disconcerting. Although, no one need advise her on the effectiveness of silence. "We are grown-ups," she adds, more weakly than she might have wished. But she can take an admonishment, on behalf of her company, a stern knuckle rap, even if she was not the actual instigator of this afternoon's abrupt and perhaps reckless change of plan.

A far more troublesome thought suddenly occurs. "And I take full responsibility," she asserts swiftly, looking into the man's cold, narrow eyes. "I gave the orders. It was my idea."

"I don't doubt it," says Gavin Silk.

The man's smile reminds her of that of a torturer. Not that she has met many torturers, certainly no smiling ones, other than the odd film director. But she imagines that they do smile now and then if they're enjoying their work.

"Let me put it another way." More smiles. Dear Lord, the man really is milking it. And she hasn't had her dessert, which she always rather enjoys. "I'm responsible for the health and safety of my residents. Yours included. And I'm afraid it is my considered opinion that your little 'entertainment' would be highly detrimental to both."

Elspeth stares at him. For the first time today, despite Leviathan, she really does feel nauseous. Bile rises in her throat like fire.

The man now appears to be stifling a grin, which is no more attractive than his other facial contortions.

"I can't believe this," she says, appalled. "You're actually stopping the show?"

"And wasn't that usually your forte?"

In the Green Room, the same residents who were looking so cheerful just minutes before are now doing more impressions of old has-been entertainers than Barry Prince could manage in an entire one-man performance.

Only Mr Chips is smiling, but this is painted on, and a dropping of the head soon signifies that he doesn't really mean it.

Even Zelda Gatley is gutted, and she hadn't wished to be in the show in the first place. Which only indicates to Elspeth just how far this company has come.

Stanley, who appears to pick up on things in Dustingford even if he is way out of earshot, enters the room like an actor who has missed his cue and is forced to hurtle onstage at an unscripted pace.

"I told him it was all me, but he said I was on my way out, anyway... You're not going to let him get away with it, Elspeth!" He swiftly corrects himself. "Miss Quest."

"I'm powerless, Stanley." She doesn't need to correct herself, as the man is staff.

"And I'd just had an idea for my solo," mourns Jacob Bloom. He looks towards the equally disappointed Mr Jackson. "Well, *we* had."

"Old and helpless," sighs Rex Markham. "After all, that's why we're here, isn't it, loves?"

"*Oh, bollocks!*"

They turn as one to the connecting door between Green Room and Dining Hall. Lisa Silk stands in the doorway and has heard at least the tail end of the discussion.

"*Lisa!*" admonishes Stanley.

Everyone stares at her like the grandparents she never had. She did have grandparents, on her father's side, but they were nothing like this lot and a bit of a dead loss to be honest.

Now they're just dead, which is not a fate she would wish to contemplate for her friends here, although they are all beginning to look as if they'd at least entered the waiting room.

"Well, I'm sorry, but you're not just any old wrinklies. You're… special old wrinklies."

Ignoring a term that she is not alone in finding unpalatable, Diana challenges the currently defiant young woman. "What's so special about us, dear?"

Lisa simply stares at them all – elderly actors, entertainers, speciality acts and pretenders – then says one word. Which, to most of the assembled company, isn't even a word at all.

"*Duh?*"

The residents repeat the word or sound to each other, at differing volumes and a variety of intonations, but are patently none the wiser.

Lisa, who is on her final warning after refusing to answer her father's repeated calls this afternoon, and who really should be more careful, looks to Stanley. The handyman has no idea what she is on about, but he surely knows that right now he is paying an excess of interest on his borrowed time. He can't actually fathom why he hadn't been summarily dismissed already. So, he simply takes a seat and awaits what Lisa Silk has to say.

It isn't at all what any of them had expected.

scene thirteen

Dustingford Hall is pleasantly quiet when Gavin Silk and his problem child pull up in the director's small but immaculate car the following morning, in order to take over from the night staff and commence their day.

The frost on the lawns and on the ivy-clad stonework glistens in the metallic, early morning sunlight, giving the still lit-up Victorian house an almost Dickensian wintery glow. Even the silver tracery of cobwebs on the peeling windows tilt towards the atmospheric rather than simple neglect, but the man whose byword is focus takes absolutely no notice.

"Remember," he tells the young woman, "I can make no more allowances for you. Nor would I wish to. Final warning, Lisa. And now that you don't have this ridiculous 'concert' to think about – something I really should have nipped in the bud weeks ago – you can devote yourself to less frivolous and considerably more purposeful matters."

"Whatever," says his daughter, but the man has already slithered in through the former mansion's heavy, oaken doors.

As is his custom, Gavin Silk, after checking in with his staff, makes his first port of call the dining room so that he can greet his residents and, more importantly, so that they can observe him taking commendable responsibility for their care and nourishment. It also enables him to give his 'charges' a verbal heads-up on the programme for the day, be it yoga (which most of them hate because the woman is a sadist), an art class (which most of them disdain because the man is an amateur) or a talk by a visiting celebrity (which they uniformly despise because the speakers are rarely top-drawer and the whole thing just makes them feel even more over the hill.)

There might even occasionally be an old and classic film, although the latter activity can be singularly fraught, if it happens to involve residents who might have become romantically entangled with the partners of other residents during the course of production, which has occurred more than Gavin Silk would have previously ever thought possible. He still recalls showing a vintage Shakespeare to the elderly first wife of its star, a man who had found wife number two as an ingenue on that accursed filmset.

As he walks into the room, the director is so involved in perusing his daily bulletin that he completely fails to notice the unusual echo from his footfall and the fact that the large chamber is completely empty. The tables are all set for breakfast, but it is painfully clear that no one has bothered to turn up.

Eventually, he looks up from his sheet to confront the unprecedented silence head-on, then spins round to Lisa, who appears equally baffled. Striding into the kitchen, he finds his employees sitting around, drinking coffee and munching toast. Their collective shrug suggests that they are to be no help whatsoever.

Yet he still asks, "*Where is everybody?*" because surely this is the first question any rest home director might pose in the circumstances. Perhaps not always so politely.

As thoughts career between a catering-provoked rebellion and a mass-suicide pact, Gavin Silk strides back into the lobby, snapping his fingers behind him for the benefit of his daughter and least-favoured employee. (Mind you, with jolly kidnapper Stanley Grainger still around for a few more days, it's a close-run thing.)

The first-floor corridor is equally deserted, as father and daughter make their bemused way between the uniformly closed rooms.

They suddenly notice, as he turns a corner and moves very slowly towards them, the remaining Jackson.

He doesn't look like he might be remaining for long. His tap-dancing legs, usually so flexible yet assured, are wobbling ominously.

At first, Silk wonders if the man is attempting to encapsulate drunkenness in a mute yet precisely choreographed routine: the stumbling legs endeavouring but failing to tap a straight line, the still lithe body, usually so fluid, almost but not quite capsizing. *It's rather well done*, thinks Silk, before noticing the man's face. Surely, no amount of talent can make a naturally dark-skinned man look so very wan and pallid.

As the dancer reaches Silk, he stumbles. Instinctively, the younger man reaches out to catch his reeling resident, but the remaining Jackson waves him off in alarm and continues on his way.

"He didn't look too good, did he?" says the director.

"Seen worse," says his daughter. "But usually with pennies on their eyes." Which is a touch too graphic, thinks her dad, and curiously old-fashioned.

He is still wondering whether anyone actually does this as he knocks on another random door. A tired and less-than-chirpy voice bids him enter.

Lying prone in his bed, the covers pulled up to his unshaven chin, Cyril Dodds looks far from well. The bird in bed with him looks equally poorly and not just because it has been carved from old and now fading wood.

"Good morning, Mr Dodds," says Gavin Silk, attempting

what he considers cheer, as he tentatively approaches the small and over-occupied bed.

"Is it morning, Mr Silk?" asks the ventriloquist, blearily. "Hard to tell."

The man's equally sickly bed companion now utters the legendary catchphrase, with an appropriateness possibly unparalleled in his long and illustrious career. And, unusually for him, does it without moving his lips. "We've not been well."

"What is going on?" demands Gavin Silk of the surrounding walls but receives only silence in return.

He decides that he will proceed to the next-door room, as Miss Appleyard is refreshingly normal, for an actress. But his brisk knock is answered by a voice that is ominously frail.

"Who is it?" creaks the occupant.

Gavin Silk opens the door. After a brief stare, he beckons Lisa over to check out what has met his gaze. When they have both seen all they need, they nod an apology and back away.

"She looks worse than Cyril Dodds," whispers Silk, in some alarm.

"She looks worse than Mr Chips," amplifies Lisa, which doesn't really help.

The story is the same in each room that they visit.

In fact, the narrative quite possibly gets worse with every room, but this may simply be the effect of its being cumulative. As Gavin Silk knocks on, then opens, each door in turn, he finds elderly actors and entertainers either splayed out on disarrayed beds, drenched in perspiration, slumped on the covers like aged Chattertons, lifeless arms dangling, or very noisily throwing up in en-suite bathrooms.

By the time they arrive at Barry Prince, they are far from surprised to discover the old gentleman collapsed in a chair, proud hair in limp disarray, running through a medley of classic death scenes from movies, like an entire boxed set of the famously sick. His Janet Leigh in *Psycho* is perhaps the most disturbing, not to say baffling, as the ailing man has had to resort to the chillingly spiky Bernard Herrmann score.

Jacob Bloom just looks dead. So, no change there.

Events appear to be reaching their nadir when the director knocks on the door of Zelda Gatley. Very warily, they open up to find the tiny woman writhing about on her floor, arms flailing, mouth foaming, eyes careering around her head like pinballs seeking a maximum score. Silk just looks at Lisa and rolls his eyes, as if to say 'trust her!'.

"What is going on, Lisa?" he asks, not unreasonably.

"Search me," says Lisa.

"Probably indigestion from all that bloody candyfloss," says her father, although he realises that he is probably clutching at straws.

They hear a croaky voice from behind them.

"Or, more credibly, from your shepherd's pie last night."

At this, Gavin Silk freezes.

Very slowly, and with a sense of his morning Weetabix surging, the director turns to find Elspeth Quest, charity case and bane of his undeserving life, in her flowery and rather elegant dressing gown. Yet it appears to have been hurriedly thrown on, sash at a dangle, without her usual regard for appearances. Indeed, the old woman looks quite drained, verging on wretched, and is leaning heavily on her stick.

"Don't be ridiculous, Miss Quest. I had some of chef's pie myself. It was quite edible."

"Praise indeed. Well, of course, I'm no doctor. Legionnaire's Disease? Ebola? No…" Silk can tell, even before the elderly actress opens her mouth, that she is segueing seamlessly into what he refers to as 'one of their godawful quote modes'. "*Something very rare and not at all hygienic, being criminally allowed to fester and breed, to the obvious detriment of the celebrated old folk, who've given so much pleasure to millions over so many years,* says Dustingford Hall's newest and most famous resident, Elspeth

Quest. MBE. Star of—"

She starts to cough quite violently, as if she is trying desperately to rid herself of her tonsils. Lisa goes immediately to her aid, but Elspeth nobly shakes her off.

"Forget about me, dear. I've had a good life. Save the others."

Amongst Gavin Silk's skills, of which he would confirm there are many, is that of knowing when one is beaten. The director is beaten. And he knows it.

"Well, I'm no doctor, either, Miss Quest. But what do you 'amateurs' think might encourage a swift recovery?

Ignoring that ever-wounding word, Elspeth Quest wraps her gown more tightly and elegantly around her slim frame and smiles bravely up at him.

scene fourteen

"*No one starts at the top and a lot of us drop, before we can reach the heights,*

But with a gallon of pluck and a barrel of luck, we can see our name up there in lights…"

Elspeth Quest has her head in her hands but at least her fingers aren't in her ears. Having seen some early, reassuring evidence over the dinner table that memorable roller coaster evening, she would have to admit now, as she watches them perform, that her cast members are finally exhibiting signs of being part of a team. If challenged, she might be exercised to say a team of exactly what, but she cannot deny that there has been progress over the past week.

Which is probably just as well, as the show opens (and closes) in four days.

Elspeth is not thinking about what happens to her after this.

Or what further excuses – well, outright lies – she can provide to explain her not returning to her grandly restored and now structurally sound Kensington residence once Christmas and essential redecorations are taken care of. Sometimes, she verges on wishing that she had simply been straight and honest in the first place and perhaps a mite less disdainful. But whilst Elspeth Quest is famously assiduous and indeed fervid in her search for the psychological underpinning of any character she has chosen to play onstage or screen, however large or small, she has never been one for unfettered self-analysis in life as we know it. So, she is parking all these thoughts for the moment. The show alone is the thing.

"*Four fucking days, people!*" she cries, encouragingly.

Whilst her attention is focused firmly on the stage (which, she has to admit, Stanley has constructed rather well, with generous attention to accessibility and safety, especially considering the paucity of funds and disinterest of management), the younger members of staff are putting the finishing touches to the backdrop. Their attempts at the masks of tragedy and comedy appear a touch idiosyncratic, resembling as they do a woman fleeing some sort of domestic abuse and a man high on synthetic street drugs, but 'DUSTINGFORD FOLLIES' looks the business, writ large in Day-Glo red and now, on the third stab, spelled absolutely correctly.

"I am so sorry, all of you," she tells the cast, "but I'm afraid it's still looking a bit, well, am-dram."

The full company onstage gasp as one.

Rex's Ex – whichever one it is today – immediately raises her hands from the keyboard. There is no greater insult in the world of theatre and entertainment than to be compared with those dedicatedly enthusiastic but often seriously limited people around the country who crave the limelight but quite prudently, haven't given up their day jobs. And hopefully – at least in the mind of this exasperated and exhausted producer/director – no sharper spur.

"You've only got two bloody feet, surely you can remember which one goes where!" She flashes a weary glance towards the choreographer, but the woman isn't looking and has cataracts, anyway. Her ears are fine, however, so she is fully aware that there is work to do. "Jacob, dear, had an idea for your spot, by any chance? Mm?" Before Mr Bloom can answer with anything more than a slight nod, Elspeth is onto the next item on her extensive list. "Lisa, nobody naps between now and Saturday, unless I say so. And Horlicks is off limits until the end-of-show party."

Jason, on his ladder, looks down at Lisa. They exchange a secret, conspiratorial, younger-generational smile, which most of the cast pick up immediately, because – although these youngsters can't quite believe it – the Dusties had actually been young themselves and where now dyspepsia and incontinence simmer, fires once did burn.

Rehearsals proceed in this manner throughout the day, with only a short break for lunch and quite a few for necessities.

Although she dares not express this too loudly or too often, Elspeth is just starting to believe that – after three more days of utterly merciless hectoring, relentless humiliation, heartfelt encouragement, veiled threats, consummate direction and a certain amount of tearful pleading – they could just about have something that vaguely resembles a show.

Possibly.

scene fifteen

Elspeth Quest is admiring herself, as best she can, in the illumination-free bedroom mirror, from which she cannot see reflected even a sliver of south coast sea. Not that she likes to dwell on these things. She is anyway far too consumed by how she might look onstage, in the once formidable dress that she is now trying on.

She has often heard it said, usually by those outside her chosen field, that actors tend not to dress particularly well when they're on their own time, as their tastes are adulterated or perhaps simply exhausted by the sheer amount and variety of costumes they are obliged to go through on duty. She has observed this to be an almost incontestable truth, at least as regards most of the performers whom she knows, but she is relatively certain that Elspeth Quest is the acknowledged exception to this rule. The frock she is currently investigating is surely a case in point. Whilst purchased some while ago for occasions one might regard as rather special, she is in no doubt that it will be equally as eye-catching on this Saturday's special stage.

"Oh Romeo, Romeo, wherefore art thou Romeo…"

She wishes she at least had a balcony to her room, like bloody Marguerite and the unduly favoured residents on the other side of the building, as the weather is bound to warm up some day. But, of course, there isn't exactly a lot to see round this side, save for the occasional sighting of doctor, dentist, chiropodist or undertaker.

A knock on the door interrupts her flow.

"Come!" she commands, although there is nobody she particularly hankers to be knocking. Except, perhaps… "*Enter!*" she says, a touch louder.

Enter Stanley, holding a bunch of newly picked flowers.

"Are you still contagious?" he asks with a smile.

"I believe you mean infectious. That was the effect for which I was striving. Contagious is when you touch."

Stanley comes closer, weaving between the corner of the bed and the small room's only chair. He sets the flowers down and then, to Elspeth's surprise, he strokes her cheek very gently, whilst staring all the time, and with some intensity, into her eyes. He wonders why he has never noticed what an interesting shade of blue they are. Almost grey, yet containing a strange light, as if someone behind these eyes is shining a tiny torch through them. She appears confused, her usually pale face immediately reddening. Yet she doesn't move away.

"I really don't think this is appropriate, Mr—"

"Why?" asks Stanley, the kindly smile with which he entered remaining on his face, as if to signal that very little is about to deter him. "Because I'm 'below stairs'?"

"Oh, for goodness sake," she says. "I'm not exactly aristocracy. The world of weekly rent collectors and outdoor plumbing is hardly unknown to me." She shakes her head. "I'm an old lady of-of seventy-nine, Stanley."

"Haven't you ever had a toy boy, then? I thought all you actresses—"

Elspeth Quest is quite convinced that there are any number of smartly glib responses to this. Yet she can't think of one at the moment. Not whilst feeling so flustered.

"I-I have to practise my part. You understand. I've been so busy rehearsing the others that—"

"Can't you ever stop, Elspeth, just for a moment?"

"*Stop?* With my show less than four days away. Are you insane?"

Stanley, who quite possibly is insane, holds her face in both his comfortingly warm hands. And kisses her. The shock of this bold, not to say brazen, overture doesn't prevent Elspeth from suddenly, and to her own dismay, clasping his strong, weatherworn fingers with her own considerably smaller ones. As if to keep them there. She wants to apologise for their chill. Circulation has never run kindly in her family.

"What are we doing?" she asks, edging away. "You've got your life here. Your family. I'm... moving on."

She berates herself for suddenly thinking of *Lady Chatterley*. Swiftly followed, like a particularly crass double feature, by *The Go-Between*. And then, she berates herself even more for forever seeing her life as simply another form of performance art. *Can't I ever just inhabit reality*, she asks herself. *Just for five sodding minutes!* Patently not.

"No, you're not, love," says Stanley.

"What do you mean?"

His smile becomes knowing, yet without a trace of superiority. "You're here for the duration, aren't you, pet?" Elspeth says nothing, which is all the response he needs. "I've worked at Dusty Hall a long time, Elspeth. I can spot the 'lifers'. Don't worry, I won't tell anyone. Not that it's anything that has to be hidden, if you ask me. We all get old. And lonely. And needing someone to take care of us. But I have to warn you, your pals around here might just have the odd suspicion... when that curtain goes down."

"I never think beyond my next performance," says Elspeth Quest. "Which is, as you well know, this Saturday night. So, if you'll excuse me, Mr Grainger..."

She returns to her mirror. He stands for a moment, looking uncharacteristically redundant. Finally, he turns and makes for the door, gripping the handle like a wrench.

"I'll leave you to your Romeo, then."

She follows the closing door in her mirror. Flustered. And alone.

scene sixteen

"Final dress rehearsal in ten, ladies and gents... *minutes*!"

The cast, or at least the majority of them, are hovering around the dining room. Some stand, whilst most are slumped in whatever chairs have been rescued from the piles already stacked and shoved against the walls.

The men and women are all in evening dress, items of clothing which fortunately most had brought with them into the home, although it wasn't totally clear to those staff or family members assisting the newly arrived exactly what events in a rest home in a remote backwater of southern England might occasion their use.

Lisa Silk is never quite certain that everyone, or indeed anyone, hears her calls to action, loud as they are, as those who should be listening out for them tend, on these crucial days, either to be nervously chatting at an unnatural volume or completely absorbed in worlds of their own. So, she usually follows up these general entreaties with a more targeted approach, gently tapping each member of the cast in turn and speaking directly into their eyes and ears. Many of them retort by telling her that they are not bloody deaf, which she happily accepts, although she knows that this is quite often a matter of pride and doesn't signify for a moment that they have actually heard her.

She has to admit that this first brush with the world of 'professional' theatre, ramshackle and superannuated as it may be, has thoroughly impressed her. She is still not a huge fan of Elspeth Quest – and why would she be – but she graciously concedes that the snappy old woman most probably does know her stuff. As indeed does her unsung understudy and personal assistant, lovely Miss Appleyard, whom Lisa has observed being able to qualify Elspeth Quest's often overambitious stage directions and mollify those who might have been stung by her words. This sweet old lady, with her cheery round face, is never less than encouraging and is responsible, in her own mild-mannered yet still decisive way, to create some sort of running order out of chaos. Lisa sometimes wishes it were this woman, and not her father, at the Dustingford helm.

Professionals aside, the novice stage manager is also rather proud of her own immediate friends and colleagues. Jason and crew have done a stellar job with the tiny stage and its painted backdrop. They are currently hard at work on the lighting, which is beginning to get there. It will never be rock concert mind-blowing, but there are some well-placed 'spots' and it will switch from darkness to light and back again more than adequately.

Jason, who reckons he knows about these things and has managed to borrow and scrounge quite ruthlessly from the local theatre, is consistently warning his fellows not to try any tricks. Just this morning, Lisa heard him over breakfast recalling one of his mother's recent am-dram efforts, something about Noah and his ark, where the guy on lights had decided to impress everyone on opening night by projecting a perfectly fluffy white cloud unannounced onto the sky blue backdrop, just as the curtains were opening for the second act. It did indeed look magical and would have remained so, had the first words spoken, by an elated Noah himself, not been something to the order of 'what a wonderful day – not a cloud in the sky'. The subsequent laughter had rather diminished the effect. "So, watch what *they're* doing, not just what you're effing doing," he cautions. Lisa feels she couldn't have put it better herself.

Stanley has been just as busy.

His stage has been shifted a few feet forwards to allow for rudimentary dressing rooms. These are by no means the height of luxury, but with judicious curtaining, a basic modesty is preserved. And, of course, the residents have their own bedrooms just up the rear staircase, with en-suite bathrooms, mirrors and the profusion of professional stage make-up that Lisa has over-ordered, on the instruction of – and with financial assistance from – her betters.

Before the dress rehearsal, the usually sanguine Stanley draws Lisa aside in a state of rare excitement. He wants to demonstrate the stage curtains he has rigged up, using heavy material of a rich red that has been donated by a store in the town and an intricate pulley system of his own devising. Yet, as he winds the curtains in and then eases them out, Lisa notices with growing concern that each process is taking an age to complete. The performers on the night would be hovering there like lemons.

She can see the sweat appearing on the handyman's face as every muscle tightens with the effort. His arms are trembling, and the sounds of exertion are almost painful. Lisa has never consciously noticed Stanley Grainger, one of her best friends in this world, growing older. And she doesn't want to think about it now. Yet the stage manager in her knows that she must.

"I think the curtains are bloody brilliant, Stanley. I'm gobsmacked. But I really can't have you stuck by that pulley all night, not when I'm going to be needing you for all the other jobs." She can't actually think what all these other jobs might be, but she will. "Just pick one of your lads. No worries," she suggests, casually adding, "I'll give him his cues in good time."

Lisa has no idea whether Stanley simply accepts all this at face value or has picked up on the innate sensitivity and practicality underlying her decision, but he can't totally disguise the relief on his face. Even as he masks it with a nod of professional agreement.

As dress rehearsal is about to start, only a half-hour after the final ten-minute call, she finds Jason hefting a huge Christmas tree onto the stage.

"What the fuck's that?" she enquires.

"What's it look like?"

"I mean, what's it doing on my stage?"

"*Your* stage? Well, ask the stage owner's dad." She just looks at the young shifter. He sets the tree down for a moment, as he rightly senses this might not be the speediest of exchanges. "He says you can't have a Christmas show without a tree."

"Oh, like he's the expert. Anyway, this isn't a 'Christmas show', Jase," she responds, channelling Elspeth Quest. "It's a regular show that just happens to be on at Christmas."

The tree-hefter, who is not versed in such niceties, shrugs and resumes his planting. But not before turning to ask her one final, pressing question.

"Here, 'darling', isn't there a play you're not supposed to say the name of, cos if you do, people die?"

"Mention any play to us and that could happen," mutters Jacob Bloom, who is standing nearby.

"Oh, come on, Mr Bloom," calls Stanley, who is giving the base of his precious curtain a final trim with some garden shears. "Aren't you a bit excited? Big night tomorrow."

The chatter around the room immediately ceases as the cast stare at the handyman in horror.

Rex Markham takes it upon himself to speak for the community. "You have no idea, have you Stanley? About the fear."

"I was in Northern Ireland," he confides, "during the troubles."

The ensemble just shakes its collective head.

"Nothing like it," comes the chorus.

*

Her father is on his computer when Lisa finally pops in to see him at the end of the long day.

"Hi," she greets him but receives no reply. She sits down opposite him and continues. "They don't want a Christmas tree on the stage."

"Can't have a Christmas show without a Christmas tree," responds Gavin Silk, without looking up.

"One of them got a pine needle in his eye and it's brought on another one's asthma."

"You're making things up again," sighs Gavin Silk, sending off his email.

"Bad dress, great show."

"What?" asks the director, looking up for the first time and wondering who exactly is wearing the bad dress. It could be any one of them, so far as he is concerned.

"It's what they say," explains Lisa, realising there is no reason the man should be as steeped as she in the arcane jargon of the theatre. "If the dress rehearsal is bad – which it was just now, it was really, really shit; everything went wrong that could go wrong and some other stuff did too – then the show will be terrific." She ponders. "Or really, really shit. But hey, know what? At least it has brought them all together. Made them—"

"Forget about *them*, Lisa. They're... old news." He leans forwards across his anally uncluttered desk, causing her instinctively to lean back. "All I care about is that this... enterprise gets it out of *your* system. Right out." He stares at her, but this time more thoughtfully. His voice has lost its edge if not its mission. "It's enough, Lisa. You know that, don't you?"

To his surprise and perhaps even to her own, Lisa Silk nods

resignedly. "Yeah. Yes. I do."

There is clearly more to be said. Further and possibly deeper discussions, between father and daughter, albeit unchanging in their focus. But these are no concern of Elspeth Quest as she steams in, with neither knock nor apology.

Despite the obvious smartness and faded elegance of her wardrobe, the elderly woman looks worn and frazzled. Gavin Silk might almost feel some empathy for her, if only he were the slightest bit capable of such and didn't dislike her quite so vehemently.

"Lisa," she commands, "I need to go over the cues with you. Dining room? Now!"

Lisa nods and immediately gets up.

"Bad dress, great show," says Gavin Silk, with what passes for a smile.

"Don't talk crap," says Elspeth Quest, with no trace of a smile whatsoever.

scene seventeen

The twenty-seven hours between the conclusion of Friday's calamitous dress rehearsal, of which least said the better, and the tentative opening chords of Dustingford Follies 2019 are up there with the most emotionally fraught of Elspeth Quest's long (and, she fears, rapidly shortening) life.

After the intensity of this final day's rehearsal process, she sits spent at her dressing table in the tiny bedroom, already surrounded by the tattered boxes of stage make-up she has brought from home and which she intends to apply tomorrow evening with her customary aplomb.

Having resolved to allow her cast these several hours just to recoup and relax until the big night itself, as further rehearsal could be counterproductive and might possibly kill them, she decides to make a list of everything that went wrong and a considerably shorter list of those things that can just about be put right on the day. She determines to be as honest and as realistic with herself as she can.

There really isn't a great deal she can do about the age of her cast and the infirmity, or at least physical limitations, of the majority. (And, sadly, the diminishing mental agility of some.) She can and has encouraged them to go over and over their lines and routines, even in their sleep, which is intermittent anyway. A nocturnal visit to the bathroom should and must be considered an opportunity rather than an inconvenience.

Thanks to Stanley and his boys, there are microphones at every conceivable angle, and she is vaguely reassured that unless the audience is as hard of hearing as the performers, they should be able to pick up most of it. Whilst the cues themselves are less than West End slick, the stage management is surprisingly adequate and the lighting should at least provide the audience with the opportunity to watch their elderly relatives, ex-clients and dear old friends ignoring absolutely bloody everything she has drummed into them over weeks and weeks of personally crucifying rehearsal.

There she goes again. Elspeth – *stop!*

She finds herself careening between a mortifying panic that the show, on which she, and to a lesser extent everyone else, have been working their asses off, will be a sheer and utter travesty, a humiliating disaster for all concerned, and a sense of genuine pride that she has taken a group of elderly, once celebrated people, whom she had discovered living almost entirely in the past, and given them perhaps one final taste of magical, ineffable, heart-stopping present. Which, in that same distant past, was all they ever truly lived for.

It's like being on an emotional Leviathan, she concludes, far more wrenching and stomach-churning than any man-made amusement park ride.

Yet, as she stares into her dressing table mirror, at that once passably attractive but now, to her eyes, sadly decaying face, she can't help but think that she – Elspeth Quest MBE, esteemed member in her time of both the National Theatre and the Royal Shakespeare Company, Olivier winner and BAFTA nominee, patron of everything and Dame in all but Name – might actually be full of shit.

Mercifully, a knock on the door prevents her from sitting too long on her own with this rare shard of introspection. She finds herself wondering if it might be Stanley. "What is *that* all about?" she asks the slightly blushing but still wrecked lady in the mirror, with a perturbation she can quite happily do without right now.

Elspeth swiftly taps some errant strands of depressingly flimsy hair back into place and calls over her shoulder towards the door.

"Come in, for pity's sake." She catches the solemn face of her visitor in the mirror. "Oh, Jesus!" she says.

"No. Detective Inspector Malhotra of the New Delhi Police," says the man.

"What can I do for you, Derek?" she asks, still facing the mirror.

"Sanjeev," corrects Derek Hirst, with a sad smile. "It is actually what I am able to be doing for you, Miss Quest."

Elspeth, who has never actually met an Indian person who talks like this (but admittedly didn't know that many when this pretend one was a radio star), turns to discover the small gentleman looking quietly confident, a polite smile on his pale, barely wrinkled face.

"For *me*?"

"Indeed. I am asking of you the opportunity to be appearing in your esteemed and wonderful show."

Elspeth can't help wanting to burst out laughing at this unexpected proposal, especially in today's febrile atmosphere, yet she also finds herself not wishing to offend the man, whose sanity as well as career have clearly seen better days.

"I'm afraid – Inspector – that the running order has been very carefully worked out. Such a pity, but I'm sure you understand that to disturb it now might undermine, not to say unnerve—"

"This I would sincerely not wish, dear lady." The man is shaking his head, a gesture Elspeth decides he must have added to his repertoire at a later stage, as head shaking is not an acknowledged radio technique. She wonders exactly what manner of speciality act he could be offering her.

"However, I have been continuing my investigations into the death of Mrs Elsie Turks. The very wealthy Mrs Turks."

Of course, you have. "She was a juggler, Inspector," says Elspeth Quest, with her infinite patience, adding, "But then, aren't we all?" She wonders why she bothers, yet slowly realises that this 'diversion' is actually calming her down. She really *must* tell – who can she tell? To her surprise, one person springs to mind.

"Her late husband wasn't in what I believe you call show business," explains the man, patiently. "He was a very wealthy Scottish gentleman. An industrialist."

"Forgive me, Inspector, but didn't I hear you say that the death of poor Miss Turks was completely natural?" Elspeth Quest hasn't done an Agatha Christie since early rep but this line she had just heard herself uttering sounded remarkably like one she might well have given in Rotherham.

"Indeed. She was quite unwell, poor lady, and it was only a matter of time."

"So rather fortunate for her son, wasn't it, that she passed without changing her will? He didn't have to bump her off at all." *Why am I getting into this?* wonders Elspeth Quest.

"As you rightly say, Madam. And her son, her one and only child, is very generously donating a portion of that large inheritance to this illustrious home."

"Well, a happy ending! And we all like those, don't we?" She realises that she is beginning to sound rather patronising but reassures herself that the poor man is totally dissociated so probably won't take too much umbrage.

At this, the detective inspector allows himself a small, indulgent smile. "This may be how it appears... to the lay person. But the Delhi-ductive mind is never sleeping. I have been doing some research. Have you heard of something called the internet?"

"I do believe I have."

"Then I think you will be finding the final episode of *A Stab in the Juggler* quite, shall we say, revelatory. As will your audience. I shall make my appearance just before the lights are going down for the commencement of your second act. When everyone is gathered together once more. It will only be taking five minutes, at the most."

Elspeth Quest has no idea why she agrees to this. Perhaps simply to get this persistent little person out of her bedroom. But she finds herself nodding at him.

"Five minutes or I shall black you out."

The man flinches at this slur, so casually racist. Yet he is accustomed to such, amongst a certain type of individual. So, he simply joins the palms of his hands together in a dignified manner and bows himself politely out of the room.

scene eighteen

The Dustingford dining room, for obvious reasons, is completely out of bounds. Serious banging and clattering can still be heard emanating from what is now the stage area, echoing through the creaky walls and hallways.

So, for one day only, the cast of this evening's landmark production are enjoying, or at least consuming, a sandwich lunch in the Green Room. Save, of course, for those who are confining themselves to their own bedrooms in order to rest and to better prepare for the ordeal to come and others, such as Jacob Bloom, who may require the camaraderie and support of their fellows but are far too sick with fear to contemplate the least nourishment until after this night's main event. Even Mr Chips is shaking, and owls are renowned in their own community for their sangfroid.

"Do you know," observes Rex Markham, as he devours his cheese and pickle and attempts manfully to disguise the mounting excitement already pounding within his once rippling chest, "I've been so involved in this bloody show, I've hardly had time to think about Christmas."

"It's over three weeks yet, heart," assures Gerard Bunting. "Plenty of time."

Diana Appleyard can see that Zelda Gatley is bursting to

correct the elderly character actor and tell him that Christmas is only days away. The understudy, who is undoubtedly the calmest person in the room, shakes her head in warning and digs the would-be-actress sharply in the ribs, causing the smaller woman's piled-high sandwich plate to wobble precariously.

"Yes, plenty of time, Gerard," agrees Zelda. "Bags of it. *Weeks!* But haven't they already made the place look nice?"

The residents all nod at this. Along with the obligatory Christmas trees, including the one Elspeth Quest had insisted be removed forthwith from her stage and relocated at the entrance to her 'theatre', the entire place – inside and out – is festooned with multicoloured fairy lights, glittery tinsel and even fake snow. Gavin Silk, having been obliged to agree to this performance, has seen the good sense in ensuring that it, and thereby himself, appears more than presentable in the eyes of household-name trustees, major donors, local dignitaries and whoever else the residents themselves have invited to join in what he sincerely hopes won't be too major a debacle. Well, at least his Home will look professional.

This director has prudently decided to keep out of harm's – or at least cast's – way until closer to performance time, when he considers that a pep talk from someone in authority, someone respected, might be just the thing. Such withdrawal has been quietly encouraged by his daughter, who suggested that those residents with a part to play in this special evening require handling of some delicacy. It was less quietly confirmed by an escalating fusillade of 'sod off, why don't you?'s earlier today. Even from people he had hitherto found relatively calm and polite.

"Time for a smoke!" announces Rex Markham, briskly wiping his mouth with a napkin and standing up. His fellow smokers immediately rise, as does Zelda Gatley, forcing the last sandwich into her mouth.

"You don't smoke, dear," says Rex.

"Then it's time I started," says Zelda through moist crusts. "It's alright for you. Worst that can happen is you fall on your arses and make bloody fools of yourselves. It's more than likely I shall lose my place here and then…" Her voice begins to crack. "I don't know where I shall go."

"Some of us could die tonight," says Jacob Bloom, helpfully. The remaining and still tapping Jackson, looking even more wistful than usual, strokes the mournful actor comfortingly on the knee. Jacob Bloom acknowledges the gesture with a small smile. "Well, perhaps not die. A stroke, maybe. Or a perforated gastric ulcer… if my luck holds."

Before the cast can respond, or in some cases move as far away as possible, Elspeth Quest strides in.

"I'm not going to interrupt you," she announces, while people are still talking. "I'll obviously see you later on before the performance. But I just want you to know that whatever happens this evening, I'm very proud of you all."

"Whaddaya mean whatever happens?" asks the night's compere, Barry Prince, as Humphrey Bogart, taking out one of his cigarettes.

"He died of lung cancer," mutters Jacob Bloom.

"I nursed my poor dear lovely Molly through cancer. It's no joke," says Barry Prince, very much as himself. Jacob shrugs a sympathetic apology.

"Maybe I should simply be saying," continues Elspeth swiftly, as she feels the cloud of melancholy that is never far away from Dustingford just beginning to settle, "I want you all to go out there this evening and – well, *just enjoy your bloody selves!* Because the more you do, and the more you *look* like you do, then the more this hand-picked audience will join you for the ride."

They can all see the wisdom of this. Many of them nod their heads in agreement. But practically all of the assembled company, in that spirit of camaraderie that goes along with first night nerves, want to tell her exactly what they just told Gavin Silk.

"And how do *you* feel, Elspeth?" enquires Diana Appleyard, with genuine concern. "You know, not only having to think of the presentation of the entire show but also being such an important part of it?"

The cast glance at Elspeth, some of them wishing they too had shown the sensitivity to voice what has just been asked so eloquently.

Elspeth Quest gazes at this sweet and still rather elegant lady, albeit a tad podgy now, sitting in her usual armchair, with a single tuna sandwich resting delicately on her plate. It is almost as if she is staring at a stranger, which is curious because she has apparently known Diana Appleyard for years and the woman hasn't suddenly had a face transplant. Of course, she *has* aged, haven't they all, but the feeling is more as if she hadn't really noticed this person before or indeed thought of her as anything more than an adjunct to herself. A resource that was always to hand but which thankfully she had never had occasion to use. Like a domestic fire extinguisher. She shakes her head, as if she really can't be distracted by new sensations or crass sentimentality right now.

"I'm fine, thank you, Diana," she says. "But I could murder a bloody sandwich."

"Is somebody saying murder?" says Detective Inspector Malhotra of the New Delhi Police. Only it isn't. It is Barry Prince. But it serves the purpose of lightening the mood.

For about thirty seconds.

Until the terror returns.

act three

The Dustingford Follies,
Saturday 21st December 2019

scene one

Gavin Silk is polishing his bottles.

He realises that there is only the most minuscule of chances that a local dignitary or someone of even greater prominence will deign to come into his office. And even smaller odds that they will assess his hobby, the joy of his life, practically the reason for his existence, as anything other than weird. But if there is one thing he has learned from being in charge of a residential home for actors and entertainers for some years, it is that absolutely nothing is off the map.

"*What are you doing?*"

The director spins round, as if he has been caught in some illicit act. In evening dress. His daughter is certainly giving off that impression.

"I'm... so, how is everything going?"

"The mayor has arrived. And I can't be dealing with him."

"*The mayor!*" He checks the large ship's clock on his wall. "But the bloody show doesn't start for another... fifty minutes!"

Lisa just shrugs. "I've got to go sort out Miss Marguerite."

Her father scuttles around his desk, straightening his bow tie. Lisa has never seen her father in a tuxedo, especially one that makes him look like a nineteen-fifties cinema manager, and would never really wish to. There is something vaguely pathetic about watching him preen himself in order to greet his 'betters'.

"Is everything alright out there, Lisa? I felt when I gave them my little pep talk earlier that they weren't really listening."

"You probably only felt that because they weren't really listening." She waits a second until this registers. "You're not in their business. You're not of their world."

"And you are, I suppose."

"Yeah. I sort of am. Least until 10.00 tonight."

He picks up the wistfulness in her voice, but it only adds a jolt of anger to the apprehension he is already beginning to feel and which the ritualistic bottle-polishing was meant to allay.

Stronger than anything, however, is the sense of total impotence. A mounting realisation that whatever happens this evening is entirely out of his hands. Whilst paradoxically, he must still ensure that any credit that might accrue, should the event miraculously go better than expected (and not be the unmitigated disaster that everyone, including the cast, is apparently telling their fellows that it will most assuredly be), bloody well ends up in his account.

"Well, I just hope that awful woman hasn't put too many foolish ideas into your head," says Gavin Silk. Lisa wonders why he is continuing with what would appear now to be a totally redundant conversation. She decides that she doesn't need to be here for it. She has a stage to manage. "Between you and me, charity cases are the worst."

She pauses, her hand on the door. "What charity cases? What are you talking about?"

"You know," he sighs frustratedly. "That woman."

"Miss Gatley? Zelda?" She realises that this can't be correct but also that she's the only resident who might fit the bill.

"What? *No!* One thing about that deceitful old minx is she pays her way. Lord knows how. She'll be paying her way right out of that door when she cocks up whatever she's doing tonight. As she undoubtedly will. I'm talking about your producer. Director. Star turn. Whatever she calls herself."

"Miss Quest? You're having a laugh. She's minted. Isn't she?"

Gavin Silk realises that, in his justifiable anger, he might unforgivably have betrayed a confidence. He can't ignore the look of wide-eyed astonishment on his daughter's reddening face. "This goes no further, Lisa. Stays in the family." He gives her one of those smiles that she can't stand. Not that there's an abundance of ones which she can. "But *now* can you see how precarious that world really is?"

"You'd better say hello to the mayor. He's got a silly costume on as well."

*

At a quarter to eight, cars are still drawing up.

The kitchen staff, who have provided those cast members willing to take solid nourishment just sufficient to sustain them throughout the evening's entertainment without provoking unscripted interruptions, have all been paid to stay on and serve interval drinks and tasty nibbles to the guests. The qualified carers will attend in their usual capacity, should anything untoward occur.

It has been impressed upon his employees by their boss that these aren't simply the usual crowd: visiting relatives doing their duty by elderly parents. There are important people about to walk through those grim Dustingford doors: the rich and famous involved in the entertainment business and the benevolent trust, as well as major donors, who have to remain convinced that their money is being well spent. They say that even the generous son of that poor lady who couldn't stop juggling has agreed to come, and you don't often get the recently bereaved rocking up.

The staff wonder what Silk thinks they might get up to without such warnings. Spit in the hot mulled wine, swing on the mayoral chain? "So, I can't ask any visiting celebs to sign my knickers, Mr Silk?" asks Nancy Fowler, in a spirit of genuine enquiry, to which Gavin Silk fails to respond.

The cast – all of whom are already fully costumed, made-up and assembled behind Stanley's magnificent red curtain, some standing, some still seated – are shivering with something compounded by fear but not totally composed of it. There is pure adrenaline scooting around here too as they anticipate the big opening number, which was intended originally as the big closing number but will now serve as both, as it is all about survival and making it through.

Their ears, as alert this evening as those of nocturnal animals (albeit with acoustic zinc-air batteried support), pick up those oh-so familiar sounds that have lingered forever in their minds, like the hum of a radio in a distant room, but which they haven't heard for real and up close in so many buzz-free years.

The chatter of an audience taking their seats.

The coughing that they hope and pray will stop once performance commences, although it usually doesn't. The rustle of programmes that Lisa has had printed and has personally deposited on every dining room chair, which lists the names of the performers and the hopeful running order of the various items, with the sensible caveat that all this is subject to change. She had noticed that the name Elspeth Quest MBE appears so many times – as producer, director, deviser and star – that she is surprised the woman hasn't claimed co-writing credit for the Shakespeare stuff as well.

A few of the residents behind the curtain begin to cry.

One of the stagehands, a kindly young lad, wants to offer them a none-too-clean handkerchief, but it is Jason who holds him back, with a shake of the head. To his own surprise, he understands exactly what is happening. He knows that this isn't simple sadness, maybe not even sadness at all, and that it must be allowed to run its course.

"Hear that?" says Rex Markham, perhaps unnecessarily but they can all understand.

"I never thought I would ever hear it again," says Barry Prince, too moved to be anyone other than himself.

"Hear what?" asks Jacob Bloom, who soon realises that his own hearing aids are down. Fortunately, he has a brand-new pack of batteries lodged in every pocket of his dinner jacket.

Diana Appleyard emerges cautiously from the rear dressing room area onto the stage, wishing to share some of this precious moment but also wanting to give the cast the encouragement she knows that they need. Encouragement she has been so assiduous in providing throughout the rehearsal period but in so understated a manner that they possibly absorbed it, each of them in their own way, without necessarily acknowledging or registering its origin. She was even doing it minutes earlier in the crowded dressing areas as she assisted members of the company – most of whom had costumed in the privacy of their own rooms – to put the finishing touches to their make-up and not spill too much on their collars. Hands that are shaky at the best of times weren't suddenly going to firm up for the occasion, however expert the technique.

"I think you all look lovely and you're going to be absolutely splendid," she says.

Rex Markham turns to her. "Don't you wish you were on with us, darling?"

The genuine kindness in his still roguish eyes touches her beyond measure. And makes her rather sad. "Oh no, Rex. I'm fine, thank you. Doing what I do. Helping this show on the road."

Diana laughs a touch nervously but can't quite meet his sceptical gaze. She finds herself pondering on how he went through so many women or perhaps how so many women let him go. No wonder Elspeth has insisted on making him her Romeo.

Instinctively, she looks towards the piano, which the curtain doesn't entirely obscure. Both former wives sit at the keyboard, clearly about to take turns as pianist and page-swiper. She has to smile as she recalls the animosity that has been a feature of the home for so long. Diana wonders if this new rapprochement, perhaps one of quite a few amongst the company, will stay the course or even survive the evening. What might happen when they see Rex and Elspeth in the rather late bloom of young love?

Her thoughts are brusquely interrupted by Cyril Dodds, as he commits the cardinal sin of sneaking open the curtain. This can only be to cast an early eye on the audience before bright lights and pure terror blind everything from view.

"*Cyril!*" she whispers sternly, then adds an 'am-dram!' in order to nail with chilling precision the sheer gravity of his crime. But now, she can't believe her eyes, nor indeed can the audience believe their own, as the spherical head of a small owl appears to gape out from just inches above the man's balding pate, and bulging mechanical eyes scour the hall like a searchlight. The duo achieve their appreciative laugh before Elspeth Quest strides out and drags both of them firmly back to obscurity.

"Shame on you, Cyril Dodds," is all she needs to say. The receding owl stares contritely up at her. "*And* you!" she adds. "You both know better than this." By this time, she has entirely ceased to wonder why she is addressing a wooden bird and that no one else finds it the least bit peculiar.

Rex gazes at his future Juliet in delighted admiration. Elspeth Quest – in the finest evening dress she could pack, with masterfully pinned and tactfully arranged hair, glinting like sun on rain-dampened granite – April in Aberdeen as her old Scottish hairdresser used to call it – and make-up, as always, discreetly immaculate – is seeming every inch a star.

"Look at *you!*" he says, in far from unwelcome admiration. Before she can will him to wax lyrically on for just a moment longer, he teases, "Don't you want a peek, love?"

"I never peak too soon," says Elspeth, with a smile.

But the tightness of this particular smile is all the evidence Rex or her company need to tell them that their producer/director/star is every bit as anxious and apprehensive as they are. And possibly half a dozen times more so, considering how many roles are ascribed to her in the programme. In fact, Gerard Bunting had mumbled earlier, on first seeing the printed sheet, that it's a miracle they don't just call it 'Elspeth's Folly' and be done with it.

The producer suddenly begins to look around the stage and into the wings at some speed, causing all the others to do the same. Save for Gerard, who is currently in a corner mumbling quietly to himself and seeming rather perturbed.

"Where the hell is the girl?" she demands. "Five minutes to fucking curtain. She should be onstage, book in hand and ready... *Lisa!*"

"Perhaps she's finding room in the car park... for the hearses," says Jacob Bloom.

As Barry Prince and the others groan, Agnes Wu, the ancient choreographer, who is onstage at her own insistence for a cameo appearance in the first number, swings her flower-garlanded Zimmer frame smartly round and catches the elderly doomster on the shin. He mentions something about her giving him DVT, but she thinks he's talking about a film and takes no notice. The tap-dancing Jackson, who looks very dapper and hasn't stopped moving since he came onstage, eases nimbly between them and offers his friend a comforting smile.

As she can't do a roll call without shouting, which would be unprofessional towards her audience and might unduly alarm the company, Elspeth collars Diana to count heads and ensure that everyone who is meant to be onstage is actually there, in full costume and make-up and correctly in place for the opening number.

Elspeth Quest might be forced to admit that a few of the bow ties would fail the spirit level test and – despite Diana whatsit's best efforts – not every element of make-up would pass muster. Yet, on inspection, her little troupe is looking not half bad. This audience is hardly going to be hostile, and provided most of the company manage to remain upright, they just might get away with it.

She only wishes that she herself weren't feeling quite so sick with anxiety. For some reason, tonight's event feels far worse than almost any first night she can recall and she really can't explain why this should be. It's hardly as if her career depends on it. Yet she feels that something, as yet not definable, truly does.

She can hear Diana Appleyard whispering in her ear. "*We've lost Zelda!*"

Elspeth sighs, as if Zelda Gatley personifies one of those little things God sends to try us. Before the director can stomp crossly off to retrieve or garrotte her missing cast member, Diana touches her concernedly on the arm.

"Elspeth, are you okay?"

Elspeth, who really doesn't look that okay, gives her understudy one of those rictus smiles. "I'm fine, Diana. Fine. Aren't I always?"

Diana nods somewhat wistfully, as the more important of the two women leaves the stage.

scene two

Lisa Silk guides the wheelchair very carefully towards a makeshift dressing room, which is situated just behind the painted backdrop that Stanley and his gang have only recently completed.

The elderly star has no intention of taking part in the opening number, she doesn't do ensemble, but she does believe in being firmly in place at the start of any show or performance, even if she is not appearing until the very end. This has been almost a code of honour with her and has earned Marguerite the begrudging respect of her peers.

It has been a great many years since the formidable performer found herself anywhere other than top of the bill, but she never forgets the long and tortuous road she has travelled to wind up here. The words of the song that her fellows are about to attempt in less than ten minutes will therefore have particular resonance for her and a certain freshness, as she hasn't attended any of the rehearsals at which she might have heard it being destroyed, mangled, adulterated and finally – hopefully – just about almost nailed.

"Are you nervous, Miss Marguerite?" asks Lisa, as she parks the wheelchair in front of a barely adequate standing-mirror.

"Nerves are for other people, dear," explains the old lady.

"When you get to my age, they worship you just for surviving."

Lisa reckons that this applies to absolutely everybody in the cast but keeps this to herself. She needs to get back onto that stage as swiftly as possible and ensure that everything happens which should be happening and as little as possible that shouldn't. Fortunately, she trusts Jason on lights, his mates on sound and whatever else they're up to and, of course, Stanley to be the rock he has always proven to be. Not that she has seen much of her northern rock for a while, but she knows that he is around.

And, anyway, as her charge has already begun to hum 'I'll see you again' by that Noel somebody, Lisa is pretty certain that at least one cast member won't be listening to anything else she says right now.

So, it takes the young care employee by surprise when Miss Marguerite addresses Lisa's reflection, just as she is turning to go.

"*Well* – have you decided yet?

"Eh? Decided? What about?"

"Your future. Obviously," says the older woman, with some impatience.

"What future, Miss Marguerite? Well, yeah. I have. Sorry, but I've really got to go."

Marguerite turns in her chair to look directly up at the confused young girl. "It is up to *you*, Lisa," she says, in an unusually gentle tone. "Nobody else. It's your life. Now go – *go!* You're needed out there. The show comes first. Last. Always. Just don't miss my bloody cue."

Lisa stares thoughtfully at the elderly lady for a second or two, then scoots off. As she goes, she can hear the still poignantly beautiful sound of an old legend humming.

Landing round the corner, on the still-curtained stage, Lisa is certain that she can smell the make-up. The paint and the sawdust. The excitement. She can see that not everyone is in place, but thankfully, those who have bothered to turn up are standing pretty well where they ought to be. Some relatively upright, others leaning resolutely on sticks. One on a decorated Zimmer, which is a new one on her. And each of them trembling no less than she would have expected.

"Zelda Gatley?" she asks.

"Fuck knows," says Gerard Bunting.

She glances towards Diana Appleyard, who is at her spot in the wings, book in hand, ready to prompt anyone who needs it. Lisa Silk has no doubt that this could be the most onerous task of the night.

Looking downwards, she catches a glimpse of the Exes, sitting cosily beside each other at the piano. The first designated pianist is just starting to play in order to lull the apparently capacity audience into the mood, whilst subliminally signalling to all one hundred and fifty three of them that they had better cease all that jabbering, coughing and bloody unnecessary rustling right now.

Lisa can't see her father, but she can certainly recognise his voice and sense the unusual trepidation within it as he greets and glad-hands those guests most generous to the home and pivotal to his own career prospects. She supposes that she can hardly blame him. It's his job and one on which she also clearly depends. Lisa just wishes he could be slightly less of a supercilious prat in the doing of it.

"Well, good luck, everyone," she says, quietly.

"It's break a leg, darling," mutters a familiar voice behind her. She turns to find Stanley walking across his stage, bulging tool-belt proudly on show. He carries a large hammer in his hand for no good reason that Lisa can ascertain, other than he clearly feels it's the thing to do.

He appears to be searching for something. Or someone. "Where's Elsp-Miss Quest?"

"Well, she's not in the opening number, cos she's too posh," explains Lisa. "Or *pretends* to be," she adds obliquely. "So, I can only think she's slapping poor old Miss Gatley around."

"Don't think much of her, do you, petal?"

"Not until she gives me one sweet solid reason why I should. And the old crow could die before that happens."

"Did somebody die?" asks Jacob Bloom, whose hearing aids appear to be just fine now.

*

Gavin Silk is indeed working the room.

He is delighted to see that the large, newly converted dining hall is filled to bursting point. Every local dignitary he has chosen to invite is here, mostly with partners, alongside some highly important trustees, who are apparently household names but not in his household, as he rarely watches TV, hates the theatre and is allergic to the smell of popcorn. Even more gratifying, although not without its own pitfalls, is that some of Dustingford's most generous donors are also in attendance. They are clearly on-site to ensure that their hard-inherited money is being well-spent and that everyone, especially the press, is aware of exactly who has been donating it.

To hear Gavin Silk talk, and there are plenty who are doing just that (whether they might care to or not), one would believe that this supremely gifted man not only runs Dustingford Hall single-handed but is the éminence grise or, at very least, the muse behind tonight's stellar entertainment.

"They were going to attempt a Shakespeare," he laughs, "but I soon guided them towards a more festive and, let's just say, less ambitious presentation." When quizzed on exactly which of the Bard's masterpieces was in contemplation, the man moves swiftly on.

Quite naturally, there are persons in the audience with whom he is utterly unfamiliar. These are most probably friends and relatives of cast members, for whom this may well be a first and possibly only visit. He must remember to include them in his closing address/appeal. (He has been persuaded by virtually everyone, including curiously the kitchen staff, out of making an effusive welcome speech, for reasons into which he doesn't wish to delve too deeply. So, he has gone with individual welcomes, which in truth was probably the better option.)

As the tinkly you-can-start-sitting-down-and-shutting-up-please piano music begins to register, Silk plonks himself near the front, right next to the Worshipful Mayor, and prays that his 'Dusties' don't let him down. Except, of course, for Zelda Gatley, who will inevitably be doing just that.

She can leave on the morning train.

*

"I'm not coming out, Miss Quest. There's no use you begging!"

Elspeth Quest needs this like a hole in the head. In fact, trepanation is exactly what she'd like to do to Zelda Gatley right now. She once played the wife of a medieval surgeon in a TV costume drama, so she knows the rudiments.

"I have no intention of begging, Zelda. I'm appealing to your sense of team loyalty and respect for your fellow artistes."

"But I'm not an artiste, am I?" comes the plaintive voice from behind the door. "I'm an impostor, who shouldn't be here. I'm a fake, about to be booted out. I'm crap, Miss Quest."

"Be that as it may," says Elspeth, who is in no mood for debate. "I fought for you; we agreed on your number; and you're in the show. So, step up and park those nerves – I want you on that bloody stage in five minutes." She starts to go.

"It'll be my last," says the voice.

"It'll be everyone's fucking last," mutters Elspeth Quest, as she moves at some speed down the corridor.

scene three

There is a hush of sorts as the lights go down.

Save, of course, for those still twinkling on the Christmas Tree by the entrance, which Silk has insisted can't ever be switched off or early leavers could trip in the darkness, smash their heads and sue.

All over the reconfigured dining hall, smartly dressed people are suddenly informing each other in some excitement that the show is about to commence, although one would have thought that all the indicators, both visual and aural, are making this reasonably obvious.

At this juncture, a knowing audience might well assume that the curtains would open wide to reveal… something. But instead, as Rex's Exes take a break from the piano, a single spot hits the far edge of Stanley's crimson plush, and Barry Prince leaps out from the wings (or as near to leap as he is able). The light catches his still impressive thatch of variegated silver-grey hair as he beams some serious wattage out towards his visitors.

The elderly entertainer waits for the wave of recognition to travel his way and for the ensuing round of applause that should be its natural bedfellow. Gratifyingly, it isn't too long in coming.

"No, no, stop," he says eventually, although he senses that they already have. "You're too kind. As the late and much missed Brucie Forsythe would say, 'nice to see you....'" He pauses for a chillingly anxious moment, until some members of the audience, in fact quite a respectable number, complete the famous catchphrase.

"*To see you – nice!*"

Behind the curtain, Barry's fellow cast members can sense that their dear friend and compere for the duration is nervous. Not just nervous but patently hungry for an affection that he rightly believes is no more than his due. Why else would he be preambling his impressions, which genuinely aren't so wanting, with solid clues as to their provenance?

Elspeth Quest, watching from the wings with one eye on the still Gatley-lite ensemble, sighs to herself. That a woman of her eminence, a champion and stalwart of both classical and contemporary theatre, should be holding her breath as to whether a pretend actress will actually turn up for the first time in her life onstage and an impression of a deceased game show host – performed by an irritating eighty-one-year-old man – is finding favour with a non-paying audience, just confirms to her how far she has descended. Whilst at the same time, spurring her on to elevate the proceedings in its penultimate moments the only way she knows how.

"Now, I don't have to tell you lucky people that I'm Barry Prince, Prince of Voices," here he segues into a passable Prince Charles, "and the voice of princes, too! It is my greatest pleasure, this fine winter's evening, to welcome you to the very first – and more than certainly the very last – Dustingford Follies!" He points to a middle-aged man near the front who looks as if he has just been handed a smile and is tentatively trying it on for size. "Not like the Follies you're used to, eh, sir?" He has become Frankie Howerd now, or someone pretending to be him. "Not like the Folly Bare Jerseys. Oh don't!" Instantly transforming into Tommy Cooper, he asks the man, "Hey you, where are you from?"

"Worthing," replies the man.

"I'm sorry," says Barry Prince.

"*Worthing!*" repeats the man, only louder.

"No, I heard you, sir," says Barry. "I'm just sorry. Ha ha ha… it's the way I tell 'em!"

Behind the curtain, the cast members are finding the wait excruciating. In fact, some are finding the simple act of standing in place unbearable. Yet the laughter seeping through from the unseen beyond energises them even as it reassures.

Gerard Bunting mutters to himself as he feverishly scrutinises a page ripped from his portable Shakespeare. Standing beside him, Rex Markham rests a kindly hand on the old actor's shoulder, but both his eyes remain fixed on the as yet unencountered audience. On Rex's other side, Jacob Bloom remains absolutely rigid.

"How do you think it's going?" he whispers to Rex.

"If I get the reaction he's getting, I'll shoot myself."

"It's not that bad, is it?"

"I'm doing Romeo."

"Oh, yes," recalls Jacob. "Got anybody here tonight?"

They can see Elspeth in the wings, standing next to Diana Appleyard. Their director is giving them a furious, lip-zipping gesture. Diana endorses this by simply shaking her head.

"My old agent," whispers Rex, meeting his Juliet halfway. "Some pals. A child or a wife or two." He notices how swiftly Jacob Bloom's rarely rapturous countenance becomes overwhelmed with sadness.

"We're your family, Jacob," says Rex.

Jacob Bloom looks down the line until he locates the remaining Jackson. The old dancer can't hear him but gives him a brief cheering-up routine with still nimble feet. He then has to shrug an apology to Elspeth because, of course, tonight he has his tap shoes on.

"Anyone seen Zelda?" asks the choreographer, who hates

the balance of one of her routines being thrown. She receives a communal shaking of heads, rolling of eyes and the odd 'Jesus wept!'.

Whilst the audience, including the man from Worthing, are still mercifully laughing, a more boosted Barry completes his introduction by doing the late Prime Minister, Harold Wilson, complete with pipe. "We have a wonderful show for you this evening, ladies and gents. We don't have Jerry Lewis. We don't have Jerry Springer. We don't even have Jerry Seinfeld. But we do have... Jerry Atrick!" He waits as that one receives its appreciative round, then concludes in full Churchillian mode. "We have nothing to offer you but blood, toil, tears and sweat cos all your inheritances have gone to pay Dusty Hall for our room and board!"

Finally, an enlivened Barry Prince makes his exit to humbling yet intensely gratifying applause.

Lisa, on the opposite side of the stage to Elspeth, waits until the compere has joined his fellows for congratulatory pats on the back, then nods to the pianist to commence her intro to the opening number. As the music starts, the busy stage manager taps Stanley, who is standing beside her, hand on pulley, muscles taut, on full alert. He has insisted with a smile that it is 'curtains' for him and that she mustn't worry – he's well up to it. There was little she could say.

The handyman looks across to Elspeth. For a moment, their eyes meet. He nods a gentle greeting but she either doesn't notice or is in too professional a mode to allow such diversions houseroom. Diana, who does notice, sends the kindly man a polite smile, as if this is simply another task that falls within her remit.

The piano builds.

The curtains open.

Their opening, in a manner far more stately than brisk, happens fortuitously to suit the tableau they are unveiling.

Just as the final section of the night's smartly turned-out ensemble is about to reveal itself and a delighted applause is building, Zelda Gatley comes scurrying into position on her stick, zombie-pale and shaking like a sapling in the wind. She narrowly lodges herself onto the very end of the front and predominantly female line, as if she has been waiting there all this time and is only breathless because of age and excitement. Her fellows can only hope that these nerves, so apparent and familiar even to them, don't send the tiny woman's voice soaring several decibels over the edge into shrill, glass-cracking mode.

With few overt signs of jealousy, the cast soon begin to realise that, wherever the audience may look, its collective gaze will always be drawn back to a small, elderly and not very significant-looking man, who grips onto neither a walking stick nor a neighbouring cast member but a large, grinning, eye-rolling bird made entirely of intricately carved wood. Who – true to form – comes into his own after dark. Cyril Dodds might as well have brought a newborn puppy or a chubby baby onto the stage.

These rapturous whoops and cheers, of the kind an audience usually holds in reserve until a number is actually or at least practically concluded, are starting to raise the roof before the performers can even commence their song. The Exes sensibly keep playing the intro until the cast can regain their composure and the overly ecstatic crowd is able to calm itself down.

"What a reaction," whispers Diana Appleyard.

"We used to get standing ovations," mutters Elspeth Quest. "Now we get ovations for standing."

Diana Appleyard, who has never had a standing ovation in her life, nonetheless smiles as she begins to mouth the lyrics of the song with her cast. To her own surprise, Elspeth finds herself observing this with some interest, as if this woman, who is now singing softly but with unfailing accuracy, has suddenly appeared on her radar, rather than having been by her side all along.

No one starts at the top and a lot of us drop, before we can reach the heights,

But with a gallon of pluck and a barrel of luck, we can see our name up there in lights...

Turning her attention back to the stage, Elspeth Quest takes a good look at the stalwart little company she has commanded, stretched, cajoled, bullied and hopefully encouraged over these past few fraught and frenetic weeks. She dares to smile. Right this moment, considering all the limitations and restrictions, she truly reckons that they are doing her – and of course themselves – proud. Their grip may be a fraction weaker these days, but they do appear to be holding on as best they can to the melody and indeed to most of the lyrics, albeit a touch croakily. They are, above all else, professionals. Save, of course, for Zelda Gatley. All she is holding onto with anything resembling confidence is her stick.

Even Agnes Wu's choreography, whilst hardly ambitious, can at least be recognised as such. Naturally, that strange tap-dancing fellow is on his own trajectory, but as it was a trajectory that apparently made both him and whoever he's so patently missing famous, she can hardly complain too much.

Elspeth knows that her attention should be firmly and solely on the show, as it has been almost religiously in her performing life, yet for once, she simply can't prevent herself from wondering what will happen next. And not simply here onstage, which despite a far from dispiriting opener, is still very much of an unknown quantity. She's thinking of her own life once that curtain comes down for the last time.

Nothing much, she suspects. Or fears.

She can sense Stanley Grainger watching her from the other wing. Lifting her eyes, she gives him a small nod. Only to see his own eyes drop and an embarrassed look appear on his face. For some inexplicable reason, this rarely experienced coyness touches her heart.

The producer/director/star turns away to catch Rex Markham observing her with some interest, even as he is singing his ageing lungs out. *Do folk in other old age homes go through as many emotions and dramas in a single day*, she wonders, *or is it just our sort?*

"The work may be hard and the way may be rough,
But whatever it takes, we can take it.
We know at the end that the journey's our friend."

Sentiments, trite as they are, that still somehow capture the industry in which they had all, over many preceding decades, happily found themselves. She offers a small prayer that its vaguely derivative tune and disingenuous Broadway uplift will see them all through to approximately half past nine this evening. And after that, who knows?

"And we are the ones that will make it."

scene four

"Now, you know what you have to do, Mr Bunting?" asks Lisa, once again.

Whilst the scheduling of this fine elderly actor so early in the show might not have been the most organic choice for the overall balance and flow of the evening, Elspeth – with Diana Appleyard's more empathic input – had already concluded in the first days of the rehearsal process that to make the man wait and indeed force him to observe his more assured fellows in action, could be both unnerving to him and destructive to the entire proceedings.

This does, however, involve a lot of nifty handiwork from Lisa, Stanley and crew. In the brief time that a reinvigorated Barry Prince is merrily trawling through the golden age of Hollywood out front, Roman columns of painted cardboard are being erected at strategic intervals behind the curtain. It is a tribute to the team's efficiency that the task is completed well before the man has even reached Technicolor.

When Barry has finally trundled off, having been thrown more than one 'wind it up' signal from his tiresome producer, the curtains slowly open to reveal Gerard Bunting leaning casually but not too heavily against one of the pillars. The applause that greets him is truly gratifying yet, a professional to the end, he knows not to acknowledge it with even the tiniest nod and simply to ride on its post-crest wave.

He commences his speech with a huge and impressive confidence. If the audience are slightly thrown by it not actually deriving from one of the Roman plays, they certainly don't show it. And the function of the columns, which might at a pinch be found at an historic British pile of a later era, will become apparent soon enough.

"*This royal throne of kings, this sceptred isle,*
This earth of majesty, this seat of Mars
This-this…"

He suddenly turns his head towards the wings. Lisa recognises instantly that the dying John of Gaunt is already beginning to wane. She is aware that this is a speech Gerard has insisted on doing, apparently has 'down to the letter' and indeed has given many times to some acclaim. She also knows that he is an old man, albeit a courageous one, whose memory is failing him on a lot more than just those Shakespearean speeches he hasn't performed, recited or even thought about for years.

She raises a single finger, the agreed signal.

Gerard Bunting immediately seeks out the number one, which is writ large in red Magic Marker on the back of his nearest column. Under this, and equally legible, are the next few lines of the speech. Fortunately, he has hit his customary faltering point spot on.

"*…this other Eden, demi-paradise,*
This fortress build by Nature for herself,
Against infection and the hand of war…"

Looking once more to his little helper, he finds her this time with two fingers held up. The digits are locked firmly together so that he would have no cause to mistake the gesture for something else. With her other hand, she points to a downstage column, secretly signalling John of Gaunt's second way station on his final journey. He makes for it as if such movement is inherent in the speech itself.

"*This happy breed of men, this little world,*
This precious stone, set in the silver sea..."

It is with a mixture of sadness and apprehension, but also genuine pride, that the actor finally completes his inspiring-whilst-expiring speech and his personal tour of the English stage.

"*This blessed plot, this earth, this realm, this England.*"

Gerard Bunting is not so naïve as to believe that the applauding audience has absolutely no notion as to what has been taking place, but they must surely admit that these were 'things done well and with a care'.

Even Gavin Silk, who rightly assumes that it has been his own daughter engineering this, and indeed the surprisingly smooth running of the show thus far, prides himself that the problematic young woman is finally showing some of his own resourcefulness and practicality. Essential qualities in a conscientious care provider.

*

Directly behind the stage, Diana Appleyard and a shivering Zelda Gatley listen to the show on the tinny loudspeaker that Stanley has kindly rigged up. Although they could probably hear most of it unaided.

Diana is holding the terrified woman's moist hand and trying patiently, yet with understandable urgency, to calm her. Or at least reduce the shaking so that the little pretender can physically step onto the stage once more, this time on her own. Not that Diana has any confidence that the woman will be anything less than abysmal. If there is hidden talent here, it has been concealed extremely well.

"Gerard seems to be doing fine," she says, reassuringly. "Zelda?"

Zelda Gatley grips the fingers of Diana Appleyard's right hand so tightly that their owner fears for its survival. "I couldn't bear to leave this home, Diana. My home. And... all of you."

"Oh, you'll be fine, dear," she lies. "I'm sure of it."

"It's okay for you," says Zelda. "You're just the understudy. I'm a star."

*

Gerard Bunting is also perspiration-heavy, as he walks at a dignified pace from the stage, but for far more fulfilling reasons. He and Lisa can still hear the applause resounding around the packed dining hall as he almost falls into the slim young woman's surprisingly firm and supportive arms.

"That's it, Lisa. Finally, all over, thanks be to God. Never again!"

"Listen to that applause, Mr Bunting!"

"I could do an encore," says the actor, turning swiftly back to the stage.

*

The elderly Shakespearean doesn't really need a percussive peck on the fleshy part of his shoulder to shift out of the way, nor indeed a quip that 'these wings aren't big enough for both of us'. Yet he receives both, as Cyril Dodds steps perkily, but anxiously, into his allotted position behind the closed curtain to await his turn at bat.

"Variety!" mutters the classical actor with disdain, as he trots off in some relief to find a seat and await the final curtain call. He wonders if he might have postponed, at least for a while, his inevitable transfer to that other home, the one whose name they dare not speak, in the adjoining county.

Yet he finds himself strangely moved and not the least bit

envious, as he hears the instantaneous reaction to one of Britain's finest, and quite possibly its oldest, surviving ventriloquists.

"So, how've you been?" asks Cyril Dodds, as the applause tails off.

Mr Chips turns his head around painfully slowly to stare at the little man – which itself gains a laugh – then, just as deliberately, turns again to look back out at the darkened audience, through huge and glassy brown eyes.

"I've not been well."

Now, it's Cyril's turn to stare at the audience. The silence is palpable. Until recognition and recollection gradually filter through the crowd like an elusive scent. As the older ones amongst them remember. And acknowledge.

Heartily encouraged, Cyril and his avian pal launch briskly into the night's main business. "I'm sorry to hear that, Mr Chips. What did you do for it?"

"Well," says the owl, thoughtfully. "I went to a dentist and a tree surgeon."

"A dentist and a tree surgeon? So, what did they say?

"Told me my bite's alright but my bark's getting worse. Hotcha!" This time, the laughter is immediate and both parties savour it. "Have you seen this audience, Cyril?"

"I can't see a thing, Mr Chips."

"Can we have the lights up please, Stanley and co?" demands the owl. "So we can see what sort of dummies we've got out there."

As messages and hand signals fly around, the main lights in the converted dining room go up. The acts onstage take a sneaky opportunity to inspect their audience, whilst the audience snatch looks at each other. Cyril, who of course has already snuck a swift peek before the show, spies Gavin Silk sitting near the front with the mayor in all his chains of office. The ventriloquist reckons it's a close-run thing between the two as to who looks the most up himself.

In another row, Cyril Dodds, and anyone else peering out from the wings, might spot an elderly and obviously Orthodox Jewish gentleman, who looks somewhat bewildered and well outside his comfort zone. And a few might ponder on his proximity to that far younger man, with whom they had observed Elspeth Quest having a brief but clearly problematic conversation on a family and friends tea afternoon some weeks earlier.

Stanley certainly notices them as he makes his own survey from his winding perch. Sitting next to the younger man – whom he recalls as being Elspeth's son, although the bond was clearly far from close– is a rather attractive Asian woman in her mid-thirties.

"Would you look at this lot!" says the unimpressed owl, his head revolving almost 180 degrees as he scans the room.

"What about them, Mr Chips? They seem alright, aside from being a bit stuck up." Cyril Dodds looks directly at the mayor. "Mind you, I see at least one of 'em must've thought it was fancy dress."

"Well, between you and me, Cyril," opines the owl sadly, as the laughter recedes, "I reckon most of them needn't bother going home!"

The audience roar at this, as only the publicly abused and ridiculed can. From the wings, Elspeth observes the act with some appreciation, without stooping to take even a furtive look at the evening's house.

Stanley watches her warily from across the stage, wondering whether her own eyes will be tempted to stray before the lights go back down and how she might react. After some seconds, an untempted Elspeth notices the handyman staring at her rather intensely from the other side of the stage and swiftly looks away.

"Now, I know you didn't pay to be insulted," continues Cyril Dodds. "Cos old Chips here just told me you didn't bloody pay at all!"

Although there is still plenty of time, with quite a few acts to go, Lisa Silk feels that it might be a kindness, perhaps even a responsibility, to look in on the star of the evening.

Yet truthfully, she reckons that *all* the residents taking part in tonight's little show are stars. Perhaps even Zelda Gatley, if they can only manage to drag her from the pokey dressing area and manhandle her onto the stage. And provided she doesn't just stand there like a shoplifter suddenly surrounded by store detectives, with the purloined knickers still in her hand.

It would appear to be what the oldies would call a 'racing certainty' that in a matter of minutes, the little fake actress will reveal her true colours and that Lisa's dad will be enjoying a deliciously quiet smirk in his seat. Whilst all around him, the poor audience will most probably be squirming at the downwards plummet this hitherto delightful and disaster-free show has taken. With its director, Elspeth Quest, suffering the biggest squirm of all.

Lisa Silk knows that smirk and wonders, for a moment, if she herself will ever experience the squirm. She realises, to her shame, that this might be the first time she is fully taking on board what every single resident of Dustingford Hall – actors, performers, even stars – must have endured on so many occasions in the course of their long and inevitably turbulent careers.

Aside, of course, from Zelda Gatley.

Marguerite has her back to the little drape Stanley has cleverly rigged up. The star can undoubtedly hear elements of the ventriloquist's act just a few feet away, which appears to be going down reassuringly well with the audience. Lisa has to whisper so as not to be picked up by the powerful microphones outside.

"You okay, Miss M? Everyone seems to be having fun out there."

Marguerite has her eyes closed. Lisa has seen this before and it doesn't always mean the elderly lady has fallen asleep. Sometimes, she is just in another place, the past, perhaps, or simply her music. She can certainly be forgiven this particular evening for wishing to compose herself before she takes to – and clearly dominates – the stage.

So, it is a few seconds before Lisa can sense that this feels different.

At first, she just touches the woman's shoulder, ever so gently, her hand gliding lightly over the soft and shiny material of the emerald gown, worn but still timelessly stylish, into which Lisa had assisted her less than an hour before. Organza the woman had called it, which had sounded vaguely rude. Then she taps more firmly.

It takes barely a moment – a step out of time in which she feels her own breathing suddenly stop, as her heart kicks into a new, more insistent beat and her stomach gives a sudden violent spasm – before she raises the heavy and still-warm arm. This is certainly not the first time she has taken a pulse nor felt its utter absence, but it is the first occasion when it feels far more personal than clinical. She doesn't need a second opinion.

"Oh, Miss M," she says.

"*Lisa!*"

For a second the voice stuns her, as if it has come from beyond the grave. She turns to see Elspeth Quest, looking unusually anxious.

"I need you to help me prise Zelda Gatley out of her chair. *Now!*" The producer is shaking her head at the way the world works deliberately to foil her, but she doesn't look half as fraught as Lisa. "Of course, she's going to be totally fucking useless and spoil my show, but, young lady, I may just have had an idea."

Elspeth is gone before Lisa Silk can speak or even nod. The young lady looks in the mirror, at her own pale face and the larger one just below, which even now boasts more colour, despite its life having so recently and permanently departed.

When she hears the familiar voice once more, she is not certain whether it is simply from inside her own head or that this most extraordinary, gifted, sometimes generous, more usually self-absorbed and cantankerous, old woman is somehow tutoring her for one very final time.

"*The show comes first. Last. Always.*"

The stage manager leaves to drag out the next star on the bill.

scene five

The curtain is closed for a scene-change.

From his increasingly uncomfortable plastic stool nearby, Stanley can observe that there is a whole lot more theatre unfolding on the drab side of the plush than there is out there in front of the audience.

Previous acts have gone down even better than expected. Elderly singers, tragedians, comics and musicians have all done themselves proud. But now, he notices that Elspeth and Diana each have a firm arm-hold on that little Gatley woman, the one who is no more a performer than he is an astronaut. At first glance, with her head down, it looks like she's champing at the bit to get onstage and be rubbish, but as he glimpses more of her face, it becomes quite apparent that if the proper actresses loosen their grip for even a nanosecond, she'll be legging it out of the building and into the sea. Stanley can't help but feel a certain sympathy for the poor woman. He has, of course, heard of stage fright, but this person looks more as if she is about to face a firing squad than a receptive and currently well-satisfied audience.

For a brief moment, his eyes meet those of Elspeth Quest once again. He catches a shoulder-sagging wince of weary exasperation that makes his heart go out to her. She has worked so hard on this show, for possibly more reasons than even she herself knows, and he would hate to watch it all go pear-shaped at this juncture.

It doesn't take a man of the theatre to work out that if the little non-actress doesn't set foot on that stage – or worse, manages to sidle on but inevitably lets herself and the side down – it will put a dampener on the evening that will be totally shattering for Elspeth and all concerned. Aside from the obvious creative nosedive, Gavin Silk would have scored a moral victory, not just over Zelda Gatley but also over the woman's recent and least-expected champion. A formidable yet clearly vulnerable person, whom the home's director patently can't abide but for whom Stanley is having certain feelings and emotions, once relegated to memory or scrapbooks, that he is quite uncertain how to process.

The handyman's evening is made no less dramatic when Lisa slips in beside him and whispers something in his ear.

"*Oh, Jesus!*" he gasps, turning to look up at the young woman.

People die in Dustingford with almost industrial regularity and perhaps it doesn't touch him these days as much as it should. He is aware, however, how much this particular resident has meant to his friend. Yet even here, he wonders whether the newly passed, and by all accounts famous star, has been recklessly drilling dreams into the susceptible young woman's head. Fantastical dreams that are only causing her more unhappiness, compounding the dissatisfaction in a life that has already been so far from calm.

And, of course, old Miss M quietly popping her clogs less than an hour before her big number doesn't exactly say a lot for that quality they all bang on about with such reverence. Timing.

Lisa looks down at this generous, simple man, who has never failed to be there for her, then nods quizzically towards Elspeth.

Stanley just shakes his head. "Not yet, petal. Not now. I'll deal with it," he reassures her. "If I'm right about who's on next, you've all of you got enough bloody drama on your hands."

"Ah… well, Miss Quest has had an idea about that. It's bonkers but whatever happens, don't you close those curtains till I say."

Stanley nods. This evening was never going to be a walk in the park, but it suddenly feels like it has become a trek up Mount Etna.

*

In that placid region just in front of the curtain, Barry Prince is concluding his current raft of impressions with a plausible Nat King Cole. Thankfully, without the accompanying make-up.

"*- but first of all please, let there be…* Zelda Gatley!*"

He shoots what he hopes is a furtive glance towards the wings. His eyesight is not great, and he refuses to wear his prescription glasses when performing, so all that he can make out are a lot of heads shaking wildly at him. Barry Prince has a feeling that the smallest and most frenetic head is that of the act in question. As a professional of long-standing, he immediately realises that it is up to him alone to divert the shit from the fan and deftly buttress the confidence of the good people out there. And even, who knows, that of the next on the bill herself.

"So… I'm, er, sure you've seen this next little lady many times over the years, guys and gals," says Barry, before realising that he has segued unwittingly into Jimmy Savile, which was perfectly fine in his time but has now been relegated to that burgeoning roster of vintage entertainers you really mustn't 'do' anymore.

The compere gives a little cough and moves almost seamlessly onto Warner Baxter, which is reasonably safe as nobody these days would recall how the old Hollywood actor sounds or what he may have got up to in his spare time, but everyone knows him for one line, which right now feels both appropriate and sadly wide of the mark. Yet even though he can't see the audience, save for the occasional glint of a mayoral chain and the odd diamond, Barry Prince knows that there's one person out there who has been awaiting this moment above all others. And for all the wrong reasons.

"Zelda Gatley, you're going out onstage a youngster, but you've got to come back a star!"

This harvests a welcome laugh from the audience, even as they puzzle over a name not a single one of them recalls hearing before in their lives.

To his relief, Barry Prince senses the curtain behind him slowly opening, giving him permission to follow its motion and walk backwards towards the enveloping wings. He claps his hands with all his might, body veered towards the larger darkness, hoping to encourage the audience to follow suit. Which, thankfully, they do, as they finally catch their first glimpse of a totally unknown and unexpectedly diminutive Zelda Gatley, standing on the empty stage, radiating nothing but insignificance, staring out at them.

Unblinking.

Paralysed.

Catatonic.

After a few highly uncomfortable seconds, a piano begins to play.

After considerably more uncomfortable seconds, Zelda Gatley's trembling right arm raises itself very slowly to point towards the ceiling. Only her producer knows that this is a gesture she was directed very specifically and often to employ several bars later in the piece and which, in its current prematurity, simply comes off like the limp-wristed salute of an indecisive Nazi sympathiser.

Still elevating her arm, Zelda begins to sing.

The voice itself might be forgiven in someone her age for being rather frail and croaky. But anyone with a mere smidgeon of musical knowledge would guess that even in her younger days, the woman would hold a tune the way a sieve holds water.

"I'm a young girl, and have just come over,

Over from the country where they... where they... *do things big,*

And amongst the boys I've got a lover," (pronounced initially as 'lohver', which of course rhymes better but is swiftly corrected because it isn't even a word)

"And since I've got a lover – yes – lover – *why I don't care a...* a fuck – *fig!"*

Zelda Gatley appears extremely proud of herself for not only having almost remembered but miraculously having managed to utter, albeit without the slightest expression or comprehension, the first verse of the old music hall song that she has been rehearsing continuously, and with some rigour, day, night and all points in-between for the past few weeks. So much so that she now seems completely spent and unable to continue.

In fact, despite all those hours of rigorously memorising relatively few lines, mortal fear is this minute – and assumedly for many minutes to come – rendering poor Zelda totally unable to recall what could possibly come next. Even whispered hints from one of the frustrated pianists – including a sotto voce rendition of *the boy I love is up in the effing gallery* – don't aid her in the least.

One can almost feel the energy being sucked out of the room, leaving the bewildered audience as dispirited as the petrified, waif-like creature onstage.

As Zelda Gatley looks helplessly out into the threatening darkness, imagining nothing other than the grin on her tormentor's weaselly face as he watches her taxi move off down that drive, she just glimpses Elspeth Quest in the nearby wing, giving a swift nod to someone out of viewpoint.

Two seconds later, Derek Hirst strides confidently onto the stage.

"I'm afraid I am going to have to be stopping you there, dear madam," he says with a quiet, subcontinental authority. "My apologies to you for interrupting one of your highly esteemed performances. And also, of course, my humblest apologies to your devoted audience."

A confused silence ensues as the younger members of this same audience attempt to puzzle out whether the interruption is unintended or ingeniously planned. And indeed, if this patently Caucasian elderly gentleman in the fraying Nehru jacket is actually daring, in this enlightened age, to put on a patently cod Indian accent. Those members of an older generation are simply trying to recall why this man's voice is so very familiar. They don't have long to wait.

"Detective Inspector Malhotra of the New Delhi Police."

This announcement is greeted with such warmth and appreciation by those many seniors out there in the darkness that the aged man onstage, who generally appears quite content yet rarely smiles, seems momentarily to glow with overwhelming gratitude.

Stanley Grainger is watching this in some amazement. He looks across to Lisa, who simply shrugs. Their joint awareness that there is an actual corpse in the closed dressing room behind them only adds a further surreal touch to the already bizarre proceedings.

"May we be having the house lights up please?" demands the detective, politely.

Jason, despite not locating this particular item on his cue list, swiftly brings up the dining room's main lights to reveal the amused and even enthralled onlookers.

"I am calling you all here to discuss the mysterious will of Mrs Elsie Turks," continues the Indian detective inspector, addressing one hundred and fifty three people who, until a few moments ago, were infinitely darker than he is. "The *late* Mrs Elsie Turks. Juggler of this parish."

The audience is quietly riveted. This is such an unexpected

deviation from any format they had been envisaging. It has suddenly transformed from a homage to sixties variety into the final act of an Agatha Christie.

The only person perhaps not quite so rapt is, of course, Gavin Silk.

The director is more than a little peeved that he appears to have been outmanoeuvred at the final hurdle on the Zelda Gatley front. Especially as all those around him are telling each other that the woman onstage has to be a jolly good sport, sufficiently assured of her esteem in an often cruel profession to allow a fellow performer to share and even usurp her limelight.

Her hitherto lamentable performance was clearly just part of the show. The couple onstage are obviously 'play-acting'.

Gavin Silk realises that he hasn't actually paid the elderly but physically robust Mr Hirst much attention. Neither recently nor indeed ever. In fact, he has quite happily ignored the harmless old actor and his being firmly locked into some sort of dissociative, politically incorrect time warp. This is mainly because the bills are settled on time and the man's little investigations, from purloined cutlery to dead squirrels, seem to keep him contentedly occupied.

He is just beginning to fear, however, that this evening may have suddenly taken the 'harmless fantasy' to a whole new and infinitely more disturbing level. Yet he finds himself powerless to interfere.

In all this unexpected excitement, no one appears to notice the sturdy, wind-roughened man with the tool-belt, as he quietly slips away from his place beside the open curtain and moves into the audience.

Nor, of course, do they pay the least attention to the director of this illustrious home, who is now craning his brilliantined head around nervously to see what the recently bereaved son of the late lady juggler, now a most generous benefactor, might be making of all this. To Silk's relief, the gentleman in question has a smile on his face, albeit not one of the most relaxed its observer has ever seen.

"It was my original surmise," explains the detective inspector, with admirable projection, "that the lady-in-question was being murdered. And why would this be? Because she had quietly let it be known that she was intending to *summon* her family solicitor down here to Dustingford Hall *in order that she might alter her Last Will and Testament*." He now pauses the dialogue to give an unexpected but welcome vocal rendition of his programme's famous musical sting, ignoring any copyright considerations. "Altering it to obliterate the inheritance of the man – her only child – who is most reasonably assuming that he is to be handed the share of the lion."

Zelda Gatley is nodding her head to the man with what looks like passionate interest and total involvement. In truth, she is so relieved to be released from her recent torment that she would have nodded her head to an accusation of illegal organ-harvesting.

"I am, however, pleased to be telling you that Mrs Elsie Turks – the extremely wealthy Mrs Turks – is dying a very sad but *one hundred per cent natural* death. She was not and never has been murdered."

The audience appear relieved but a trifle disappointed. This is hardly Poirot-standard. Only Elspeth Quest, watching from the wings, is quietly content. The show – minus Gatley, who has served her time – can now resume as planned. The little detective can return to... wherever.

"It is her *solicitor* who is being murdered," announces the radio detective triumphantly.

Shit! thinks Elspeth Quest.

Even Stanley Grainger, en route to Gavin Silk, freezes where he stands. The audience appear to gasp as one. They've been brilliantly outfoxed – this is excellent stuff. Life and artifice seamlessly combining.

"*Her solicitor?*" cries out Zelda Gatley, who has that rare talent of being able to sound like a bad actor even when she is being genuine.

Elspeth Quest feels slightly sick.

Derek Hirst, aka Detective Inspector Malhotra of the New Delhi Police, whisks a piece of paper from his inside jacket pocket. "The very day before Mr Clifford Dunstable – senior partner at Dunstable, Malvern and Clyde, a legal practice in Lewes, Sussex – is intending to visit his client – the aforementioned Mrs Turks, here in this very establishment, in order to take instruction on her will-changing – he is having a very fatal car accident on the A27. Mrs Turks herself is passing away two days later. The will is never changed. And I am thinking, this is a very convenient 'accident' for the heir apparent."

From the wings, Lisa Silk watches Stanley Grainger as he approaches her father. It takes a second or two before she registers Diana Appleyard standing behind her, telling her rather breathlessly to wind the curtain down as fast as she bloody can. The woman appears more agitated than Lisa has ever seen her.

"And that heir is – apparently – in this very audience tonight!"

Whilst everyone in the hall squints around, searching for someone who might resemble a solicitor-slayer, and Stanley reaches Gavin Silk, the curtains close on the satisfied detective and the truncated (yet elated) songstress. The current Ex at the piano cannot resist pounding out the appropriate musical sting once more.

Lisa watches as her friend tactfully informs his boss of the sad news about Miss Marguerite. Gavin Silk, already shaken by the recent onstage lunacy, nods gravely and slowly rises. Looking none-too-steady, he makes his polite excuses to the mayor and guests.

On the way back to his office, the director feels his arm being grabbed very tightly by a red-faced man in a smart blazer, who is fortuitously sitting by the aisle. Gavin Silk has no idea whether this gentleman truly is a killer, and it is really none of his concern. He does realise, however, as he sharply pulls away, that he may have a bit of explaining to do.

In the wings, Elspeth Quest is trying to quell her horror at what she has just unleashed. She swiftly realises that she has to get her understandably bemused compere back onstage. Fast! (She does, however, allow herself a little smile at having hopefully thwarted the Silk-Gatley plan.)

Whilst she can't help wondering exactly what Stanley had to impart to Gavin Silk that appeared so very urgent, Elspeth is also, of course, slightly concerned that there might be an actual murderer out there in the resumed darkness, as this kind of thing can often skew the delicate balance of a production.

scene six

"Well, ladies and gentlemen, how on earth can we top that?" says Barry Prince, who for once genuinely means it.

Out of respect for what has just transpired, he gives the audience his homage to the legendary Hercule. "I have been racking my leetle grey cells as to what weel 'appen next but all je can come up weeth is *le interval!*" Losing the Belgian, he gives a straight, "So just get up, stretch your legs, use our excellent facilities – handrails provided – and enjoy your complimentary vino and mince pies in our lovely red Green Room. Carols will be sung for you out there by the world-famous St Luke's Choir." For reasons he himself would find hard to fully explain, he concludes with a drunken Bette Davis. "Fasten your seat belts – it's gonna be a bumpy night."

The lights go up and Barry Prince, somewhat reluctantly it has to be said, leaves the stage.

Behind the curtain, Elspeth Quest is congratulating her cast. They can hear a sweet if slightly shrill 'God Rest Ye Merry Gentlemen' just starting to filter through the open doorways and fire escapes.

"Very well done, everyone," says a beaming Elspeth. "Really excellent. Even you, Zelda."

The little non-actress shrugs, clearly not convinced that she is completely out of the woods.

"I've still got my bit to get through," moans Jacob Bloom. "If the suspense doesn't kill me."

Rex Markham smiles at Elspeth. "All set to knock 'em dead, kid?"

"Ever known me not to be?" responds Elspeth Quest, returning the smile but with an enigmatic twist so brief he either fails to notice or chooses to overlook.

Diana Appleyard joins them. She appears to have calmed down since the earlier, homicidal revelation. "It's nice Oberon has a seat out front. At last."

The smile vanishes from Elspeth's face. "*Oberon?*"

"Yes. He's here. With his fiancée, presumably." She suddenly looks upset. "Oh. Elspeth. Didn't you know?" Elspeth just shakes her head. "They're in row E or F. Sitting next to a rather large, elderly man. Who looks, well, who looks sort of like a rabbi. Oops, sorry, is that 'un-PC'?"

They don't see Jacob Bloom as his face takes on a shade of white that one might not have thought possible on skin that still lives.

"Well, let's just pray there are no more surprises," says Elspeth, attempting to regain that celebrated and much envied composure. She finds Lisa giving instructions to Jason and goes to tap her gently on the shoulder. "Very well done, dear. In fact, both of you. How's Marguerite? I know she doesn't like to be disturbed before a performance."

Lisa immediately looks round for Stanley. He must still be with her father. "She's... resting, Miss Quest."

"Aren't we all, heart?" says Rex.

"We still have a while," says Elspeth. "I told them the interval should be at least twenty-five minutes. And *no* mingling! I shall be up in my room if anyone needs me."

They all nod as she goes.

"The poor girl looks exhausted," says Gerard Bunting, still flushed with triumph.

"This life does take its toll," sighs Zelda Gatley.

*

Elspeth Quest can't have been lying on her bed for more than three or four minutes when a knock on her door appears to wake her.

"I shall be down in five!" she calls, a bit crossly. "And I am never late."

"It's just me, petal," says Stanley.

"Oh… the door's unlocked."

He finds her moving towards the window, although there is nothing out there to see. But after his talk with Gavin Silk, he knows that there soon will be.

"Happy?" he says.

"Should I be?"

"I would have thought so. *And* proud. It's going really well, Elspeth."

She shrugs. "Save perhaps for one of our cast accusing an audience member of murder. That has to be a first."

Stanley smiles. "The poor guy came rushing into Silk's office when I was in there. He was practically screaming that the solicitor was eighty-two and had a stroke at the wheel. Doubt he's going to be giving much more to this place any time soon."

Elspeth seems amused. Yet there is something about the man's face that disturbs her. She realises that his eyes, usually so filled with warmth, aren't smiling at all.

"Why were you in Silk's office?"

Stanley appears hesitant. "One thing at a time. How are you… with your, y'know, Juliet, is it?"

"My vanity project," she laughs. "In a few minutes, I am about to give what will undoubtedly be my last ever performance." She shakes her head. "And then it ain't over till the old lady sings." She registers Stanley's silence, which again isn't of his normal, comfortable kind.

"It was… decent of you to put her on at the end," he says, uncomfortably.

"I'm a hard act to follow, Mr Grainger."

"I think maybe you can call me Stanley. Considering."

"I have to go downstairs," she says, with some urgency. "Considering what?"

"Considering how I feel about you. And how I think you feel about me."

Elspeth moves towards the door. "I'm a leading lady in my closing scenes. I don't need… complications."

"Bit too real for you, am I?"

"There's a watchword in my business. It's called timing. I'm afraid yours is considerably off."

"Tell me the best time to care about somebody. I'll try to fit in."

She glares at him but yet again there is something in his manner, an unease she doesn't normally associate with this man. Or with why, despite everything, she finds herself so partial to him.

"What aren't you telling me?" she asks.

He is silent for a moment. When he speaks, it is in an even more subdued tone, yet curiously, his accent appears more pronounced.

"Miss Marguerite, she won't be going on."

"Don't be ridiculous. That woman has never missed a…" In an instant, she understands. "Oh… oh shit! Well, we can simply end with me and Rex and then we all go straight into our closing number."

"Hey. Hey, girly. This isn't you."

She pauses. Shocked. She has no idea whether the man is

entirely correct in his assessment. Yet she finds herself hoping that he is.

"The poor lady," she says, more gently. And thinks that she probably means it.

"I've asked Lisa to take her back to her room. Before the-the company finds out. Except for maybe Miss Appleyard. Mr Silk is, y'know, making the arrangements."

"Right. Good. Yes. And we *must not* tell the audience, Stanley. No way. It isn't proper. And it will just make a lot of them fret even more about their own relatives here." She laughs wryly. "Marguerite always was one for a big ending."

"You can still have a big ending," says Stanley.

She stares at him, then opens the door and walks out.

*

Standing behind the curtain, Jacob Bloom is too anxious even to try and recognise who Barry Prince might be approximating in front of it.

"If you're a guy with lead in his pencil, I'm the gal to keep it sharpened," comes the vaguely familiar voice.

Jacob looks at Lisa, who is moving softly towards him and offering up as much encouragement as she can muster.

"I've no idea who he's meant to be, either," she whispers, recognising his puzzlement.

"But, ladies, if there's one thing an older man can do, you're bloody lucky. And talking of older men, Miss Mae West is proud to present, together again for the very first time…"

The piano begins to play a tinkly melody.

"I don't think I can do it, Lisa. Not this. Not with *him* out there in the audience," murmurs the elderly actor.

"Who?"

"My brother. The rabbi. How did he even *know—*"

"Your brother's a… no idea, Mr Bloom." She hears a familiar

tapping and finds the remaining Jackson by her side. "Here's your partner. *Sshhh!* Now, break a leg."

"With my osteoporosis, that's a foregone conclusion."

"That wonderful thespian – that's not rude, darling, behave yourself – Jacob Bloom," announces their compere. "And our very own maestro of tap. The tap-meister himself – the one and only Jackson Brother!"

The curtain opens. The music builds.

To generous applause from the audience, many of whom are clearly familiar with the names announced, albeit not as a double act, the elderly actor walks slowly on from one side of the stage, whilst in from the other, with far greater agility, dances the remaining Jackson.

The chosen number is 'It's never too late to fall in love', which at least some of those watching happily recall from the classic and oft revived British musical hit *The Boyfriend*. Although, not necessarily performed quite like this.

Jacob delivers the song with an unsurprising confidence and respect for the lyrics, penned as they are to be sung by an elderly and rather lecherous man to the far younger woman for whom he has fallen. As he half speaks and half sings the well-crafted words, the other equally senior citizen taps out a rhythm that has its own singular attraction, yet fits the song and its sentiment perfectly.

Those watching from the wings are relieved that at least this number is proceeding pretty much as in rehearsal, perhaps even better, although they would probably admit to having initially found the choice of material slightly unexpected. Yet what they hadn't fully anticipated, and what might also be surprising the audience, is that the two performers, in their own particular and rather dignified way, are quite clearly delivering its message to each other.

Very occasionally, Jacob Bloom glances out into the audience, but he can't yet make out his brother. A fact which actually brings him some relief, as he doubts that the elderly scholar, however he came to be here after so many years of estrangement, would have been expecting this.

Even as he is singing, Jacob Bloom realises, to his great surprise, that he really doesn't care.

scene seven

Elspeth Quest and Diana Appleyard are seeing to it that neither they nor anyone else intrude on the curtained area where Marguerite was assumedly resting and, so far as the cast is concerned, continues to do so.

The actress/director is simply sitting quietly in an adjoining 'cubicle', whilst her former understudy, squeezed in beside her, tackles another of the myriad crosswords she has completed over the decades. *It almost feels like old times*, thinks Diana, without a huge nostalgic rush.

As the applause dies down for the evening's most unusual and possibly most touching new double act, Lisa Silk slithers into their tiny, purpose-built nook.

"Miss Quest?"

Elspeth gives a start, as if she has been voyaging somewhere and summoned swiftly, perhaps reluctantly, home.

"Oh. Sorry. You're on – with Mr Markham – in a minute or two. Depending on how long Mr Prince is doing this time."

"Could be weeks yet," says Diana Appleyard.

"Mr Grainger and his guys have done a lovely job with the…"

Lisa stops, aware that Elspeth Quest is staring directly into her face. The young woman wonders for a moment if her dark eye make-up has smudged, which it can so readily do when she has been sweating a bit. And she has been sweating more than a bit this evening, what with sudden deaths and unravelled murders and fake actresses and unexpected declarations of love. Not to mention the odd tear. All parcelled up with the tricky concealment of any bulletins relating to the sad demise of the night's anticipated star turn, at least until after the final curtain call. *Rocky Horror Show* was never like this.

"I'm not going on," says Elspeth Quest, quietly.

"Pardon?" says Lisa.

"You heard me. I'm sorry, Lisa."

Diana Appleyard looks up from her crossword, as if her ears might be playing mischievous tricks. Lisa Silk is just staring helplessly.

"Elspeth – what's wrong?" asks Diana.

"What do you think is wrong? It's been too long—"

"Diana," says Diana.

"That was a fucking pause! *Jesus!* I'm shell-shocked, Diana. My nerves are shot to pieces after the past few weeks, not to mention tonight. I look like bloody Juliet's granny. And I just heard my son's in sodding row E. Or F!"

"But everyone's waiting for you, Miss Quest. That's probably why they've come," pleads Lisa frantically.

"I'm damn sure it's why they've come. I'm sorry, Lisa. Unprofessional, I know, but if I go out there now, they'll have to wipe me off the floor."

Lisa is at even more of a loss now than when she first discovered the late Marguerite. *Bloody hell!* She simply stares from one elderly lady to the other. Finally, the only possible solution romps home.

"Miss Appleyard?"

"*Me?*" exclaims Diana, perhaps a trifle disingenuously. "Oh. Oh no – no, I couldn't, Lisa. I never have, you know. She never missed a performance."

"Well, I'm missing one now," insists Elspeth Quest. "I'm in a blue bloody funk. Please don't make it any worse for me, Diana. It's mortifying enough as it is."

Elspeth stands up. Holding back the tears, she begins to unzip her dress. "It'll be a bit tight on you, obviously," she explains, "but—"

Diana Appleyard also stands, wondering seriously whether she is about to collapse back down again. "Very well, Elspeth. For the sake of the show. I know the words, naturally. And we've already lost poor Marguerite. But I won't give half the performance that you'd give."

"No one expects you to," says Elspeth reassuringly.

Lisa and Diana stare at her, then the stage manager rushes out.

*

Barry Prince is just finishing off his James Cagney when he sees Lisa in the wings showing him two fingers, which he thankfully reads as his instruction to fill a couple more minutes. Fortunately, Al Jolson is there when you need him. Slightly less fortunately, the compere, who has unquestionably been the rock for this show, is not young and is clearly approaching total exhaustion. Which is probably why the audience are treated slightly bafflingly, but not unenjoyably, to that legendary blackface entertainer's soulful version of 'I Belong to Glasgow'.

Meantime, behind the curtain, Diana Appleyard is scuttling into the wings, fastening up Elspeth's best but tightest frock and looking pathologically terrified.

"I don't need this," she quietly tells the world. "I really don't. Not after all these sodding years."

scene eight

The audience doesn't require much prompting.

When the curtains finally creak open to reveal a small, Italianate balcony, with an apron beneath and a mercifully short set of steps concealed behind, the delighted spectators are there. Even before Rex Markham makes his entrance, applause resonates around the packed hall. And when he does turn up – looking so dashing in his immaculate tuxedo, a white silk scarf flung with artful casualness around his neck, concealing his less than juvenile throat – the crowd goes wild.

How does the old guy do it?

He still looks the business, after so many years away from it. Even with his less than perfect hearing, the former matinee idol can pick up the buzz around the large, packed chamber. He reckons he can almost catch the gasp from two of his ex-wives, still seated at their piano, but suspects that this could simply be his still robust vanity thankfully kicking in once more.

Moving slowly, but with an unexpected (even to him) grace that belies his years, he finally reaches the balcony.

"*He jests at scars that never felt a wound,*" he announces from the still lonely stage.

The silence is almost too long and charged for him to bear. Rex Markham can feel a slight panic just beginning to work its way into his already trembling frame. It instantly reminds him of other panics, far greater ones, and why he chose to forsake a life onstage for what he considered the far less petrifying world of film and Hollywood. He starts to wonder if poor Elspeth has become stuck – or indeed unstuck – on the steps.

Then Juliet appears.

And the panic he has been feeling is replaced in an instant by an even more profound sense of shock. A reaction patently mirrored in the audience, as they attempt to check their programmes in the dark, wondering who this far from unfetching but totally unknown elderly lady might be.

Rex Markham, ever the gentleman and never less than professional, simply gives a terrified Diana Appleyard one brief but clearly encouraging nod and proceeds as if all is absolutely fine. Curiously, he believes this might also be the truth. Although, he does wonder what the hell has happened to Elspeth Quest. Only a plunge off Beachy Head or a case of alien abduction would have kept this particular Juliet from their tryst.

"But, soft! What light through yonder window breaks? It is the east, and Juliet is the sun."

As he looks at her, as Romeo would undoubtedly gaze at his Juliet, drowning in her beauty and their love, Rex Markham is clearly not displeased by what he sees. Diana Appleyard, one of his dearest Dustingford friends and a woman with whom he chats and smokes each day, really does look quite lovely. How come he has never noticed this before?

For her part, Diana Appleyard, having interrupted his florid opening speech with the requisite 'ay me', only briefly wrenches her adoring eyes from this graceful poetic youth, for so he has become, in order to peer towards row E or F and check out what on earth poor Oberon Quest might be making of this. But all is darkness.

"O Romeo, Romeo! Wherefore art thou Romeo?" she eventually enquires quite beautifully, in the knowledge that

most of the audience are probably doing it with her. The voice that carries to the very back of the hall is still girlishly sweet yet with a rather more mature potency that brooks no interruption. *"Deny thy father and refuse thy name; or, if thou wilt not, be but sworn my love, and I'll no longer be a Capulet."*

As they watch, huddled in the wings, the remaining members of the cast are gradually losing their astonishment at who isn't on the makeshift stage in front of them and becoming fully enraptured with who is. They are all well aware of the chemistry that can happen when actors become the roles they are playing. Indeed, many have seen it at work. The company, to a man and woman, are slowly and miraculously being convinced that this is what they are witnessing right now. At their age. In this home. And maybe not for the first time this evening.

Perhaps the magic that Elspeth Quest had summoned to her cause, whilst trying to persuade them to do *The Dream*, is somehow happening this extraordinary midwinter eve after all. Enchanting players and audience alike.

"Shall I hear more, or shall I speak at this?"

And there is the legendary Marguerite yet to come.

How fine can this evening get, they and their audience marvel.

*

Once the rapturous applause for the Shakespearean lovers has died down, and it does take a while, Barry Prince, his impressive hair now a tad dishevelled, bow tie at ten to four, returns wearily but gamely to his favourite position in front of the curtain.

For this round, he sports a Groucho Marx moustache thickly pencilled above his upper lip and holds an unlit cigar in his right hand.

"And I thought it was only Romeo and Julieta cigars that smoked," he quips, waving his prop with gusto. "In case you hadn't noticed, that *wasn't* Elspeth Quest. Don't worry, the dame is fighting fit, and you'll see her at the end. I think she just felt she had enough to do, putting this whole *tzimmes* together. We're none of us chickens, you know, although we can still give a cluck. Her part was taken, along with her frock, at extremely short notice, by her lovely understudy, Miss Diana Appleyard.

"But now, ladies and gentlefolk, we got something *really* special for you. There are a couple of little gals here – you know 'em both from stage and screen – who've been working their stockings off to support us all – maybe they're support stockings! – by rattling the ivories so beautifully. So, this is their turn in the spotlight, as they play some music just for you. Let me present Rex's… er, no, Miss Margo Creeley and Miss Christina Pickworth. And if you give these dames the right key, they'll play in any flat!"

*

As two of his ex-wives happily collaborate at the piano, Rex Markham is still staring at his erstwhile Juliet.

"What happened out there, love ?" he asks, quietly.

"I have no idea, Rex," says Diana Appleyard.

"Well, whatever it is, they should put it in pill form instantly." The old actor smiles at the former understudy. "Are you doing anything after the show, Juliet?"

If one of the ex-wives begins to thump her keys with added vehemence and the other swishes her pages more audibly, it may simply be the nature of the piece.

scene nine

Elspeth Quest is still unfrocked when Stanley Grainger pops into her tiny dressing room.

"Oh, sorry," he says, edging out again. "I shouldn't have—"

"It's alright, Stanley. I'm quite decent."

"You've been quite decent for a while," he says, moving back in.

"What do you mean?"

The man just smiles, the amusement fully back in his eyes. Then, he shakes his head, in disbelief perhaps. Or wonder.

"It's not like you to be oblique," says Elspeth.

"Okay then," he says. "*Stage fright*? You!"

Elspeth begins to protest but realises almost instantly that this is a man who can see both through her and into her, with a precision that would be chilling, were it not so filled with its own genuinely disarming warmth.

"I gather the two young lovers performed only too well," she says, finally.

"Apparently so. It was very generous of you, Elspeth."

"And I'm not a woman famed for her generosity."

He doesn't disagree, as he suspects that her assessment in this is quite correct. "Never too late," he says. "Bet your son would have been disappointed."

"He watched me often enough as a child. If he had wished to see me more recently, he could have bought a ticket."

"But he came this evening."

"And saw our devoted understudy. So, he should be well-pleased." She stares up at him. To his surprise, the look on her face is one of genuine enquiry, as if she is more than a little lost. Her words confirm what her face, softer than it has seemed all evening, already tells him. "So, Mr Stanley Grainger, now that you're a seasoned man of the theatre, advise me on what we do?"

"How do you mean, pet?"

"Our top of the bill is regrettably lying-in-state upstairs. Do I come on – to huge applause, obviously – and say, 'terribly sorry, ladies and gents but Miss Marguerite is…' I don't know, 'sadly indisposed'? Or shall our little company just move seamlessly and, so far, obliviously into our closing number? Which, incidentally, is pretty much the same as our opening number, save that we all look a helluva lot more exhausted."

"There is another option, Elspeth."

"Oh no, I'm sorry Stanley, but I am *not* going on now and doing a solo. It will look as if I ducked out of being Juliet just so I could end up being Marguerite." She smiles, wryly. "Not that I have her voice. She told me that all too clearly, you know, when she had me unceremoniously removed as a youngster from our only joint project."

"Oh, did she now?" says Stanley, with an interest that is almost flattering. "And did you respect her opinion?"

"How do you mean?"

"Well, you know, like she was one of those judges on the contests everyone watches on the telly these days. Even here."

"Much as it pains me, Stanley," confesses Elspeth, "the late Miss Marguerite was a far more astute judge of talent than any hack off the television."

Stanley Grainger says nothing in response to this. He just stares straight into her sad but still sparkling eyes. And through to her wise brain beyond.

scene ten

The ladies at the piano have been playing for far longer than expected. Fortunately, thanks to sensible parenting and early musical education, they are up to the challenge and able to switch roles with aplomb at appropriate intervals. Rex Markham and Diana Appleyard remain prudently out of the way.

Whilst all this is going on, Gavin Silk has been in his office ensuring that the usual arrangements for when one of his residents sadly, but not unexpectedly, passes away click smoothly into place. Fortunately for him, although perhaps a source of regret for her, the late Miss Marguerite had no living relatives or next of kin.

Sequestered in what his employees refer to as his 'bottle-bank', the director has missed the revelatory Quest-Appleyard substitution, which might have intrigued him. He realises that it would be diplomatic, however, to return to the concert before the lights go up for the last time.

On balance, despite initial reservations and one of his more recent benefactors being accused onstage of inheritance-induced homicide, he decides that the concert has left him firmly on the credit side and most probably done his standing in the community and, more importantly, with the Trust, far more good than harm. Admittedly, the little fraudster in their midst has gotten away with it – for now – but even allowing for this subterfuge, his daughter's organisational skills have been a source of some paternal and professional pride, boding well for her own future in the field of social care. He just hopes that she can avoid actors and their ilk, in a way that he unfortunately cannot.

Silk arrives at his seat just as the ladies at the piano are gratefully winding down. He senses from the collective sigh of relief around him that they may have exceeded the appropriate duration for such a performance by some margin. The audience is clearly hungry for what is to come. Simultaneously, he realises that they are all in for further disappointment, as the evening's top of the bill is not simply taking an understandable age to assemble herself but unfortunately gave her final appearance earlier this evening.

The applause, when the thoroughly exhausted and politely perspiring ladies finally take their bow, is rightly appreciative. As it settles, the audience clearly expects their hardworking compere to return for his concluding intro.

"Who's the old bugger going to be now?" mutters the mayor to the recently returned director. As Gavin Silk can't recognise one from another, he will be no better informed once Mr Prince has started.

"Thank you, Margo and Christina," says Barry Prince, in his normal and rather melodious voice. "Well, ladies and gentlemen, you've been a truly great audience. In fact, you've made a wonderful impression and I hope I have too. So, no more funny voices from me this evening…" He waits patiently for the audience to catch up. "Take your time – all we have to do in a rest home is wait." Finally, he hears the heartfelt communal 'aah' he has been seeking. "You're too slow, I mean, too kind. Thanks again."

He goes off to slightly mystified applause as he hasn't introduced the next historic and assumedly ultimate act. The curtains remain closed. In the darkness, the audience check each other out to discern any mutual puzzlement.

And then they hear it.

A voice, pure and unaccompanied.

A song so familiar, at least to the older members of the audience. Yet somehow, enticingly fresh.

"*I'll see you again...*"

The curtains slowly open.

Bathed in a single spotlight stands a very pale young woman with spiky black hair. She wears faded blue jeans, with a slight rip in one of the knees, and a checked lumberjack shirt. Her eyes, darkened by make-up to contrast dramatically with the possibly enhanced whiteness of her skin, appear to gleam in the cool light that one of the younger members of staff is shining with some sensitivity upon them.

The audience is clearly mystified, yet just as obviously enthralled. Not a single cough, shuffle, rustle of sweet paper or programme disrupts the silence. A silence that is like an almost tangible energy, enhancing the poignant bittersweetness of the song and the pure, crisp yet husky voice that transports it.

No one is more still and silent than the tall man with the thin moustache sitting somewhere near the front, yet not so near that the singer can pick him out. Not that she is looking at or even aware of the audience. The young woman is clearly in the music, in the song, in the unforced stillness of herself. And in the remembrance of a tricky old lady who taught her so much and gave her such faith.

Whilst perhaps not quite forgetting another old lady, one still very much alive, who came through in the end and did okay.

The applause, when it comes, surpasses any that has gone before.

The young woman appears stunned.

Audience members – at least the younger ones – are starting to stand. And not because they're leaving.

Lisa looks to one side of the stage and then to the other.

In both sets of wings, all that she can see are faces of people she genuinely loves, beaming with a mixture of pride and astonishment. She has hardly told any of the residents of her ambitions or perhaps, more truthfully, her dreams. Nor have they ever asked, being far more immersed in recounting their own past glories than contemplating another's future.

A word she has never thought she would hear, or at least not applied to herself, comes sailing through the darkness, spoken in a voice she doesn't recognise and endorsed by dozens more of equal unfamiliarity.

"*Encore!*"

Almost before she can process it, a voice she actually does recognise sings, or rather shouts, through the chorus of approval.

"It means 'again'!" yells Gavin Silk, to his own surprise as much those around him.

"*I know what it bloody means!*" she blurts back, before telling herself that her late mentor would have probably chosen better moments to have a row with her father.

"Sorry." She laughs. "Sorry, dad." Which only makes her audience warm to her even more. "I'm afraid I don't have my guitar with me," she says, hesitantly. "I wasn't expecting to... so, I'm gonna have to sing the next one – what's the word..."

"A cappella," comes from the wings.

"Yeah, whatever. And this isn't one from Noel whatsit. This is one from – er – me."

And the young woman begins to sing.

"*Sand – loving you is like sand. You slip through my fingers, you don't leave a trace. You'll say that you'll stay, but you just wash away. Like sand... sand...*"

Whilst most of the people listening with such intensity in the darkness would agree that it certainly isn't Noel whatsit, it is certainly something worth listening to and encouraging. Which they do, first with their silence and then with their whoops and cheers.

These continue through her clumsy but heartfelt bows, her acknowledgement of further encores (without overstaying her welcome and leaving her new public asking for less) and her stunned but elated skip offstage into the arms of Stanley Grainger, at least one of which he has to extricate in order to wind out the curtain.

After more than a few moments, as the applause gradually subsides, a new person walks onto the stage to meet her audience. She is at least a half century older than the one who has gone before. And she is fortunately now fully clothed, in attire oddly similar to that which 'Juliet' had been wearing only fifteen minutes earlier.

The cheers this time are as much of recognition as appreciation, although a body of work like that of Elspeth Quest does merit its own substantial slice of acclaim.

The woman's eyes, despite her best efforts, find themselves seeking out not the place next to the mayor but further back, row E, perhaps, or row F. But all she can see is Jason's almost dazzling lighting, as it shines directly into her face.

"Thank you," she says finally, with a gracious smile, her small hand tapping gently and a touch shakily on her heart. "Thank you so much. But this isn't about me. For once! No, this evening I would like to pay tribute to a wonderful performer. The great – the truly legendary – Marguerite, who, unfortunately, wasn't able to make this performance but has given so much pleasure to so many for so long." She looks towards the wings and smiles. "And who certainly knew musical talent when she saw it." This receives some appreciative applause as the audience gradually takes on board the history of what it has just witnessed. But the producer is already moving on. "I'd also like to pay tribute to the finest company I've ever had the pleasure and indeed the privilege of working with."

With both hands, she beckons the entire cast onto the stage. As the curtain opens, they form two ragged but discernible lines behind her. She beckons once more, with some insistence, and Lisa Silk slips in somewhat sheepishly to join them.

"I'm not talking about talent," she says and receives stage moans from her company. "I'm not *just* talking about talent." Which results in stage sighs of relief. "Ladies and gentlemen, I have been playing what passes for real people for almost sixty years." She looks briefly to see Stanley, on his perch beside his pulley. "Yet it took some genuinely real people to finally teach me how to become one offstage." Enough said. She steps back into the nearest of the two lines. "This is for Miss M."

As the piano plays with commendable gusto once more, the ensemble reprise their big opening number. But this time, despite the hour and all that has gone before, the unscripted drama onstage and off, the elderly professionals (and Zelda Gatley) perform it with an energy they didn't know they could still muster. No nerves, no fear. Just heart. And soul. And love.

No one starts at the top and a lot of us drop, before we can reach the heights,

But with a gallon of pluck and a barrel of luck, we can see our name up there in lights...

The
Eleven O'Clock
Number

Encore!

Whilst many of the invited guests leave immediately after the performance, pausing only to congratulate Gavin Silk on his Home, his staff, his residents and, above all, his talented daughter, some relatives and friends linger on in the Christmassy Green Room for more hot mulled wine but thankfully, fewer carols.

One such lingerer, choosing not to warm himself with a drink, shows less reluctance in accepting the unfamiliar but far from unwelcome warmth of a hug from his long-estranged brother.

"I didn't think you'd ever come to see me," says Jacob Bloom, with tears unashamedly speckling his still made-up cheeks. "Especially on a Shabbos." To which his brother, the retired rabbi, can only offer a regretful, and perhaps even remorseful, shrug. Because he had never thought that he would either. (And, fortunately, the nights are so dark these days that the Sabbath went out some hours ago.)

"Oh, by the way, Avram," says Jacob, with more confidence than he might have expected himself to muster, "this is Ernest Jackson." He turns to introduce the remaining Jackson brother, who stands beside them, moved but for once unmoving. "Born Efram Jacobovitz," adds the elderly actor, unconvincingly.

"In your dreams, Jakie," says the rabbi sternly. But then, to the relief of both men, he laughs. "And, my dear brother, who do you think sent me the ticket?"

*

Lisa Silk has been organising the after-show tidy-up.

This includes clearing some of the shell-shocked but elated cast off the stage and ushering them either back into their own rooms for a lie-down or on to the Green Room to suck up some love, compliments and most probably more than one steaming glass of mulled wine.

When she is finally able to join her fellows, Lisa is met with an unalloyed warmth, to which she is quite unused. Or perhaps, she now wonders, it was always there but she was too suspicious or wrapped-up in herself even to notice.

She looks around for her father and unsurprisingly discovers him with the mayor and the Chairman of the Board of Trustees. At first, she resolves not to interrupt. The resolve lasts about ten seconds, after which she makes a beeline for the grey and, from past experience, unbearably tedious trio.

"*Well?*" she challenges, "What did you think?" She is smart enough to know that her father wouldn't dare to be his usual self in front of these guys. Or at least not his usual dad-of-Lisa self.

"Think?" he says, surprised by the full-frontal assault but also unusually thoughtful. Even more unusually, the man smiles. This is not the most attractive sight on the south coast nor even his own most flattering facial posture, but right now, it works for her. "Well… I suppose, no, I think… I have a feeling, Lisa Silk, that I may be obliged to – let's say – re-evaluate. Yes. It looks dangerously like I'm going to be running this madhouse on my own."

In full view of the local royalty, Lisa gives the man a huge hug. She can feel his body stiffen, as if from disuse, but the gesture is not wholly unrewarding for both parties. Nor is what her unmistakably proud yet understandably cautious father says next. "But Lisa, please, don't be like… like some people. Don't ever mistake your work for your life."

The young woman suspects that Gavin Silk is not talking simply about those around her, veterans steeped in the profession into which she might soon be taking tentative and hugely scary steps. So, she simply nods in understanding.

"Now, where's that mulled wine?" she says, with a ragged laugh. Because she knows that if she stays where she is any longer, she will unquestionably break down.

As Lisa slips away, she almost knocks over Zelda Gatley, who looks energised by the night's activities yet still utterly terrified. The elderly credit fraudster says nothing to her former stage manager but almost physically accosts Gavin Silk.

"*So*, how was I?" she asks, nervously.

The director, currently the most pivotal person in her life, stares down at her. Didn't someone only just ask him this?

"Well, I'm no expert, Miss Gatley, and of course you were quite rudely interrupted, but in my humble opinion, from what little I saw, you were terrible."

"*Dad!*" says Lisa, overhearing.

"So, you'll probably just have to rest here a while longer, Zelda," continues the man, "until you get better."

Lisa watches the birdlike old lady as she processes this. When the words finally sink through the panic, a huge smile appears, first of the day or perhaps the week, on her tiny, pinched face, as her usual colour returns.

"I shall probably die before that happens!" says Zelda Gatley, joyfully waving her stick and making for the mulled wine. "Oh, and my first name is really Doreen."

*

To no one's particular surprise, although disappointing perhaps to some of his older admirers in the audience, who are still hovering, Rex Markham has found a quiet corner with Diana Appleyard, understudy no more. They stand quite close to each other, despite an absence of overcrowding.

"Where've you been all my life, Diana?" he says.

"Oh, for fuck's sake, Rex!" says his leading lady.

"Sorry, love. Old habits."

The pop of a champagne cork causes them both to turn.

Slumped into their usual armchairs but bunched up against a wall to open up more space, Cyril Dodds, Barry Prince and Gerard Bunting are looking distinctly knackered but utterly elated. Even Mr Chips looks bushed. They have all swiftly drained their mulled wine to allow room for better things.

"I think we should take this on the road, don't you?" says the owl. The others, even Cyril Dodds himself, just stare.

*

Despite the hint of December frosts and a biting breeze off the sea, Elspeth Quest stands with her only child, shivering on the terrace. Stanley has strung fairy lights over the trees and they can even spot some illuminated mistletoe. Elspeth has never been much enamoured of this particular season, yet tonight is causing her to have belated second thoughts.

"*Ill met by moonlight, fair Titania*," says Oberon Quest.

"You remembered."

"Oh yes."

Elspeth's eyes turn to the attractive woman standing at the doorway, trying not to eavesdrop but plainly wishing to be introduced. The older woman's eyes move from this person's sweet face to somewhere slightly lower down.

"I notice you're going into production yourself."

Oberon smiles and beckons the woman to join them, murmuring her name. Before she can fully do so, Stanley arrives from the dining room, having just finished up whatever he felt needed doing to ensure the residents' safety in the morning. He immediately sees that Elspeth is occupied and alters his trajectory.

"Stanley, please," calls Elspeth. "Don't go. This is my son, Oberon. And his er, er, Anchal. Whom I am meeting for the very first time." She smiles warmly at the younger couple. "Stanley and I are… very good friends."

Oberon Quest has been around plays and players for enough years in his youth to appreciate subtext. He simply nods. "So, maybe this wasn't such a bad move after all."

Elspeth, who has never told her son that it was a bad move in the first place, is impressed both with his insight into her character and the swiftness of his uptake. Perhaps she didn't do such a godawful job after all, despite the strain and the estrangement. She hopes not. She does know that she owes a lot to Diana Appleyard. Both for today and for so many times before. Elspeth hopes that this evening has repaid at least some of that debt.

When she looks at Stanley and observes how he is gazing back at her, that endearing softness blending with such strength in his oddly moist eyes, Elspeth has to agree that maybe becoming an old Dusty hasn't been such a catastrophic reversal.

How bad can it be, she muses, with a first grandchild on the way; a shining young star to nurture and advise; old and new friends on tap; a hopeful rapprochement with a beautiful son; and also, perhaps, with a smarmy, thin-moustached adversary?

And a gentle old man tap-dancing, far less wistfully these days, on the Christmas-lit lawn. This time, not on his own.

All I need now, thinks Elspeth Quest, grabbing a warm glass of mulled wine, *is a fucking sea view*. Is that honestly so much to ask?

acknowledgements

I would like to thank Petra Fried and Andy Baker of Clerkenwell Films who set this whole ball rolling.

And my wonderful representatives Christina Pickworth of Imagine Talent, Sarah Arnott and Cameron Cubbison of Zero Gravity who always saw my story's potential.